OATH OF **VENGEANCE**

BOOK TWO
OF THE VIGILANTE DUOLOGY

A BRAD MADRID STORY

OATH OF **VENGEANCE**

BOOK TWO
OF THE VIGILANTE DUOLOGY

A BRAD MADRID STORY

GLYNN STEWART
TERRY MIXON

**FAOLAN'S PEN
PUBLISHING**
faolanspen.com

This edition published in 2018 by:

Faolan's Pen Publishing Inc.

22 King St. S, Suite 300

Waterloo, Ontario

N2J 1N8 Canada

ISBN-13: 978-1-988035-57-4 (print)

A record of this book is available from Library and Archives Canada.

Printed in the United States of America

1 2 3 4 5 6 7 8 9 10

First edition

First printing: November 2017

Illustration © 2017 Jeff Brown Graphics

Faolan's Pen Publishing logo is a trademark of Faolan's Pen Publishing Inc.

Read more books from Glynn Stewart at faolanspen.com

―――――

CHAPTER ONE

―――――

The pirates were good. Too good.

Brad Madrid, owner and commander of the Vikings platinum-rated mercenary company, watched the boarders' progress through the concealed security cameras with concern.

The intruders had to believe the JoveCorp automated freighter was empty of people, just like the other seven they'd plundered in the last three months. His people had boarded it in space well away from prying eyes, using codes provided by the company's security department.

Even though this ship was supposedly unoccupied, that didn't necessarily mean it was unguarded, even without his mercenaries. This ship—like all the rest the pirates had hit—had computer-controlled weapons clusters at various key locations. Ones Brad had decided to leave active so he could see how the pirates managed them.

With aplomb, it turned out. The twenty men in the pirate boarding party maintained surprisingly good order as they advanced into the ship. Easily as good as Saburo Kawa's people. That was going to annoy his combat team leader enormously.

The pirates watched each others' backs, checked every hatch and

1

compartment, swept corridors before entering them, and destroyed every automated weapon on the ship before it could fire on them.

Every single one.

That level of information suggested JoveCorp Security had a traitor in their midst.

The casual competency of the troops suggested something else to Brad. He'd presumed the people pillaging the automated freighters were Cadre. He'd thought no one else would've had the sheer nerve to pick off the damned things between the diver bases in the outer edges of Jupiter's atmosphere and the refineries in high orbit.

Only, Cadre pirates weren't this precise or capable. Most of the troops that paid allegiance to the Terror were just scum stiffened by a cadre of the Terror's core thugs—hence the group's name. Even those bastards, while more disciplined than normal pirates, were *nothing* like this.

"Commandos," Brad's companion in the cargo crate hissed. Trista Doary was the attractive redheaded second-in-command of Saburo's combat team. "They have to be commandos."

Brad considered that and nodded, trusting her helmet's light-enhancing systems to show his gesture in the pitch black of the box. While the term itself might not be technically true, these men had the feel of Commonwealth Marines. Well-trained ones that had worked together before.

They might not be commandos—the cream of Commonwealth combat forces—but compared to the run-of-the-mill Cadre forces, they might as well be. What in Dark were they doing there?

Time to find out.

The pirates hadn't been scanning the cargo. They'd been more concerned with destroying the automated weapons. That mistake was going to cost them.

If they had scanned the cargo, they'd have found five of the large crates didn't contain Helium-3. They'd been loaded empty, unbeknownst to the diver crews and the loaders alike.

Each now contained two heavily armed and highly skilled merce-naries who were a match for Commonwealth Marines in training, discipline, and skill. And, while it was true his people were outnumbered two to one, they had the element of surprise.

Brad activated his com. "Go! Go! Go!"

Even as he spoke, Brad kicked open the side of his crate and lunged out. There were four commandos in his cargo hold. They confirmed his guess about their quality by instantly diving for cover, but it was already too late.

Brad put two flechettes through the pirate nearest to the door with his rifle and then dodged to the side as Doary opened up with her automatic shotgun. Another commando collapsed, his chest ripped apart.

A third came up with his mono-blade snapping to life. Brad danced out of the way of the first lunge easily, but the man brought his blade back quickly. He was trained in this and wasn't too bad.

Brad dodged again and hurled his rifle at the man. He was far too close to bring it to bear, and it was slowing him down.

With a single slash of his glowing blue blade, the commando cut the expensive rifle in half, sending the pieces clattering across the deck.

All of that was impressive but kept the pirate from focusing on the real threat.

Doary stepped to the side and unloaded a three-round burst into the commando. The result was an exceptionally gory death.

He was glad he wouldn't be the poor bastard cleaning this up.

Brad drew his pistol and went looking for the last commando. He needn't have worried. The man's corpse was sprawled against the container he'd tried to hide behind. The first blast of flechettes Doary had fired had ripped his arm off and shredded half his chest.

That combat shotgun was a scary weapon, especially when you didn't know it was coming.

He verified that all the pirates were dead, while Doary provided cover. As he did so, he activated his com. "All teams, Viking Actual. Four enemy down here. Report."

"Three here," Saburo replied.

"Two here." "Four." "Three."

Brad added up the reports. "We've still got four on the loose. Saburo, take your team and Raffi's to secure Engineering. Duncan, you and Lance take your teams to secure Comp Central. I'll take Doary to block them from retreating to their ship."

Assorted *affirmatives* came back and he killed his transmission. "Let's go, Doary."

The pirate ship had latched on near his cargo bay, so it only took them a few moments to reach the hole they'd cut. At the sight of it, Brad gestured Doary to halt and scanned it. It didn't look booby-trapped or occupied. He gestured her forward again, covering her with his pistol.

Half a moment later, a scuffling noise behind them set him in motion. He dove forward, taking Doary down to the deck as a grenade bounced around the corner and detonated.

The explosion picked the two of them up and tossed them down the corridor past the breach. They hit the bulkhead hard.

Brad swore as he grabbed the pistol he'd dropped and rolled to cover the corridor behind them. Doary's arm was twisted at an impossible angle. His helmet display showed she was unconscious but in relatively good health. How long that would last was anyone's guess.

Two commandos came diving around the corner. One rolled to a stop and opened fire with a pistol while the other ran for their ship. Flechettes whistled down the hallway, and Brad returned fire, hugging the deck for the minimal cover it offered.

Flechettes ripped through the left arm of his combat suit and he hissed in pain, but his shots were better aimed. The commando racing toward him crumpled to the deck in a bloody heap.

Ignoring the pain as best as he could, Brad began firing at the other pirate just as two more commandos lunged around the corner and opened up with their own weapons.

Brad snarled and dropped one with a rapid series of shots across the torso. Before he could fire on the second, the man's fire forced him to roll across the corridor.

He came to a stop against the bulkhead and got the bastard dead center in his view.

Before he could fire, the pirate ship blasted free of the hull. The living pirate that Brad had been forced to ignore had made it into the ship and taken off without his companion. That wasn't very sporting.

Emergency blast doors slammed shut in front of Brad to protect the ship from pressure loss. The commando he'd been about to shoot died abruptly as it cut him in half. Yeah, he definitely didn't want to see the cleaning bill.

Brad activated the channel to the freighter's long-range com. "*Heart*, this is Madrid. Status?"

"We've got the pirate ship heading away from you fast," Jason Finley, *Heart*'s tactical officer said crisply. "Orders?"

"Kill him."

"My pleasure."

———

Two hours later, Brad sat in *Heart of Vengeance*'s wardroom with a bandaged arm, watching the recording of the short engagement between *Heart* and the pirate ship. It hadn't been a fair fight and the pirate vessel had died before he could escape.

"The bugger was fast, sir," Jason said quietly. "He was pulling twelve mps squared, easy. We only had him in range for a few minutes. If I hadn't gotten lucky with the first salvo, he might have gotten away clean."

"Is it just me or did that ship seem to be in better condition than most Cadre ships?" Brad asked slowly. "And more capable."

John Marshal, their pilot nodded. "He sure was. Why send something that fast just to get He3 off a freighter? Sure, it's valuable, but it's not worth *that* much."

"People like that don't just do things for no reason," Shelly Weldon, their communications officer, said. "From what I overheard on the combat channels, they were high-class fighters. Why even send them? Was the Cadre expecting a fight?"

"I have no idea," Brad admitted. "But I intend to find out. We're going back over to the freighter. Keep an eye out for trouble while we're gone.

"Also, give us a heads-up if any JoveCorp ships come our way. I really don't want them looking over my shoulder while I try to solve this mystery."

"Will do."

He took one of the shuttles back over to the automated freighter and met Saburo. Their combat team leader hadn't been injured in the fighting, for which Brad felt certain he'd eventually get some smug comment.

"What have you found?" he asked as they started walking.

"About what one would expect from a boarding party of military types, which makes it unusual for pirates. Nineteen bodies, all in combat armor and heavily armed. Their gear isn't branded. Home-built, but someone fed the Marines' latest designs into their nano-forge. Definitely better than the usual crap the Cadre favors."

"Do we have any ID on the dead?"

"No, and I don't expect that to change anytime soon. We just don't have access to the kind of databases these people would be in. They're ex-military. Some of them, anyway. Others might be mercenaries.

"We stripped them down and looked for tattoos. Those can tell you a lot about someone's history. Marines favor certain ones and often have unit blazons somewhere on them, particularly if they served in a prestigious unit.

"Like I guessed, these people are ex-Marines. Six of them had the same unit blazon. One I didn't recognize. A total of eleven were marked. The others might not like tattoos. Or have had them removed."

Brad scowled. "What in Darkness would ex-Marines be doing working for the Cadre? Any idea why they were stealing He3?"

"I'm not sure they were," the troop officer said slowly. "I think they had a completely different reason for being on this ship. Take a look."

The two of them entered one of the cargo holds. Saburo's people had laid the bodies out for inspection. Their gear was arrayed off to one side. It was eerie and a bit grotesque.

"Look at these packs," the Asian man said with a gesture.

There were six packs opened on the deck, with their contents arrayed beside them. The small, square blocks were familiar to Brad: Composition Fifteen, a high-energy explosive the Vikings occasionally used to destroy things they couldn't leave behind.

To say acquisition of it was restricted was an understatement. The amount of carnage even one block could create was impressive. A quick count showed more than a hundred kilos.

"Holy crap," Brad muttered. "That's more than enough to wreck the freighter. Talk about overkill."

"I don't think that was their plan," Saburo said with a shake of his head. "I think they wanted to blow up something else.

"Based on the weapons and armor, as well as the amount of ammunition they have, I think this group intended to board the JoveCorp refinery and wire it for destruction. They'd use their little ship for a fast getaway when they were done."

Brad shook his head. "No way the people at the refinery could miss the condition of this ship. The telemetry would show compromised hull integrity and loss of defensive weapons clusters."

"It would," Saburo agreed, "if that data was being transmitted. They have gear for reprogramming the outgoing data stream. No one on the refinery would see a thing until it was far too late.

"The first people to get eyeballs on it would be flight control. If they're in the Cadre's back pocket, no one would know anything until it was far too late to defend the refinery."

Saburo idly scratched under his torso armor. "With surprise on their side, these people could easily take out the defensive security teams. They all expect to have some warning of an incoming attack. Not this time."

That scenario was horrifying. What did the Cadre have to gain? He knew that they had to be behind it. No one else was this bloody-minded.

"You might be right about the people in flight control," Brad admitted. "We should see if our arrival brings someone out of the woodwork.

"The freighter is still on course for the refinery. Our little fight wasn't in line of sight, so any traitors won't know there was any trouble. We'll move one of the assault shuttles to cover the breach. Can you reprogram the outgoing telemetry to show no damage?"

The other man nodded. "One of my people can. It might be a good idea to set up a defensive perimeter inside the freighter to apprehend the first people on board, just in case. What will you be doing?"

"Waiting to see if anyone starts running," Brad said grimly. "I'll contact MacDonald once you dock. I won't give him any of the details over the com, though. He'll just have to wait for me to get there."

And Brad had no doubt the man would be seriously pissed. That was his default mode. This time might be worse.

He allowed himself a wry smile. If finding his freighter all torn up and filled with mercenaries twisted his tail, he'd really go ballistic when Brad told him that the Vikings wanted a bonus for saving his ass.

CHAPTER TWO

BRAD HAD BARELY STEPPED off the shuttle at the refinery when Jake MacDonald, the head of JoveCorp Security, tore into him. His approach reminded Brad of the powerful storms on the planet below: intense, powerful, and implacable.

"What the Dark was that all about?" the man demanded pugnaciously. "I got people screaming at me about you assaulting JoveCorp personnel and damaging one of our ships."

"We had reason to believe that an attack on this facility was imminent," Brad said coolly. "And I'd say we detained JoveCorp personnel, but I'd rather explain in private."

That caused the belligerent man to pause his diatribe and look around the crowded landing bay. While no one seemed to be listening, any number of people were passing by closely enough to overhear what they were saying. It wasn't hard at MacDonald's volume.

The other man grunted. "Maybe that's not such a bad idea. Let's go."

Brad hadn't brought any of his people with him. MacDonald was the kind of man who seemed to revel in conflict. Particularly in front of people he deemed to be his subordinates, whether they worked for JoveCorp or not.

The trip through the crowded corridors of the refinery was tense. Brad chose to walk slightly behind the security chief to discourage any conversation. From that vantage point, he could see how tense MacDonald's shoulders were.

The lift that took them to the executive level was mostly empty, and Brad suspected the junior managers they met there actually got off before they reached their intended destination. The tension was that palpable.

As JoveCorp's chief of security, Jake MacDonald had a spacious, well-appointed office. It also seemed he had a fetish for marbles.

Row after row of glass spheres with the most amazing designs sat in display cases for visitors to examine. They ranged in size from the tip of his pinky to several that were the size of a closed fist. One looked like Jupiter. It was stunning.

Once the door was closed, MacDonald turned on Brad. "You've got five minutes to convince me you didn't just stab me in the back. If you don't, I'm going to throw your ass off this refinery and file a complaint with the Mercenary Guild. And you'd better believe they're going to take this seriously."

A younger Brad might've gotten back in MacDonald's face, but he only smiled. The last three years had certainly given him better self-control, though he imagined the angry man was going to test him sternly.

"Do you really think that a platinum-rated mercenary company would attempt to hijack an automated freighter, deliver it to the refinery where it was expected, and then hold the employees that boarded at gunpoint? Doesn't that seem a little far-fetched to you?"

"Educate me. What in Dark is going on, Madrid?"

Before he could respond, MacDonald stalked around his desk and sat down with significantly more force than was required. He laced his fingers in front of him and planted his chin on his thumbs, staring at Brad with cold eyes.

Brad picked a chair and sat without an invitation. He knew one wasn't coming, and he wasn't going to ask.

He wasn't going to stand like an employee called onto the carpet or sit in one of the handy chairs directly in front of the desk, either. Those kinds of tactics were meant to intimidate people.

Instead, he chose one off to the side, leaned back, and crossed one leg over the other.

"The first part of the mission you hired us for went off exactly as planned," he said as if there were nothing wrong. "Things went off the rails when we saw who actually boarded the freighter."

With as few words as possible, Brad described the commandos and the Vikings' defense of the freighter. He watched the security chief closely, though he really didn't expect to catch any kind of awkward reaction. The man was an ass, but he wasn't a traitor.

By the time he was finished, MacDonald's face was one of stunned astonishment.

He leaned back in his chair, making it creak. "Commandos? Why the fuck would anyone send people like that to raid an automated freighter full of He3? That just doesn't make any sense.

"They wouldn't get any resistance other than the automated systems. And those certainly haven't caused the pirates any problems in the past." The last was added in a grumbling tone.

"That's why we came into the refinery the way we did," Brad said. "We're pretty sure you've got a mole inside your security department and probably another one in the flight control center.

"We think they intended to board the refinery and sabotage it. With the amount of explosives we found, they could've destroyed every critical system and taken this refinery out."

MacDonald slammed a fist on his desk blotter. "But why? Sure, JoveCorp has made a lot of enemies over the years, but this is over the top. And why do the other six raids they pulled off? Why not just do this the first time and make sure we didn't hire someone to stop them?"

Brad shrugged. "I can't begin to guess. In hindsight, they might have been warmups or intended to keep the endgame hidden. I'll get you our surveillance data from the action. What's going to jump out at you first is how they knew how *every* defensive weapon was placed. Someone in your department gave them complete specs for the freighter.

"If you think differently, you'll have to look wherever you think the information came from. As for the flight control people, the commandos probably intended to leave their ship on the hull. They had to get away somehow. That means they expected to get past whoever was on duty today."

The security man grunted and nodded. "We always have two people in flight control. Both of them are discussing today's events with my people. If one of them is dirty, the odds are really good they both are."

MacDonald considered Brad for a long moment. "I'm going to check every bit of information. I'll examine the bodies and equipment, too. If it all checks out, I'll pay you your fee."

"You'll do better than that," Brad said bluntly. "We were hired to protect your freighter from pirates. These commandos were a significantly more difficult nut to crack. I've got injured people—including myself—that would never have gotten hurt on the mission that you pitched.

"Then there's saving this refinery. We went far above what was called for in the original contract when I'd have been justified in pulling back. I want a bonus."

MacDonald laughed. "You're crazy. Why in Darkness would I do that? I hired you to protect my freighter, and that's exactly what you did. No more. No less."

"You could do that," Brad admitted levelly, "but then you'd have to deal with the consequences."

"What consequences?" the security chief asked warily.

Brad favored him with a wide grin. "The Vikings are a platinum-rated mercenary unit. If I start spreading the word that JoveCorp is understating the risks in their contracts or failing to pay bonuses for going above and beyond what was expected, then you're going to start getting other people negotiating harder and maybe turning down work from you. Is that really how you want to play it?"

MacDonald surged to his feet. "JoveCorp doesn't let little turds like you extort money from us."

"If you think this is extortion, you shouldn't be negotiating contracts," Brad said bluntly as he rose to his feet. "Why don't you talk it over with a few of the executive vice-presidents and see how they see matters?

"Meanwhile, I believe this concludes our business. I'll get my people back to our ship and we'll be on our way. Good luck in your mole hunt."

———

Rather than heading directly for Io, Brad redirected *Heart of Vengeance* to Ganymede. While he wouldn't be there long, he really wanted to pass the information they'd gathered to Fleet Security, and that meant a visit with Lieutenant Commander Jean Greer.

She was Fleet's designated contact for Mercenary Guild officers in the Jovian system, and he'd worked closely with her during the Slavers conflict three years earlier. She'd also introduced him to Agent Kate Falcone of the Commonwealth Investigative Agency.

Truth be told, Brad wanted the information he'd gathered about the Cadre's use of ex-Marines—if that's truly what they were—passed on to both groups.

The young Fleet officer immediately agreed to meet him at her office when he commed, so Brad left his crew with a few hours on their hands to blow off steam. He trusted they wouldn't get into too much trouble, but hinted that Saburo should keep an eye on Marshal. It paid to cover all the bases.

He had to surrender his weapons when he reached the Fleet offices. As always, that bothered him, but he wouldn't win that fight.

A petty officer cleared Brad into the building and led him to Greer's office. She was waiting at the door.

Once they were alone, she shook his hand and looked pointedly at his bandages with a raised eyebrow. "Run into trouble?"

"You might say that," he admitted. "Trouble Fleet Security needs to know about."

"Ominous. I have a stash of alcohol for visitors, and the sun is over the yardarm, as they say."

To her obvious surprise, he nodded. "Scotch, if you have it. Straight."

"It must be serious. Have a seat while I get us fixed up."

He settled into a chair off to the side of the room and watched her fix the drinks: straight scotch for him and a fizzy water for her. She was on duty, after all.

She handed him his drink and sat beside him. "Tell me what happened."

Brad took a sip of his drink first and nodded. It was decent.

"JoveCorp hired the Vikings to stop pirates from hitting their automated He3 freighters. They've lost six in the last four months. The last two had a bunch of their security people on them. After that didn't stop the attacks, they called me.

"Only, we didn't run into pirates. These people were a lot better than that. We think they were ex-military."

He laid out what he knew and then told her what he suspected. The amusement that had been in her eyes when he'd arrived was long gone by the time he finished.

"That's intensely disturbing," she admitted. "I'll be able to check if they were ever in the Commonwealth Marines or Fleet."

"I assumed so." He handed her a data chip. "This has everything: recordings of the combat, still images of the bodies, and more of the weapons and equipment. We left all of the hardware and physical evidence with JoveCorp Security, so you might have to pry it out of their hands."

She scowled. "I've worked with MacDonald before. Or, should I say, I've worked around him? I'd better make that call now."

Brad took advantage of the lull to finish his drink. He took the glass back to the bar and rinsed it out. Then he joined Greer at her desk.

She looked up from her console. "I've requested he turn everything over and added his bosses to the distribution list."

"Does that help?" he asked as he sat again. "The man seems remarkably stubborn."

"He is, but I think I'll come out ahead in the end. Let's see if we can discover any information about these people in Fleet's database."

She flinched a little as she loaded the images. "I can't imagine how you do this all the time."

"You get used to it," Brad said with a shrug. "Not to sound callous, but these people don't deserve your sympathy. Very few of the scum I'm hired to deal with do."

"I suppose," she agreed reluctantly. "Let's run them one at a time. The facial recognition software we use is pretty damned good. Bets on how many hits we get?"

Brad considered that for a long moment. "Twelve out of nineteen."

"Dark, I hope not."

There ended up being fifteen hits, but two of them came from Fleet's links to the civilian network on Ganymede. Twelve of the dead men were ex-Marines, and the last was a former Fleet officer.

Greer sat back and stared at him in subdued shock. "You're on to something. I just can't imagine what it is."

"Whatever it is," he said softly, "it's Fleet business now. And, if you could pass it along to the CIA, I suspect that would be helpful, too."

The corner of the woman's mouth came up. "Hoping to work with Agent Falcone again?"

"I'm not planning on working this particular problem, but if things go all to Everdark, I certainly wouldn't mind having her at my side again."

The Fleet officer nodded. "I'll ask someone in the agency to pass the information along. No matter who they send—and they'll send someone—I feel pretty confident they'll be good. You did good work passing this on to us so fast. Fleet thanks you."

"My pleasure," he said as he rose to his feet. "I'll leave this in your capable hands, then. I need to get back to Io and see what other crises have developed in my absence. Thanks for your help and for the drink. I appreciate both."

CHAPTER THREE

BRAD LEANED back in his office chair and watched the Jupiter-set on the massive viewscreen built into his wall. It was beautiful. Too bad the sight of the massive gas giant slowly sliding behind Io couldn't wash the bad taste of their last mission out of his mouth.

Silhouetted against Jupiter's light, and against the dimmer glow of Io itself, parts of the massive Io Yards complex began to fall into shadow.

The massive orb slowly reduced itself to a mere corona around one edge of its moon, then vanished. Technically, Jupiter-set was really an eclipse, but given the regular orbit of the Io Yards, Jupiter rose and set in a time frame that gave the yards an effective twenty-six-hour day.

It also meant he'd worked late. Again.

He'd just spent over two grueling hours on the line with Jove-Corp's head of security. As he'd expected, Jake MacDonald had agreed to pay the bonus for saving their refinery—and, reminding Brad why he worked for the man despite his attitude, it had been significantly more than expected.

Exactly as expected, however, he'd bitched and complained at length about paying up.

Brad didn't feel at all guilty. JoveCorp had gotten more than enough value to warrant the increased payout. And his people had more than earned the extra money.

Putting the stress of the call behind him, Brad glanced around his office, finding relaxation in the familiar features. He'd purchased the three-room suite on Io Yards Node Seven just over a year and a half earlier when he'd finally given in to the inevitable and formally home-ported *Heart* at the Io Yards.

It made sense. They'd been in space over a year at that point, and it was always Io they came back to when the missions were done.

His wrist-comp beeped. It was a short text message from Shelly.

Don't forget the anniversary.

He snorted. She'd insisted on organizing a party to celebrate the third anniversary of *Heart*'s formal commissioning. Trust her to remember the date. She probably had it in her wrist-comp's planner.

Brad sighed and closed the files from the mission. Thank the Everlit that was behind them. He'd already put out feelers, looking for new contracts. They wouldn't be idle long. Platinum-rated mercenary companies were always in demand.

The sound of voices in the outer office made him turn to face the door as it slid open. Shelly came right in with Jason on her arm.

"I knew I'd find you in here," she said triumphantly. "The party is officially getting started, sir."

Brad inclined his head. "Go on, then. Enjoy yourselves."

"You need to get out. Brooding like this isn't healthy."

"She has a point," Jason said apologetically. "Every time we finish a contract, you bury yourself in this office and stay here. This is your party, too."

"And if you don't come willingly," Shelly continued with a grin, "I've got Marshal outside to physically drag you out of this office."

"You should've brought Saburo," Brad said wryly. "Don't I get a say in this?"

"I'm adding *social director* to my list of titles," Shelly said, favored him with an even wider grin. "So, when it comes to social events, what I say goes. Now, you need to change."

He examined the pair. Shelly wore a dark green dress that hugged her curves and seemed to slink with her economical movements. Jason sported the Vikings' signature midnight-blue jacket with faint gold piping over a shipsuit of the same shade.

A suit which was, Brad felt like pointing out, virtually identical to the one he currently wore.

Jason's left shoulder sported a stylized viking, and the right had a patch displaying a fist holding a beating heart, as did Brad's uniform. The latter represented *Heart of Vengeance*.

The collars of Brad's dress uniform jacket held the silver triangle of stars that marked him as a Guild captain, and he wore the short gold chain of a company commander. And, of course, he was armed with his pistol and mono-blade. Weapons were part of everyone's standard uniform in the Vikings.

He eyed his communications officer. She was supposed to be armed, but he couldn't imagine where she'd stashed a weapon in that dress. In fact, it was probably a good idea not to consider that too closely.

"I just need to grab my jacket," Brad said mildly. "It's not as if I was slumming around in shorts and a moth-eaten sweater. And if I need to be better dressed than my uniform, what kind of party is this?"

"We've rented a small dance hall," she told him. "Marshal! Get that case in here."

John Marshal, their pilot and executive officer, drifted into the room with a sheepish grin and extended a carry case to Brad. The case contained a uniform jacket just like the one Brad normally wore, only this one also held a number of medals.

The Guild didn't normally issue medals. As a rule, mercs weren't rewarded for actions taken under contract with anything other than the money they'd earned. Only when they acted without prearranged payment did mercs acquire medals and similar awards.

Brad was one of the most decorated mercs in the Sol system and refused to wear the damn things.

He weighed the odds of declining the outfit, but Shelly's expression said she was spoiling for a fight over this.

He sighed and gave in. "Fine. This *one time*."

That made her grin. "I win! Now hurry up. I have a friend at the party I want you to meet."

For a moment, his expression threatened to sour. At some point during the first year of the Vikings' existence, she'd taken it upon herself to try and "fix" his singleness. Her efforts had been uniformly disastrous from his point of view. His poor dates had held a similar opinion, he suspected.

Something must've bled through into his expression, because she held up a hand. "Nothing like that. I've learned there are some things in the universe I can't change."

Brad shook his head and took the jacket out of the case. This was probably going to be a real pain in the ass.

———

Thirty minutes later, a transit tube delivered them to the hall Shelly had rented. A small cluster of people waited for them in the corridor.

Both of the combat team's female members were there. Trista Doary wore her dress uniform and a cast on her arm. The other woman— Adriana Macaulay, one of their new hires—wore a long white gown that showed off her heroic physique.

Marshal had brought his current lady friend, a short redhead whose name Brad hadn't caught. It hardly mattered. He had a tendency to turn up with a different woman every time he was expected to bring one, so keeping track was pointless—though Brad *usually* tried to at least catch their names for the time he spent with them.

As they approached the door, the distinctive tone of a corridor car's warning horn sounded and everyone quickly made sure they were clear of the lines marked for the car's use.

A taxi came to a stop, disgorging a statuesque brunette in what was clearly a dress uniform of some kind, but one Brad didn't recognize offhand.

The woman barely had time to pay her fare before Shelly caught her up in a hug. Since the communications officer was barely a hundred and sixty centimeters and the other woman was taller than Brad, they made quite a contrast.

Shelly quickly led the other woman over to where Brad and Jason were standing. "Jason, you've met Michelle, right?"

Jason took the taller woman's hand and bowed over it. "Indeed I have. It's good to see you again."

Shelly turned Michelle to face Brad. "Captain Brad Madrid, meet Captain Michelle Hunt."

Brad took the woman's proffered hand and shook it. "Captain Hunt."

"Just call me Michelle. The title is just a courtesy. I'm a diver pilot."

He nodded in understanding. Divers were little more than life pods, tanks, and magnetic scoops. They dove—hence the name—into the surface of the two largest gas giants and brought back valuable gases. Like the He3 JoveCorp had been losing.

Following up on his suspicion, he smiled. "JoveCorp?"

He didn't think so, but he wanted to be sure. JoveCorp employed most of the divers around Jupiter.

She smiled and shook her head. "SaturCorp out of Blackhawk Station."

Brad couldn't stop his eyebrows from rising. SaturCorp was one of only two corporations working near Saturn. Both of them worked out of Blackhawk, which was the only inhabited location in that planetary system. The ringed giant fell into the odd gap between the populations of the semi-lawful Outer System and the utterly lawless Fringe.

"When Shelly found out I was on station, she invited me to your party," the woman continued. "For which I'm grateful. I was starting to look forward to going back to Blackhawk. That only happens when I'm *really* bored."

Brad understood. *Heart* had called at Blackhawk's massive refineries and fuel tanks a couple of times. The station was about as plain as physically possible. The list of distractions aboard the station had driven Marshal to despair. Brad didn't envy the thousands of people that called it home on a semi-permanent basis.

"Since you two don't seem to have noticed," Shelly said, "the rest of us are going inside."

Brad glanced around and realized he'd gotten so wrapped up in the conversation that he'd missed the others entering the hall, so he followed them inside.

It didn't take long for him to fade into the background. He shortly found himself propping up a handy wall. It wasn't that the music was bad or that he disliked dancing. This was just his way.

He held a beer but only occasionally sipped it as he watched his crew have fun. He was just considering taking his leave when Captain Hunt approached.

"Do you actually drink?" she asked. "Or is that just for decoration?"

Brad raised the almost-full bottle slightly. "The latter tonight, I'm afraid. I'm not much of a socializer, Captain."

"As I said outside, call me Michelle. I always feel silly when people call me *captain*, with my crew being so small."

"You're in sole charge of your ship and the lives aboard her. That's what makes you a captain, not how large your crew is."

She snorted. "I'm a diver pilot. I have a long list of regulations controlling what I can and can't do. Men and women like you are the people with true independent authority."

"I have independent authority only as long as I remain one of the most efficient killers in the solar system," Brad said with more bitterness than he usually allowed himself. "As a mercenary captain, you have to realize that when you accept a contract, people are going to die along the way to its completion."

"Not your company," she objected. "You haven't lost a single person in three years. That's one of the reasons you're the smallest platinum company in existence."

He arched an eyebrow at her awareness of his company's stature and their record.

"Shelly is a dear friend," she said with an embarrassed shrug. "I've kept tabs on the Vikings ever since she joined."

Brad raised his bottle in acknowledgment. "I'm afraid you misunderstand. While we've been incredibly lucky and managed to keep all our people alive, we've done so by killing more people than I can reasonably count.

"In fulfilling a contract, people tend to die. No matter which side they're on, there's guilt in that for the man who orders it. Not something I'd imagined myself doing when I was growing up. Independence comes at a heavy cost."

"I see," she said softly. For a moment, they stood in silence and she studied him. "You're not at all what I thought. I kind of expected you to be more standoffish, based on how Shelly described you. No offense."

"None taken. Shelly is my subordinate. That imposes a certain bias on our relationship. And the fact that she keeps trying to set me up with her friends hasn't helped us grow chatty."

Michelle laughed. "You've noticed that tendency of hers, have you?"

"It's hard to miss," he observed dryly. "She seems to regard the fact that I've kept to myself for the last three years as a horror. She claims she's given up on me, but I remain skeptical."

"She's convinced that love should not only be contagious, but aggressively contagious," she said with a smile. "She also doesn't limit her matchmaking to her male friends."

Brad surveyed the room again, noting that his crew appeared to be sufficiently distracted for him to make his escape.

"So, why are you here?" Michelle asked, stopping him from making his excuses and departing.

"Hmm?"

"All you're doing is leaning against the wall, watching people," she observed. "And talking to me, but I initiated that."

"As I said, I'm not much for social occasions."

"Ah," she said before turning away to survey the crowd herself. "They're having fun, aren't they?"

"They've earned it. They deserve to be able to relax every once in a while."

"And you don't?" she asked softly.

"I'll relax once I've achieved what I've set out to do."

"And what's that?"

"Something I'd need a lot more alcohol to discuss, I'm afraid."

"As you wish," she said with a quirk of her lips. "To be honest, I've grown less fond of large groups in the last few years too. That probably comes from spending half my time on a ship that only requires a crew of three."

Brad nodded his understanding but remained silent, unsure of where she was going.

"Shall we head out?" she asked after a long moment, a twinkle in her eyes.

He found himself smiling. This was an unexpected turn, but not unwelcome. "Sure."

"Will Shelly expect you to say goodnight?"

"No. She makes sure I come to these things, but doesn't expect me to stay all that long."

Michelle flashed him a bright smile. "Then why don't you grab us a cab? It'll keep her from swooning in delight at her potential match-making coup. I'll join you in five minutes."

CHAPTER FOUR

BRAD WOKE to an unfamiliar weight on his arm. Smiling gently, he luxuriated in having Michelle's warm body curled in his embrace.

They'd gone for dinner after the party and talked. The restaurant was near Brad's apartment and they'd ended up there, drinking. He wasn't entirely sure who had made the first move, but it hadn't been long before they'd found more pleasurable pursuits on their minds.

He smiled lazily, knowing that everything was right with his world for the first time in a long while. As he did, he felt Michelle shift and stretch.

"Good morning," he said softly.

She startled and then relaxed. After a moment, she rolled carefully to face him.

"Good morning," she replied, her voice equally soft. Then she kissed him.

Events were proceeding in a highly satisfactory manner when a buzzer cut through the quiet of his apartment. Brad came up for air and swore.

"Com call," he said. "I'd better take it."

She sighed but helped him disentangle himself from her and the sheets. The buzzer sounded again as Brad jumped out of bed, desperately trying to find something decent to throw on. As the buzzer sounded for a third time, he grabbed a bathrobe and belted it around his waist.

The buzzer was sounding for the fifth time as he finally sat at his desk and ordered the console to accept the call. Hiroshi Kawa's face appeared on the screen.

"Good morning," Saburo's father said with a smile as he took in Brad's robe. "I hope I didn't wake you."

"Morning, Hiroshi. Not exactly."

When Brad didn't add anything, the older man shrugged. "I wanted to catch you before you left for your office."

"You've succeeded. I assume there's a specific reason?"

"Indeed. It brings me great pleasure to inform you that the basic work on hull number nine-kay-kay-gee-six-seven was completed last night. She should be fully outfitted and ready for commissioning within thirty days."

Hiroshi wasn't just Saburo's father. He was also the owner of one of the premier ship-building and repair firms in the Io Yards. Since he'd rebuilt *Heart of Vengeance* after Brad had captured it from pirates and slavers, it had been a certainty the Vikings would use his services to expand.

Brad grinned. "As always, your people have performed miracles. That's wonderful!"

"I'm going to take a shower," Michelle whispered as she passed the desk. "Join me when you can."

Her voice was pitched low, but something must've gotten through the com.

The older man's eyes widened. "My deepest apologies," he said, inclining his head. "I hadn't considered that you might have company."

His tone didn't sound sorrowful at all. In fact, his expression indicated sly approval.

"It's not what you think," Brad said somewhat desperately. He didn't want Shelly to find out so soon.

The older man's lips quirked. "It hardly matters *what* I think. If there's a woman in your apartment—which certainly seems to be the case—I'd imagine talking business is not the weightiest matter on your mind. We shall speak later."

The tiny old man winked and cut the call before Brad could say another word.

He turned to Michelle. She stood there, gloriously nude.

Her expression was somewhat abashed. "Sorry. I didn't think I was loud enough for the com to pick up. What was that about, anyway?"

Brad grinned, suddenly unconcerned about word getting out. It wasn't as if he was ashamed. Far from it.

"That was my builder notifying me that the Vikings' new ship will be commissioned in a month."

"Oh?" she asked, raising an eyebrow. "That's good news! Give me details!"

"She's a destroyer. Brand spanking new and she incorporates the best equipment money can buy—and a few things that money *shouldn't* be able to buy."

"You have to be pleased. A destroyer sounds really big and power-ful." She smiled seductively. "I get all worked up when something big and powerful comes along. You know, I think the shower can wait. This calls for a celebration and I know just how to do that.

"Besides," she purred as she drew him to his feet and peeled his robe off, "I want to leave you wanting more when I ship out for Saturn this afternoon."

———

Brad was unsurprisingly very late getting to the office. He felt as if everyone would guess why, and knew he was even blushing a bit. He covered it by briskly summoning his senior staff into the conference room.

He sat at the head, of course. Shelly, Jason, and assistant engineer Jim Shoulter filled the right side of the table. The left held Saburo, Trista, and Mike Randall, *Heart*'s chief engineer. John Marshal sat at the far end of the table, as befitted the ship's executive officer.

"All right, people, to business," Brad said. "I received a call this morning from Hiroshi that our new ship is one month away from commissioning."

That sparked a lot of celebratory conversation that he had to eventually calm with a few knuckle raps on the table.

"As you'd imagine, that will mean we need to reorganize. I've been thinking long and hard about it and I've made a number of decisions. Some of them will not be popular, but I think they will be what's best for the Vikings."

That caused a bit of consternation. Each of his officers glanced around the table at the rest, likely gauging if anyone else know what was going on.

"No, I haven't discussed this with anyone," he confirmed. "I'm sure it will come as no surprise that I'll take command of the new ship. When I do, Marshal will come with me as executive officer and command pilot, Randall will become her chief engineer, and Saburo will be our combat team leader."

Brad watched his words sink in. Marshal seemed momentarily stunned and then narrowed his eyes in a glare at Jason.

"Eyes on me, people," Brad said firmly. "I need our most experienced people on our most powerful ship. I also have to see that *Heart* is well taken care of. I'll be happy to address your individual concerns, but let me finish first.

"I'm inclined to hire someone from outside to command *Heart*. Jason will move up to serve as her executive officer as well as her tactical officer, and Shelly will serve as her pilot. Marshal says you've passed your certifications with flying colors, so well done. Jim will become *Heart*'s chief engineer and Trista will be her combat team leader."

He glanced around the table. "We'll have a lot of new folk coming in to get us back up to full strength. I'll work with each of you to make sure you're involved in the process as it concerns your departments."

Marshal cleared his throat. "Why aren't you giving me *Heart*? I've got the experience to command her."

His glance at Jason implied the tactical officer didn't. And, sadly, he didn't. Not yet.

Jason's eyes slitted and his lips compressed. "At least I'll be sober when trouble comes calling."

"Enough," Brad said, his tone cutting off Marshal's response before he made it.

He shot Jason a stern glare. "I won't tolerate that kind of disrespect to a superior officer."

The young man sighed and slumped back in his chair. "I was out of line, but I wasn't alone."

Shelly looked as if she was going to inject herself, so Brad held up his hand. That would only make matters worse if more people—particularly an aggrieved party's lover—leapt to their defense.

"No, you weren't," Brad said to Jason once Shelly closed her mouth.

He shifted his gaze to Marshal meaningfully.

"You two have been working hand in hand for three years," he said after a long pause. "I expect better from both of you. I won't ask either of you to apologize. You wouldn't mean it, anyway. But I will demand professional behavior. Is that clear?"

Once both men had nodded, he continued. "Jason, you don't have the command experience I'd like. I'm sorry, but you'd be commanding a ship in space, and that's different than the combat experience you currently have. A stint as executive officer will season you. Once the Vikings grow again, you'll be a strong candidate to command a ship."

He waited for the tactical officer to nod before looking at Marshal.

"You have the experience, John, but not the temperament. What Jason said was out of line, but if you want to be seriously considered for command, you need to start addressing some of your off-duty behavior."

"I've never been drunk on duty," the pilot protested.

"No," Brad allowed. "That doesn't mean you haven't caused a fair bit of havoc while on leave. That would be your business if it didn't blow back on the Vikings. Which it has.

"I'd rather have had this conversation in private. Neither of you should have had to hear it with the rest of our people looking on, but you brought that on yourselves. I expect my officers to be better than this. If either of you expect to ever command a ship in space, you'd best get your acts together."

Brad looked at each person around the table to see if they had anything to add. When they each shook their head, he continued.

"Until now, I've preferred an informal system of command. The new ship is going to change that. She's a full-sized destroyer with a crew of forty-six and a thirty-man combat team.

"To prevent confusion once we start hiring new crew for her and replacements for *Heart*—and we all know *Heart* could use an extra hand or six herself—I'm afraid we're going to have to formalize our rank table."

From the shocked silence that greeted this pronouncement, none of them had considered it. Which was rather myopic of them, as it was an obvious consequence of the vastly increased size of the Vikings.

"To make it quick and simple," he said softly, "I'll just tell you the new rankings. I'll formally take the rank of commodore and the title of captain on the new ship. If it was only a single ship in the company, I'd stick with *captain*, but two ships means we need a flag officer. I hope we'll keep growing so that doesn't sound as pompous as it does now."

That got chuckles from everyone, breaking the gloom that had settled on the room.

It was kind of pretentious to have a destroyer captained by anything more than a commander, but mercenaries had their own traditions. He'd adjust.

"*Heart*'s as-yet-unknown commanding officer will be a commander by rank and a captain by title. John will be a commander as well as executive officer on the new ship. Jason, Shelly, and Jim will be lieutenant commanders. Trista is now a senior lieutenant and Saburo is a major. I figured we'd skip captain in the troop ranks to avoid potential confusion."

For a moment, the room was quiet as they digested the changes. Then congratulations and mild—but mostly joking—complaints began to fill the air. It was, after all, the mercenary way to find something to complain about.

Once he'd let that play out, Brad raised a hand and they quieted again.

"That completes my special announcements, so we can start our regular meeting. Randall, what's the status on *Heart*'s repairs?"

———

The docking port assigned to ships going to Blackhawk Station was relatively empty when he and Michelle met there a few hours later. There were only two vessels at the moment: a small liner for tourists and SaturCorp personnel, and a tanker used for ferrying gas on its way to the Inner System. It was going back empty for a fresh load.

Brad wasn't sure why, but Michelle had chosen to travel on the tanker. Perhaps that was because she was a diver pilot and had a bond with the others on that ship. Or maybe she didn't want to deal with the passengers on the liner. He'd have to ask her if she really did come back to see him when her tour ended.

He kissed her and she returned his passion with interest.

"I'm going to miss you," he said quietly when they finally separated.

"It's only six weeks," she said with a smile. "Once this dive period is up, I'll be back. I'm sure you can survive that long."

Brad knew that he could, but his life would be a lot emptier until she got back.

CHAPTER FIVE

Sarah Harmon, the Vikings' receptionist and permanent contact person on Io, smiled at Brad as he walked back into the office. "You had a call while you were out. A Mr. Justin Sloan from Senator Barnes's staff."

Brad stopped and cocked his head. A Commonwealth senator was a big deal. While each of the moons around Jupiter had a governor—who made up the planetary system's *actual* government—the Jovian system as a whole was represented by a single person in the Senate. In this case, Senator William Barnes. Whose actual job description was closer to "ambassador," but no one was going to *admit* that.

He'd never met the man, though he'd seen him at a distance once or twice. Senators didn't use mercenaries. They had Fleet and the Commonwealth Marines at their fingertips to solve vexing little problems.

"Did he say what this was about?" he asked.

"No, sir. Just that it was extremely urgent."

"Did you verify he really worked for the Senator?"

It wouldn't be the first time someone that had tried to pull something over on a mercenary company. It always paid to make sure who you were dealing with.

Even if the man did work for Senator Barnes, that didn't necessarily remove the possibility that he had his own agenda. Jack Mader had worked for Io's Governor, but he'd been Cadre for decades.

The thought of the man almost made Brad snarl. He'd spent a considerable sum trying to get a lead on Mader over the last three years, to no avail. It was as if space had swallowed him whole.

If there was any justice, the Terror had spaced the man for failure. But since no one was that lucky, Brad was sure Mader would turn up to cause him trouble one day. Probably at the worst possible moment.

"I ran Mr. Sloan's background," Sarah said. "He was hired just over a year ago and came from an internship on Mars. A call to the Senator's office confirmed he was speaking on the Senator's behalf. They said that the Senator was here at the Yard for a charity event last night on Node One and hasn't departed."

"All right," Brad said, satisfied they'd done what they could to verify this was a real contact. "Send the number he left to my workstation and I'll call him back."

A small box on his console screen was flashing as Brad sat at his desk. He brought up his internal email and pulled the contact number out of the message.

He checked his appearance in his reflection on the console screen and then initiated the call. A moment later, the screen cleared, showing the image of a wiry, dark-haired man.

"Senator Barnes's office. How may I help you?"

While Brad knew they weren't at an official office, the man had to answer the call in a way that told the caller they'd gotten the right place.

"Mr. Sloan? Brad Madrid of the Vikings, returning your call."

The man seemed to sag in relief. "Thank you for being so prompt, Mr. Madrid. The Senator has found himself in need of your services. He wishes to discreetly meet with you as soon as possible."

"My schedule is open at the moment. When works for him?"

"I can have a shuttle at docking bay K1C8J in twenty minutes."

That was fast. The matter must be pressing indeed. He'd need to hustle.

"That works for me. I look forward to meeting you and the Senator shortly."

"As do we, Mr. Madrid. We'll see you soon." With that, Sloan cut the connection.

Brad's eyebrows rose. Hardly anything made a professional bureaucrat get right to the point. It must be really serious.

––––––––

When Brad left the shuttle at the dock on Node One, he found Sloan waiting for him.

"Mr. Madrid," the man said, gesturing toward an exit from the gallery. "This way, please."

Brad inclined his head and followed.

As they moved through the sparse crowd, Brad picked out four casually dressed men keeping pace with them. Once he knew where to look, his trained eye spotted the signs of concealed body armor and firearms.

Which was a puzzle in and of itself. Even the most paranoid senator wasn't likely to send more than one guard with an aide to pick up a mercenary. Something was definitely up.

Sloan led him out of the gallery and into the corridors of the station. Brad expected them to take a fixed-route transit car, but instead he found one of the more flexible corridor cars waiting for them.

The car was unmarked, but that wasn't exactly good security. There were only a handful of corridor cars that served as anything other than taxis, and the Yard government owned most of them.

The four bodyguards followed Brad and Sloan into the vehicle. One of them sat at the controls and the vehicle gently slid into motion.

"I apologize for my brusqueness, Mr. Madrid," Sloan said tiredly. "The Senator wishes to explain the situation to you himself, and we're short on time."

The next few minutes passed in silence before the car slid to a gentle stop. The guards opened the doors and exited, but Sloan raised a hand, preventing Brad from leaving as the men surveyed the area.

Once they'd done so and stepped away from the car, Sloan gestured for Brad to leave the vehicle.

Brad couldn't imagine what threats the men were worried about. A dozen men in full body armor with battle rifles at the ready scanned the promenade outside the hotel Sloan had brought him to.

A trio of Commonwealth Marines in even more extensive body armor had set up a security post—complete with a flechette cannon— at the door and were checking all entries. It was by far the most blatant and extensive security Brad had ever seen at a civilian hotel.

Sloan quickly led Brad forward, ignoring the protests from the short line of people trying to get in, and flashed an ID portfolio. The corporal leading the Marines gestured for one of his men to take over and pulled Brad and Sloan aside.

As soon as they were out of sight of the crowd, he spoke. "You're both expected, but I must insist you surrender your weapons, Commodore."

Considering that Brad had only notified the Mercenary Guild of his new rank a few hours before, the man was very well informed.

Brad nodded, unhitched his weapons belt, and handed it to the Marine.

The corporal pulled out a scanner. "No offense, Commodore, Mr. Sloan, but I have to scan you both."

Brad submitted without a complaint. Sloan was grumpier but seemed to accept the necessity. As the Marine stepped back with Brad's weapons belt slung over his shoulder, he gestured them inside.

Two of the guards who'd met them at the spaceport followed them to the lift on the far side of the lobby. The other two were already holding the doors open. All four crowded inside with Brad and Sloan.

"I'd apologize for the security," the aide said as he punched the button for the top floor, "but it's necessary. As I said, the Senator will explain."

Moments later, the lift doors slid open again, revealing another trio of Marines. No flechette cannon this time, which was a good thing, considering the carnage one of the heavy weapons would cause if fired inside the building.

Sloan produced his ID folio again and the Marines passed them on.

He led Brad down a hallway to a door flanked by two more Marines, where he stopped.

"The Senator is expecting you."

Brad nodded his thanks, opened the door, and went inside.

The room was done in tones of dark red and black, with the furnishings clearly on the high end of the luxury scale. Though designed to seat two dozen people, the conference table held only a single man: Senator William Barnes.

His skin was a deep mahogany, resembling old leather more than anything else. His hair was short-cropped in a style that seemed vaguely military and nearly matched the skin in its shade.

Brad cleared his throat and the man raised his gaze to meet his eyes. "Senator Barnes."

"Commodore Madrid," Barnes replied, his voice vaguely scratchy. "Thank you for being so prompt. Please sit."

Once Brad had settled into a chair near the man, he continued. "Governor Johnson tells me that you're the best in your business."

"Not *the* best, I'm afraid," Brad said, "but certainly *one* of the best, yes."

Barnes nodded slowly. "You noted the security around the building? We requested the news media keep the story under wraps for at least twenty-four hours. To my great shock, they seem to actually be doing it."

He laid his hands on the table. "The reason for the security is simple. After the charity banquet last night, a team of assassins tried to kill me."

Brad was shocked that he hadn't heard something. That was bigger than big. Normally, the media would be screaming their fool heads off.

"I'm pleased to see that you survived," Brad said.

"I might have lived, but four Marines didn't. None of the assassins escaped, so we have no idea who hired them."

"And you want me to identify their employer? Wouldn't that be something best handled by the Commonwealth Investigative Agency? They're frightfully competent."

The man shook his head, sagging a little. "No. It appears the assassination attempt was a cover. While my guards were stopping the attackers, my daughter Josephine was unguarded. In that handful of minutes, she vanished."

He clenched his hands into fists and slammed them down onto the table. "Someone has kidnapped my daughter and disappeared. Fleet can do nothing without a target. The investigators are working feverishly, but I'm afraid this is something more serious than they know. I think it's the Cadre."

The Terror had tried to do something similar with Governor Johnson's son three years before, so that certainly wasn't out of the question.

"I'd still imagine that the authorities are the best resource to go after them," Brad said after a long moment. "If they don't know where your daughter has gone, then I won't have much better luck in finding her."

The Senator shook his head. "They'll find out how the bastards got my daughter out of the Yard soon, I'm sure. And I have no doubt she's already gone. Fleet can't be everywhere at once and still protect this system. They'll try to find Josephine, but that's not their priority.

"No, if I want to have someone looking full-time for my daughter, I must hire them myself. I need someone who will take the information the investigators find and pursue these bastards unrelentingly."

He sagged farther. "If it was only money, I'd pay. I'm a wealthy man and I'd trade it all for my daughter. Only, I'm sure this isn't about money. They want to force me into doing something for them, and they'll threaten my daughter unless I do it. I don't want to have to choose between the Commonwealth and my daughter."

The last was tinged with the bitter rage of an impotent man.

"I understand, Senator," Brad said gently.

"I hope you do. I want my Josephine back and I want her kidnappers dead. I understand you have a...preference for missions such as these."

Brad met the Senator's gaze and nodded. "I do. However, as much as I'm willing—even eager—to help you, there are unfortunate realities we must deal with. It might not be possible for me to find who did this and make them pay. The Cadre is powerful and no one knows where they have their major bases."

"I'll pay double your standard fee for as long as it takes," the Senator said flatly. "And double that again if you bring my daughter back unharmed. This contract runs until you find her or I give up hope. Is that sufficient for your 'unfortunate realities,' Commodore?"

Brad bared his teeth. "I think those bastards are going to regret this, Senator. I'll head back to my office and start getting my people in order. I need everything you have about the attackers and your daughter."

"I'll have Sloan send it via courier within the hour. Thank you, Commodore. Please, save my little girl."

———

The Vikings' analysts were waiting for him when he returned to the office. He'd called ahead to make sure they had the little information he knew. Time was critical.

He began snapping orders as soon as he opened the door. "Sarah, contact our people. I want them aboard *Heart* in two hours. Sooner, if possible."

She nodded and picked up her com.

"I want a complete listing of every ship that has left the Io Yards in the last fifteen hours," he told their lead analyst, Cory Delbruck. "I want names, capacities, where they were officially headed, and where the Yard's sensors say they were *really* headed. Clear?"

The analyst nodded his assent and darted for his office.

Brad turned to their second analyst, Kelly Mestiphor. "I want you to get into Yard security. They should've been conducting a search for a single young female with an unknown number of companions, probably masked.

"I want to know if they've found anything and where the group went. Match that with Cory's ship list and give me a probability breakdown of which ship they probably took."

She turned toward her office but stopped. "What's the contract, sir?"

"Someone kidnapped Senator Barnes's daughter. We've been hired to get her back and terminate the kidnappers. We should have a courier packet within the hour detailing everything, but I want to get a jump on this if we can."

The woman nodded. "I'm on it."

Brad crossed to his own office. He'd expedite getting *Heart* clear of the yards, just in case they had a target to pursue.

———

An hour later, they gathered again in the front office. The data packet was supposed to arrive momentarily, but he'd use the time to get an update from his people.

"Four ships departed the Io Yards in the timeframe you specified," Cory said as they crowded around the reception desk. "Two were bulk freighters headed to the trojan clusters, one was a gas tanker headed for Blackhawk Station, and the last was a liner also headed for Blackhawk."

"Nothing else?"

"Nothing else," the analyst confirmed. "Sensors say the bulk freighters are heading exactly where they said they were going, too. It's conceivable that they used some kind of local small craft to move the girl elsewhere in the Jovian planetary system. There are a lot of possibilities to check out. It'll take time. Maybe the kidnappers are still in the Yard."

"That's what security thinks, too," Kelly said.

"Does security have any hard evidence to back up their theory?"

"Not really. They're doing what I was trying to do and failing miserably. Do you have any idea how many teenage females wander around the yards at night? Isolating the right one in all that is almost impossible. They may succeed eventually, but I have my doubts."

"Did the freighters leave together?" he asked Cory.

"Yeah. They belong to Sostara Shipping. It's a small, independent line that does a roundabout run through the trojans, selling luxury supplies and picking up ore to sell to the refineries here."

Brad considered them an unlikely getaway probability but hesitated to dismiss the possibility. If he chose the wrong ship to chase, the kidnappers would get away.

"I don't think they could—or would—have stowed away on that sort of flight," he said at last. "Is security checking with them?"

The door opened and a young man in a brightly colored shirt over knee-length shorts came in. One of the mercenary security troops stood beside him, a scanner still pointed mostly in the direction of the envelope the courier was carrying. The trooper flashed a thumbs-up before letting the man into the room.

"Package for Brad Madrid."

"That's me," Brad said as he extended his hand.

The boy handed him a thumb reader. "Print, please."

Irritated at the momentary delay, Brad pressed his thumb to the reader and grunted when the light turned green.

The boy handed him the package. "Have a great day."

Brad opened the packet, ready to hand the data to his analysts but stopped. There was a picture of an attractive redheaded teenager on top. He handed it to Kelly.

"Go back over every bit of footage you can get from security. Find her."

———

In the end, it took three days to determine how the kidnappers had gotten Josephine Barnes out of the yards. They'd walked her right aboard the liner heading for Blackhawk Station in a brazen daylight escape. Mixed in with the other passengers, no one had thought her unusual, though the young woman had undoubtedly been drugged to ensure her docility and compliance.

Sure, they'd taken the precaution of dyeing her hair and doing something to her face to stymie facial recognition, but it was inexcusable that no one from Io Yard Security had spotted her. In fact, they still hadn't.

Kelly had spent the last seventy hours virtually living at her desk, playing all the feeds she'd gotten from security at double speed, looking for anything that stood out. Her sharp eyes had caught what the computers had missed. She'd be getting a big bonus for this one.

Brad did some quick calculations. The liner would beat them to

Blackhawk Station, even at *Heart*'s best speed. It wouldn't be by much, but they couldn't intercept the liner in space.

Calling the ship and letting them know Josephine Barnes was aboard was a risk he wasn't prepared to take, though. Drunks in the lounge were more their security staff's speed. The kidnappers had killed four heavily armed Marines and almost gotten Senator Barnes. It was far too dangerous to allow amateurs to try a rescue.

The same was true of Blackhawk Security. It was a company station. They didn't deal with killers like this. He'd have to get the Vikings there as quickly as possible and do it himself.

Of course, he could call Fleet and let them know, but then he wouldn't complete his contract. He suspected the Senator would pay him anyway, but he didn't know what ships Fleet had in the area.

He knew his own people, though. He trusted them more in this kind of situation.

Odds were that Blackhawk was a transfer location in any case. If *Heart* could get there fast enough, he could catch them in transit and free the girl. If he counted on Fleet, they might miss the departure and lose the girl for good.

That was unacceptable.

Decision made, he tapped his console and called *Heart*. Shelly answered immediately.

"I'm on my way," he said. "We've found her."

CHAPTER SIX

Brad's thought on first seeing Blackhawk Station several years earlier was that it looked crude and unfinished. The intervening time hadn't improved matters.

He wondered if Michelle was still somewhere on it, or had she already taken her dive ship down to the gas giant?

As tempted as he was to indulge himself in considering that, he forced his mind back to the task at hand. He could see about a surprise visit after they saved Josephine Barnes.

Blackhawk Station was a single sphere, sparkling with scattered lights, forming the center of an immense set of girders. Those served to link the docking ports, storage tanks, and fueling stations.

Unlike the Io Yards, the girders on Blackhawk were an open skeleton. Tiny personnel pods gleamed in the dim light reflected off Saturn, flitting between the central core and the assorted auxiliary platforms through the open construction.

As *Heart*'s passive scanners began to trawl information from those platforms, Brad noted thirty of them were forts. He'd spotted them on previous trips but gave them more of his attention this time around.

Each outgunned *Heart of Vengeance* twice over. Combined, they had enough firepower to fight off a cruiser squadron. Out here where the

Cadre was a real threat, that kind of protection was mandatory. Fleet was a long way off if trouble came calling.

He noted that the platforms were tracking *Heart*. All of them. Talk about overkill.

"Paranoid buggers, aren't they?" he observed dryly.

"Very," Shelly snorted. "Their local space control seems to be running around like a bunch of chickens with their heads chopped off —they can't figure out what to do with a warship, even one our size. And we've been here before. I can only imagine what they'd do for an unknown ship."

"Flash them a copy of Senator Barnes's authorization and we'll see what they make of it."

One of the things Barnes had given Brad was a blanket authorization stating they were acting under his authority. Mercs rarely saw something like that. Contracts normally covered authorization for lethal force and such, but rarely a complete authorization.

A minute or so after transmitting the authorization, Shelly gave Brad the expected thumbs-up. "They're letting us in. Bay A6."

"John?"

"On it." A moment later, he whistled. "Sweet. They've put us on the core itself."

"Take us in. Shelly, as soon as we dock, I want you to jack us into the computer net. We need to find these bastards."

"I had a thought about that," Jason said hesitantly.

"Oh?" Brad inquired, turning to face his second officer. "Tell me more."

"Well, you're talking about hacking into their security files, right? Why don't we just use the authorization the Senator gave us and *ask* Blackhawk Security for the data we need?"

Brad stared at Jason for a moment and then laughed. "I'm so used to doing this the hard way that it didn't even occur to me to be above-board. Never mind, Shelly. I think I'm going to be paying their security chief a visit."

———

The front office for Blackhawk Security Central consisted of a tiny room with one desk and a young man in body armor.

While the body armor suggested a reasonably high level of preparedness on the security trooper's part, the fact that his mono-blade was being used as a paperweight and his assault shotgun was leaned against the far wall suggested otherwise.

Brad finished his quick survey of the room and stepped up to the desk. Marshal stayed back a few steps.

"I'm here to see your boss," he told the trooper.

The young man looked up at him disinterestedly. "Chief Raine is busy. He might be able to fit you in. Tomorrow."

"Since you have no idea who I am or why I'm here, maybe you'd best double-check. It's important and I'm going to stay right here until he can fit me in."

The trooper sighed. "Names?"

"Commodore Madrid of *Heart of Vengeance*. This is my executive officer, Commander John Marshal."

"Business?" the trooper asked, clearly stalling for time.

"Is with the chief," Brad said bluntly. "Now, are you going to call him or not?"

The trooper started to snarl something but then thought better of it and picked up a headset. He murmured into the mic and listened to the response. With a scowl, he removed the headset.

"He'll see you. First door on the right."

Brad nodded and then forgot the man. He led the way down the hall and into the indicated room.

Chief Raine was one of those rarest of physical types among spacers: a bulky man. Where most spacers tended towards tall and wiry, the chief couldn't have been much over a hundred and fifty centimeters tall and was almost as broad across the shoulders.

Like the trooper outside, he wore light body armor. Unlike the boy, his blade was belted to his waist and his shotgun leaned against his desk, out of the way but easily within reach.

"What the fuck do you want?" he said, his calm tone at odds with his swearing.

"Your help," Brad replied with a small smile.

"And tell me, 'Commodore' Madrid, just why I should be helping a two-for-a-penny ragtag merc like yourself."

Brad calmly stepped across the room and faced the chief across his desk.

"Three reasons, Mr. Raine," he said, intentionally omitting the man's title. "Firstly, I'm a platinum-rated officer with the Mercenary Guild and a holder of the Commonwealth Black Star. I'm hardly a 'two-for-a-penny ragtag merc.'"

The chief's eyes widened in surprise. The Black Star was one of the few decorations Fleet awarded nonmilitary personnel—and it was the highest. Varieties of stars could be earned for everything from saving lives to capturing criminals, but the Black Star was awarded solely to people responsible for saving either a Fleet warship or at least a thousand lives in a single incident.

What Brad rarely bothered to mention was that he actually held two Black Stars—one for each reason it could be given.

"Secondly," he continued, "the life of a kidnapped woman is riding on the line. Someone valuable to an important man.

"Third, well. Read this."

He handed a pad, containing a copy of Senator Barnes's authorization, to Raine.

The man scanned it several times. When he finally laid the pad down, most of his cold hostility seemed to have faded.

"I see, Commodore Madrid." This time, the title lacked the heavy irony he'd originally used. "What exactly do you want?"

"Check the other file on the pad."

Raine did so and looked at the picture. "Who is this?"

"Josephine Barnes. The man with her is presumably one of her kidnappers, as he was certainly the man who escorted her aboard the liner from Io Yards. I need to know who he is, if they got off the liner, and where they are now."

"I believe I begin to understand your authorization. I'll see what my people can do."

"Quickly, Chief Raine. I have no idea what her kidnappers' objectives are, and I don't want to leave her in their hands one moment longer than I have to."

"We'll do our best," Raine said grimly. "I promise you that."

————

Barely an hour later, Raine contacted Brad aboard *Heart*.

"We've got them," he said bluntly as soon as his image came up on the main screen. "The man was listed on the liner's passenger manifest as Brian Abernathy. He got off with Ms. Barnes and four other people we're still identifying. That's probably less important, as we have a pretty good idea where they went."

The security chief grinned. "He obviously thought one pseudonym was enough, because a man using the same name rented one of the warehouse platforms."

"Which one?"

Raine reeled off a number, which Brad made note of. "I think I have a slight surprise for Mr. Abernathy."

"Wait," Raine told him. "He has a ship docked there. I don't know if it's armed, but given the situation, I wouldn't bet against it. Also, you'll need my people to get onto the platform."

"Unfortunately, Chief, your first point invalidates your second," Brad said gently. "If I take *Heart* in, I can disable the ship and board the platform—*Heart*'s stealth abilities might surprise you. However, if your people come along, the extra ships would draw attention."

Raine grimaced. "I don't like it, but you have a point. You still need one of my people to override the lockouts on the airlocks."

Brad was tempted to argue, but he *did* need the codes. Otherwise, they'd have to come in hot, and that posed a serious risk to Josephine Barnes.

"Whoever you're sending has twenty minutes to get aboard my ship or I leave without him."

"He'll be there in ten," Raine promised.

————

Nine minutes later, one of Saburo's troopers called up to the bridge. "We've got a security officer here, boss. Says his name is Lieutenant Champion."

"Have you checked with Raine?" Brad asked.

"Of course. His ID checks out."

"Send him up and clear the lock."

He turned his attention to Marshal. "Go."

"Undocking now."

The ship shuddered slightly as it undocked.

"We're maneuvering," Marshal said. "And we're clear."

"All right, Jason," Brad told his tactical officer. "Make us invisible."

Jason grinned and hit a key on his computer.

The ship was now spreading its electronic and heat signature over nearly ten times its own volume. By doing so, the signature was reduced below minimum detection values on most scanners.

"Done."

"Get us to the target platform, John."

An armored security officer entered the bridge with two of Saburo's men at his heels. "Lieutenant Leo Champion, Blackhawk Security, Commodore."

"Welcome aboard, Lieutenant. We've got about ten minutes before anything exciting happens. Take a seat."

"Thank you, sir," the officer replied before proceeding to carefully fit his lanky form into a spare acceleration couch.

Brad turned back to Jason. "We should be clear of the core. Can you get me a passive scan of the ship?"

For a few moments, silence reigned on *Heart*'s bridge as Jason played with his console. "Looks like a small tramp freighter. The kind that normally operates in the Belt. I'm not seeing any heavy weaponry, but I can't be sure unless I go active."

"Can you disable his engines without exposing the crew decks to vacuum?"

Jason regarded his console for a moment, then nodded. "Probably, but I'd rather get much closer to be absolutely sure."

"Lock in the mass driver, but stand by for my order."

He turned to Marshal. "What's our ETA, John?"

"Five minutes at this speed," the pilot told him without turning his head. Marshal had locked his hands onto the joystick primary controller and was carefully guiding the ship through the girder work of the station.

Brad glanced over at Champion and the troopers who'd escorted him up. All were in full body armor.

"I need to get into my armor. Give me four minutes."

He crossed to the tiny office next to the bridge. Once inside, getting his armor on was quick and simple, even in the claustrophobic space. He made it back onto the bridge in three minutes with his helmet under his arm.

"Current ETA?" he asked, standing beside his chair.

"Ninety seconds," Marshal said.

Brad regarded the screen for a moment. "Lieutenant Champion, join Major Saburo and his men in the boarding bay and stand by to transmit your codes, please. I'll be with you momentarily."

Champion nodded and scooted out of the bridge, his escorts right behind him.

"All right, Jason," Brad said quietly. "Activate your fire plan at thirty seconds from boarding. Do your best not to hull the crew spaces, but stop that ship."

Not waiting for a response, Brad strode out of the bridge and headed for the boarding bay. It was time to save a young woman's life.

CHAPTER SEVEN

BRAD REACHED the boarding bay in good time. Lieutenant Champion had joined Saburo and the rest of *Heart*'s squad in the chamber, which was effectively a giant airlock.

Saburo saw him coming and gave him a thumbs-up gesture, signifying that the squad was ready to move.

Brad activated his com. "All right, Jason, how are we sitting?"

"The transport is dead in the water," Jason reported, his voice pleased. "Her drives have a nice hole through the middle of the pulse chambers. We're swinging in on the main airlock and should be docking about…now."

Heart jolted a bit as she docked.

"All right, Lieutenant Champion," Brad said. "Get us in."

The security officer typed a series of commands into the computer on his forearm. A moment later, he looked up and nodded. "Done."

"We're going in, Jason," Brad said. "Be ready if we come back in a hurry. All right, folks, let's roll."

A command from Brad's computer started the boarding bay door opening. Simultaneously, the airlock on the other side opened as well.

Saburo gestured his men forward, and three of them, assault shotguns at the ready, darted into the lock. Moments later, one of them waved the all-clear.

Brad led the rest of the squad and Champion forward. The security officer looked around, checking that everyone was in, then typed another series of commands into his wrist-comp.

"Be ready," Brad ordered as the airlock began to slowly cycle.

As if to prove his words, a shotgun fired as the door passed the halfway point, blasting flechettes into the enclosed space. Fortunately, the shooter hadn't taken the time to aim, and the razor-edged darts hit an empty wall.

Brad felt several of the darts bounce off his back armor as he lunged forward. The masked man tried to bring his shotgun to bear, but Brad met it with his now-activated mono-blade in mid-swing.

The end of the barrel and part of the action went flying into the depths of the platform as a blast of flechettes from one of *Heart's* troopers nailed the kidnapper in the chest.

From the ensuing mess, Brad judged the man had been completely unarmored.

He glanced around the loading bay they found themselves in, and then turned to his squad.

"Saburo, take four men and secure the transport. If you find Ms. Barnes or any evidence that she's aboard, let me know."

Saburo gestured at the mercenary troopers. "James, Duncan, Ciro, and Rafi, with me. Good luck, Commodore.

"Same to you." Brad turned to the remaining three troopers and Champion. "That leaves the platform for us. Lieutenant, as you have the security codes, lead the way."

The security trooper nodded, pulled up a map, and headed off at a run. Brad and the rest of the mercenaries did their best to keep up.

They only made it a few corridors from the lock before a grenade came bouncing around the corner. Brad's respect for Blackhawk Security's training went up a notch as Champion immediately lunged forward with his mono-blade and neatly sliced the weapon in half.

As the halves rolled apart, a trio of men with blades and pistols out came around the corner. Champion jerked his blade into place to stop the first series of attacks as Brad and the troopers rushed forward to help.

One of the men shot the security officer in the stomach, sending him crumpling to the deck.

Brad's flashing mono-blade removed the man's arm and sliced deep into his chest just a moment too late. As the man stumbled back, coughing blood, Brad spun to face the other two just as his people took them both out with shotgun blasts.

He checked Champion, but it was too late. He was already dead.

————

Cursing, Brad raised his wrist-comp to his face. "Saburo, report."

"We've secured the tube to the transport," the Major replied. "I'm leaving two men here and moving in. You?"

"Champion is dead," Brad told him flatly. "Proceed as planned. Madrid out."

"Let's finish this," he told the troopers coldly.

The three led the way down the corridor, shotguns leveled and sweeping back and forth. When they reached a corner, one of them stepped forward, extending his weapon around the bend.

"Clear," the man said.

There was a security door around the corner and at the end of the short corridor. Brad brought up the map of the platform again and nodded to himself. This was the most likely location for the kidnapper and his victim.

Brad examined the door as the troopers covered him. By the lights on its control panel, it was locked. That was going to complicate things now that Champion was gone, but they'd brought the tools to get in. It would just take time.

To his surprise, the door chose that moment to slide open.

"Welcome," a cold voice said from inside. "I've been expecting you."

Brad considered how he'd use these circumstances to spring an ambush. And how he'd counter one.

"I wouldn't try anything hasty if I were you," the voice continued. "Your lovely prize here might become less lovely if you do."

Deciding to take the risk, Brad stepped through the door, immediately spotting a pair of figures in the middle of the bare room. The masked man who was speaking held a long-bladed knife to Josephine Barnes's throat. She was tied up and sitting in a chair.

"In fact, to prevent undue hastiness," the man said, "you'd best lay down your weapons. Now."

"Do it," Brad ordered his men. He deactivated his mono-blade and dropped it to the floor. At the man's gesture, he added his pistol to it. That still left him with a concealed pistol at the small of his back.

"Now, come in," the man said. "Let me see the brave mercenaries who've come to rescue our damsel in distress."

Brad gestured his men forward, and the three of them slowly drifted forward to flank him. They'd dropped their obvious weapons in the hall, but he knew they'd have more secreted about their persons.

"You're good, whoever you are," the man complimented them. "I'd assumed our isolation would more than suffice to prevent any attack on us. You handled my people on the platform quite efficiently."

Brad said nothing, watching the man, waiting for an opportunity. He seemed to be enjoying himself. If he let his guard down for one second…

"The silent type, eh?" the man observed. "It won't do you much good."

He dragged Josephine up from the chair. Her eyes were dull and she seemed slack. Drugged again, most likely.

"What do you want?" Brad demanded softly.

"You seem to have broken my ship," the kidnapper observed. "I'll want a new one, clear passage out of the Saturn planetary system, and a guarantee that no one will follow us."

"I can't order that."

"I'd suggest you'd best get on the com and talk to someone who can, mercenary," the kidnapper said sharply. "If I don't get what I want, I may have to start removing important parts of the Senator's daughter. I'd imagine her value goes down if she comes back in pieces."

Brad regarded the man coldly. "If you start hurting her, your leverage goes out the window."

"Actually, no," the kidnapper disagreed with a grin. "It only disappears if I kill her, which I don't plan to do. I have so many better uses for her than that."

As if to demonstrate his "better plans," the man ran his tongue up the side of the girl's neck. For half a moment, he took his eyes off Brad.

It was enough. Brad drew the hidden pistol and brought it up.

The man snapped "Drop it or the girl—"

Whatever else he was planning to say was lost in the sharp *hiss-crack* of the ten-millimeter automatic. Long before the kidnapper could react, the heavy slug smashed through his forehead and into his brain. He dropped like a puppet with its strings cut, his knife clattering to the floor.

Even before the man's body hit the floor, Brad lunged across the room to catch Josephine Barnes as she began to slump. He carefully lowered her to the floor. She had a nick from the blade, but was otherwise unharmed.

"It's all right," he murmured. "You're safe now."

She seemed to hear him, even through her drug-induced haze. Her tense muscles relaxed.

Brad used the knife the kidnapper had dropped to carefully cut her bonds. A moment later, she wrapped her arms around herself, turning away from the blood-spattered corpse of her kidnapper and sobbing.

"Trista," Brad said softly, stepping back.

The female mercenary officer removed her helmet and knelt next to the girl, cradling her head. She looked up at Brad and nodded, accepting responsibility for Josephine Barnes.

"Guard the door," Brad said. "We don't want to get caught by surprise."

After they stepped out, he picked up his blade, holstered it, and called Saburo. "We have the girl. What's your status?"

Saburo's voice came back rather breathless. "I think we underestimated the crew aboard this thing. I haven't lost anyone, but Rafi's wounded and we can't seem to press them further."

"I'll call Raine. He's got the manpower to drag them out."

"Understood, sir."

Brad used *Heart*'s com system and called Raine.

"Chief, it's Madrid," he said quietly. "I have mixed news, I'm afraid."

A sigh came over the link. "The news is always mixed, Commodore. Give it to me."

"Lieutenant Champion is dead."

"How?"

"They tried to grenade us," Brad said flatly. "He lunged too far forward to disable it and was isolated when three of the bastards followed it up."

The other man sighed. "Well, shit. What's the rest of the news?"

"The transport is disabled but is heavily defended. It seems to have a good-sized crew aboard. On the positive side, we have Ms. Barnes. We're withdrawing to our ship. She seems physically unhurt."

"I see. I presume you called requesting backup. I thought you had this all covered."

"If you don't have at least one shuttle full of troops ready to go, I've completely misjudged you," Brad said matter-of-factly.

"I have two and can have them at the platform in ten minutes."

"At which point," Brad told him, "I'll happily turn over responsibility for this nest of scum to you."

"And I will deal with them," Raine said, his voice as hard as steel.

CHAPTER EIGHT

MORE THAN A WEEK LATER, Brad stood in Blackhawk Station's departure lounge and watched his people escort Josephine Barnes to her ride home.

He'd been overruled about taking her home himself by several people. Firstly, the doctor on the station felt the young woman needed treatment that she wouldn't get on *Heart*. She'd been through a lot and Brad could see how fragile she was, even though she put on a good face.

Secondly, Fleet had dispatched a trio of corvettes to see her safely back to her father. Since she had been staying there until she was stable enough to be moved, that didn't really hurt anything.

And it had allowed him several clandestine meetings with Michelle. That was a great third reason that he hadn't felt like sharing with anyone else.

Surprisingly, there was a medium-sized crowd gathered to watch the Senator's daughter leave for the Jupiter planetary system. His people had an eye on them, so Brad wasn't particularly worried.

Trista was at point on the four-man security team. The others had spread out into a diamond around their charge as they escorted her to the Fleet corvette that had docked to receive her.

He came to a halt as they arrived at the boarding tube. Inside, he could see the Lieutenant Commander he'd spoken with this morning and two female Marines waiting to receive her. Their doctor hovered behind them.

Three of the mercenaries split off and formed a perimeter as Brad stepped up to Josephine Barnes.

"I know that we haven't known one another for very long, but I'm very happy to see you doing so well," he said. "I know your father won't be able to sleep until he has you safely home. I regret the circumstances of our meeting, but I hope you don't regret the meeting itself."

"I don't," she said in a soft soprano as she stepped in to hug him. "Thank you."

"It's been our pleasure. Have a safe and quiet trip home, Miss Barnes."

With a small wave, Josephine stepped on board the warship. A moment later, the tube closed behind her.

"Do you think she's ever going to recover?" he asked Trista softly as they headed back to *Heart*.

The woman shook her head. "Not really, but she'll come out the other side a stronger person, if I'm reading her right. The only casualty will have been her innocence."

Brad considered that as they walked and nodded slowly. It wasn't really that different from his own life. His rebirth might have been bloodier, but hers had a more intense personal pain to overcome.

She'd do it, he decided at last. Josephine Barnes was stronger than she looked. There was steel inside her that other people couldn't see. She might not be fine for a long time, but she'd reforge her life in ways no one would be able to predict. She was a survivor.

———

When Brad got back to *Heart*, Shelly intercepted him before he could vanish into his cabin. "A transmission came in while you were out. Looks like a response to your last v-mail to the Senator."

"Thanks," he acknowledged. "Transfer it to my cabin."

She inclined her head and vanished onto the bridge.

Since his cabin was only a few meters away, he reached it in moments. He settled into his chair and found the message. He activated it and an image of Senator Barnes appeared.

"Commodore Madrid," the man greeted Brad warmly. "By now, my daughter should be safely in Fleet's hands. From the bottom of my heart I thank you. While I doubt anyone who isn't a father can understand the depths of the fear I've felt for the last few weeks, you've done more than I'd dared to hope. Thank you."

The Senator's face hardened. "I must also thank you for appending her physician's reports. As I expected, it's disturbing. If I ever find out who was behind these bastards, you'll have another contract. One with much more direct and violent goals."

Brad nodded in angry agreement. The bastards had clearly discovered Josephine Barnes was a virgin early on and had chosen not to change that.

That hadn't prevented them from raping her in everything but name. That she could still summon the courage and strength to hug him before boarding the ship taking her home impressed him deeply.

"To more immediate matters," the Senator continued. "I promised double your normal rate and double that if Josephine was returned unharmed. You managed to get her back more quickly than I'd feared, and kept her from even worse harm than she's already suffered.

"In light of the circumstances and due to the value of your services, I'm paying eight times your normal rate. And, as I've left you stranded at Saturn rather than allowing for the time to bring Josephine home, I'll double the time you've spent on this contract and add a bit.

"We'll call it six weeks at eight times your regular pay. Well, that's only forty-eight weeks, if we consider it as a lump sum. We'll make it equivalent to a full year's pay just to satisfy my sense of balance. I'd take it as a favor if that extra four weeks ended up being divided among your people as a sign of my gratitude."

Brad inhaled sharply. Even after distributing the bonus to his crew, that amount of money could replace *Heart*. Well, make a sizable down payment on a base corvette hull, anyway. It could support the company, without them taking another contract, for a full year.

The Senator continued, his face serious and thoughtful. "You saved my daughter. That's a debt I can never repay with money. If I or mine can ever serve you or yours with treasure or blood, you need only ask."

Barnes raised his hand in a gesture of goodwill. "May the Everlit guide you and keep you, Commodore. We'll speak again in the future, I'm sure. Farewell."

———

Brad glanced around the conference table in *Heart*'s cramped wardroom. "All right, people, down to business. As of ten minutes ago, the payment for this mission was transferred into our accounts on Io. The Senator doubled the amount of time we spent on the contract and paid eight times the customary rate for a platinum-rated company.

"He also added an additional four weeks' normal pay to be distributed to all of our people. I'm sure each of you can come up with something worthy of that kind of spending money."

He grinned as signs of shock and pleasure appeared on everyone's faces. "This is obviously far more than we were originally promised. As you might imagine, this makes a major difference in our planned operations for the next few months.

"The most significant change is that we can now refrain from active operations until our new ship is fully commissioned, crewed, and worked up.

"Secondly, due to your excellent performance on this contract, I've decided to release you all for R&R for three weeks."

It took a moment to sink in. Everyone looked pleased, except for Jason. He was shooting Brad a dubious look.

"On Blackhawk?" the tactical officer asked.

"I see no reason to delay your well-deserved vacation until we return to Io," Brad said with a perfectly straight face.

"In other words, we're being stranded on this isolated outpost so you can see your girlfriend," Randall said.

Everyone stared at their engineer.

"Oh, don't think you were *that* discreet," the burly engineer assured him. "I saw you two a few days ago. She's a diver here, right? What was her name? Marilyn?"

"Michelle!" Shelly crowed, surging to her feet. "You and Michelle? Woooo!!!"

"And this is why I didn't say anything," Brad said dryly. "Yes, I am seeing Michelle."

"That settles it," Shelly told the engineer sternly. "Blackhawk it is. Besides, they might not have heard about your poker skills here."

Randall perked up. "That's true. It might not be a total waste of time after all."

Brad found himself smiling. "I'll admit my motives might not be entirely professional, but there are solid reasons other than my personal gratification. Senator Barnes said that if anyone identified the people behind the kidnapping, he'd have a direct-action contract for us."

That made them all smile coldly.

"Then it makes perfect business sense," Jason said. "If we can get a lead on the backers—if there are any we missed killing—before we leave Blackhawk, we'll save weeks of travel time. Maybe even a month or more, depending on where *Heart* needs to go."

Marshal glanced around the table. "I think I speak for all of us when I say that being on Blackhawk doesn't bother us that much under those circumstances."

"Good," Brad said with a smile. "Let's set up a standby watch and get to it, shall we?"

The console screen on Brad's desk swirled with the shifting colors that were supposed to relax the viewer. He regarded it with an amused glance. It never seemed to relax him. His current tranquil state had nothing to do with any screensaver.

Michelle's diver was due back in about four hours. She thought he'd be gone by now, so he couldn't wait to give her the good news.

He got up to make a cup of coffee, but his console chimed with tones indicating an in-ship call before he'd taken two steps.

A white-faced Shelly appeared in the screen when he accepted the call. When she saw him, she visibly relaxed.

"Thank the Everlit you're up," she said quickly. "We've got a problem."

"What sort of problem?" he demanded, his relaxation of moments before vanishing in an instant.

"I was running a sensor sweep—primarily passive—of the space around Blackhawk. Mainly, I was looking for Michelle's ship, to see when she was going to be back."

"I assume you found something other than her diver."

"I found her, but I found something else, too. Look at this."

His communication officer's image vanished and was replaced by a raw data dump from their infrared scanner—the longest-ranged sensor *Heart* carried. It showed an attack fleet of nearly sixty spaceships headed their way.

CHAPTER NINE

I_T ONLY TOOK_ Brad a few moments to reach _Heart's_ bridge. "What have you got?"

"I've refined the data," Shelly said. "I'm waiting for Jason to get here and double-check it, but we're definitely looking at a minimum of sixty ships. Possibly as many as seventy.

"It's not all bad news, though. I don't think there is anything heavier than a destroyer in that pack. The station should be able to handle them with their weapons platforms."

Shelly highlighted a group of eight signatures at the front of the fleet. "These ships are giving off significant power densities. I'm guessing they're Fleet-style interceptor frigates."

"Shit," Brad swore succinctly. Interceptor frigates could easily pull twenty—maybe even thirty—meters per second squared. That meant _Heart_ couldn't run from them.

"What else?" he asked.

"We've got at least ten transports. Probably a couple of hundred shock troops per, I'd guess. That means several thousand total. It looks like an attack fleet."

"This doesn't make sense," Brad muttered as he studied the icons on the screen. "That's a lot of firepower, but Blackhawk will eat them alive.

"Why in Darkness hasn't the station sounded an alarm?" he asked. "Get me Raine."

She turned away, her fingers flickering across her console. A moment later, Raine's image appeared on Brad's chair screen. He was dressed for duty and didn't seem at all disturbed about the incoming threat.

"Commodore Madrid. How can Blackhawk Security help you this very early morning?"

"What the fuck are you playing at?" Brad asked sharply.

Raine's eyes narrowed. "Would it help if I said I have no idea what you're talking about?"

"You mean you don't know about the attack fleet less than two hours from your outer defenses?"

"The what?" Raine demanded, sitting up abruptly.

"There is a fleet of sixty-plus ships approaching from around Saturn," Brad said. "How can you not know? You have active scanners running."

Raine's image turned away from the camera for a moment, looking at something, and then he turned back. "I don't know what sort of joke you're playing, Madrid, but our scanners are clear."

An icy-cold fist closed around Brad's heart. "Check the raw data."

"The what?"

"Oh, for Light's sake, check the Darkness-damned raw data!" Brad snarled.

Raine turned away again and manipulated his screen. Moments later, the blood drained from his face.

"Everlight," the man swore softly. "My own Dark-damned computers are lying to me."

He turned back to Brad, his face going red. "My apologies, Commodore. Thank you for the very timely warning. If you'll excuse me, I have to prep our defenses so that we can kick their asses."

"Understood, Chief. Madrid out."

Jason arrived just as the call ended.

"Blackhawk knows," he told the tactical officer softly. "But the fact that their scanners were hacked makes me wonder what else is wrong on that Dark-damned station. Get to work refining the data. Just in case, stay passive."

———

Ten minutes later, Brad was staring at Raine's image on the screen in horror. "All of the weapons platforms?" he demanded.

"There's a hard-coded lockdown command on all of them," Raine said grimly. "It's designed so that if one of the platforms is seized, we can keep it from firing on us. Someone sent the code to all the defense platforms. And they changed them, of course. I can't reactivate them."

Without those weapons platforms, Blackhawk was doomed.

"There's a Fleet cruiser group nearby," Raine said, his face drawn. "The Station Commandant is on the line with them right now. At best, they're eight hours out."

It would be an ugly fight if it came to that. Fleet might not win it.

"The pirates are less than two," Brad said. "How quickly could they reactivate the weapons platforms?"

"If they have the codes—which seems likely—they could have them online in twenty minutes once they take Security Central," Raine told him, his voice weary. "It can only be done from here. Just like only one of my people could've betrayed us."

"Then there's still a chance," Brad said fiercely, running through potential options.

"What do you mean?" Raine demanded, sitting up a little straighter.

"They have to capture your strongest area before Fleet gets here. If they don't, they'll probably have to run. We need to do everything we can to delay them. Can you disable the systems you'd use to reactivate the weapons platforms?"

"Yes, but it won't take very long for anyone who knows the system to cobble something together. At least it will at least add more time to the clock. I'll set it up, but I'm not going to blow the controls to the platforms unless they are about to take Central. It's always possible we can get back in."

From his tone, Brad suspected that outcome was unlikely.

"My ship and my people are at your disposal," Brad said. "Let's hope we can come out the other side alive."

He spent a few moments considering Michelle. She was down below, collecting He3. That process was always uncertain, so he'd just hope she didn't come back up before they'd driven the pirates off.

There was no way to communicate with her until she did. And if she came up at the wrong time, they'd kill her.

───────

Brad entered the bridge an hour later dressed in full armor, with his helmet tucked under his arm. Shelly was at the pilot's console.

"Where the Dark is Marshal?" Brad demanded as he took his seat.

"I don't know. He was off-ship last night and didn't come back. I've paged him a billion times but he never responded. Station security is too busy to search for him."

"Shit," Brad said succinctly. "Try this code."

He read off a series of numbers from memory and she entered them.

"What is that?" she asked.

"My override on his com. Even if he's turned it off, that code will set it off at max volume."

The communications console chimed with an incoming off-ship call moments later.

"Put it on my screen," Brad ordered, glaring at the small repeater as his pilot's image appeared. "Where in Darkness are you?"

"Residential six," Marshal said. "Did you have to set my beeper off like that? I met this little—"

"I don't care," Brad said, overriding his pilot. "Blackhawk is under attack. Can you get back aboard ship in ten minutes?"

Marshal gaped at him for a moment, and then shook his head as his officer brain apparently kicked in. "No. Res six is on the other side of the station from *Heart*."

"That'll teach you to turn off your beeper," Brad said grimly. "Meet us at Security Central. You just got drafted for grunt duty, Mr. Pilot."

"Understood," Marshal acknowledged with a sour expression. "Marshal out."

Brad turned to Jason and Shelly. "You two understand the plan?"

"Relocate to the cargo area," Shelly said. "Find some containers to snuggle up to and wait. They shouldn't spot us there if we activate stealth—even if someone on Blackhawk has told them to look for us."

Jason picked up where his girlfriend left off. "If they take control of the weapons platforms, we maintain position and wait for you and the crew. If you can get off, we'll try to slip away. If not, we'll improvise."

He shook his head. "That's not the plan and you know it. If we can't make it back, you slip away without us."

The tactical officer grinned. "You have to survive to enforce that order, sir. We're not going anywhere without you."

He sighed. "Try to keep my ship in one piece. Let's do this."

———

When Brad, Saburo, and his squad reached Security Central, they found Marshal waiting for them. He'd managed to get a set of Security armor and had an auto-shotgun very similar to the kind the Vikings used hanging from his shoulder.

He saluted. "Grunt Marshal reporting for duty, Commodore."

"You talked them into outfitting you. Good."

"They're handing out armor and guns to anyone who turns up and asks for them," Marshal said with a shrug.

"We have more armor and guns than we have people that can use them," the security chief said as he walked up. "I sent out a call for any combat-trained personnel. If you ask for a gun, I'm presuming you're capable of fighting, so you get one."

He shrugged fatalistically. "Some of them are likely working for the pirates, but a handful of extra hostiles are meaningless against any increase in my own strength."

"What's their ETA?" Brad asked.

"Less than twenty minutes," Raine said grimly. "The interceptor frigates split off from the main force and are blasting after the ships that tried to run."

Once Security had transmitted its warning, six ships—about a fifth of those docked at the Station—had tried to escape.

"Are they going to make it?"

"No way," Raine said sadly. "The pirates probably won't even try to board them. They'll blow them out of space and loop back around for the big prize."

"That being the station," Brad said softly.

"That being the station," Raine agreed. "You may as well watch from Central. Until they actually board us, I have no idea where to send people."

"Help them," Brad told Saburo, gesturing at a trio of security troopers passing out weapons and armor to a line of spacers.

"Copy that," Saburo said.

He turned and followed Raine into Central. The control room at the heart of Blackhawk Security Central was cool and quiet. Despite that, the tension in the air was tangible. A military-style vid-tank—normally used to control task forces and such—showed the station and the various ships around it.

He was pleased to note that *Heart* wasn't visible. If the station fell, that might be worth something tactically.

A massive red splotch dominated the upper-right corner of the tank, coming around the curve of the ringed planet.

"I see that you've fixed whatever was wrong with your computers," Brad said as he examined the pirates' velocity data.

One of the techs looked up. "It was a virus. We did a hard reboot from a clean chip."

"You might want to do that more often."

The tank updated. There was now a single green dot rising up from the bottom of the vid-tank, which was aligned with the surface of Saturn.

His gut turned to ice. "Raine!"

The chief hurried over and studied the tank.

"Is that Michelle Hunt's diver?" Brad asked, his throat tight with fear.

"It is," he confirmed. "She'll cross their approach path in less than a minute. She popped out of the atmosphere right under them."

"What does she think she's doing?" Brad asked, fearing it would get her killed.

A data code flashed and a small cloud, flashing white for unidentified, spread out behind the icon.

"She's venting from the diver's tanks," the tech who'd spoken before said. "But why? To get a little more speed? That won't help."

As Brad watched, the first of the red icons began to overlay the flickering cloud. Then the green icon pulsed brightly. The white cloud vanished, taking ten red icons with it.

"What in Everdark?" he demanded.

"She vented a gas cloud and then used her emergency drive to turn it into a giant fuel bomb," Raine said softly. "Holy shit."

Brad watched the green icon with his heart in his throat. Praying the pirates wouldn't be able to hit it before Michelle ducked back under the clouds.

The vector data next to the green icon changed. "She's coming back around," the tech said.

"No, no, no," Brad said. "Run!"

The icon came hurtling back at the pirates. This time, they weren't ignoring her.

She began to twist and bob through three dimensions as she tried to evade their fire. Another cloud began to develop behind her ship.

The pirates knew what that cloud was now. Their fire intensified, red streaks developed all around her ship. A single streak—a mass driver round—connected and the diver lurched.

Moments later, the icon representing Michelle's ship pulsed again and the cloud of gas exploded. When the tank updated, six more pirate ships had vanished.

And so had Michelle's diver.

CHAPTER TEN

Brad barely managed to keep himself from screaming in anguish. She was too good a person to die like this. Like Shari.

"She may have saved us," Raine said softly.

Brad spun, harsh words fighting to make it to his lips. He somehow managed to stop them.

"How?" he asked brusquely.

"A lot of the ships Captain Hunt destroyed were transports. "There were ten of them and she destroyed six."

Brad nodded slowly, taking a deep breath to help control his rampaging emotions. "So, instead of two thousand or more troops, we're only looking at eight hundred or so. That's an improvement, I suppose, but I'm still not sure we can hold."

"We just have to hold them until Fleet gets here," Raine said.

It sounded more like a prayer than a plan to Brad.

"Do we have an ETA on Fleet?"

"Morgan?" Raine asked one of the techs.

"One sec."

A moment later, a green icon appeared on the edge of the tank—representing ships not yet within its purview but known to be coming. Numbers and vectors appeared next to it.

"Five hours," Raine said, reading the information. "A Fleet cruiser battle group will eat these bastards alive, so the pirates will have to run if they can't activate the weapons platforms."

"Which means we have to hold them for four hours or so," Brad said grimly. "That's a tall order. How many people do we have?"

"Between my troops and those we passed out weapons to, probably around five hundred," Raine said. "Most are spread throughout the station, guarding their homes.

"A significant portion of my command is guarding Central Engineering. If they get control of our air, we're fucked. Including your people, we've got about eighty people to hold Central with."

The security commander grinned coldly. "Of course, we've kept the heaviest weapons for ourselves."

"Sir!" one of the techs interrupted. "They're here!"

"Zoom in," Raine ordered, turning back to the vid tank. The image expanded to show Blackhawk Station itself, resolving into a schematic. The red icons of pirate ships flitted through the girders and platforms of the station—thankfully not anywhere near where *Heart* lay hidden.

The crew of Security Central watched silently as the transports locked on. Of the four transports, two were in position to take Central.

"All right," Raine said into the silence. "Seal all emergency bulkheads in sectors thirteen through sixteen."

As he spoke, someone highlighted the sectors in question on the schematic. The green light completely severed Central from the threatened portions of the station.

"Doesn't that completely cut them off until they get through?" Brad asked.

"Unfortunately not. Highlight structural columns Alpha, Beta, and Gamma."

Three cylinders suddenly glowed white in the schematic, starting at the top of the station and dropping clear down to the bottom. Central was toward the top of the white columns.

"These can't be sealed," Raine said with a sigh. "Which makes them the key to taking Central. However, only the bridges across them have gravity."

"So, we need to hold the bridges," Brad said as he studied the schematic.

"Exactly. I want you and your squad to go with Lieutenant Simon and her people. Hold Column Gamma."

The tall woman he gestured toward nodded at Brad.

"Done," he said.

"I'll flash you all the com frequencies and encryption codes by the time you're in position," Raine promised. "Good luck."

Brad ground his grief under a mental heel as he followed the security officer out of Central. He'd mourn Michelle after he avenged her.

———

The column was an odd-looking structure from the inside. The bridges started at the same angle and plane as the decks they came from and twisted around to merge with the central platform that extended for the length of the column parallel to the walls. It was like a strange 3-D puzzle.

Of course, he didn't have much time to admire the scenery. The pirates would arrive at any moment.

He raised an eyebrow at Lieutenant Simon. "Who is leading this dance?"

"I'll let you run the show," she said quietly. "I'm not used to pitched battles."

"Whereas mercenaries fight them all the time," he agreed.

His com system updated with the station frequencies and encryption codes. He passed them on to his people.

One of the security troopers had vanished as they entered the column. He returned driving one of the transport vehicles that used the columns.

The trooper skewed the truck across the bridge, blocking almost the entirety of the five-meter-wide structure. It still wasn't much cover, considering how open and airy the column was, but it was the best they were going to get.

As his mercs and the troopers began taking up positions behind the truck, Brad's com chirped.

"Madrid."

"Commodore, this is Central. The pirates have run into the blockade in the standard corridors. They're splitting up and it looks as if you have thirty or so headed your way. It's probable there will be more eventually, but that's the immediate threat."

"Got it. Madrid out."

He looked over the troops under his command. They were as ready as they could make themselves.

"All right, folks," he said on their frequency. "The bad guys are coming, but there's only two of them for each one of us in the first round. Let's teach them a lesson they won't live to regret."

"I see something," one of the security troopers said a minute later. "They're below us."

"Everyone, hold your fire till I give the word," he ordered. He raised his head into a position where he could see the new arrivals.

A dozen men were moving across the span linking the deck below to the central span. Their movements made Brad nervous. They had far more precision than he'd have expected. On the plus side, their companions hadn't come across with them.

The enemy squad surveyed the bridge and then advanced. The truck was making them nervous, but it wasn't slowing them down all that much.

"Now," Brad said, raising his auto-shotgun just as the pirates spread out across the central span.

He only came up enough to fire. He dropped the closest pirate as the rest of the friendly troops behind the impromptu barricade opened up. The swarm of flechettes swept the bridge clean in moments while the truck protected them from the return fire.

"That was short and painless, but there'll be more," he told the troops. "Lots more."

———

Five minutes later, the rest of the pirate platoon showed up, looking for their missing squad mates. Like their comrades, they showed far too much military discipline for Brad's peace of mind. They barely seemed to hesitate at the sight of the bodies sprawled in front of the truck.

Unfortunately, the bridge came into the column from well beyond the effective range of his people's shotguns and pistols. Though hits at two hundred meters were theoretically possible, they were extremely unlikely.

Brad was doing the mental calculations to see if he might be able to use the grenade launcher one of his people carried to make the bastards' lives more complicated, when they began to advance toward the central span.

As they did, a sharp *crack* rang through the column. One of Simon's troopers who'd been relying too heavily on range for protection crumpled.

"Down!" Brad shouted, crouching lower.

Someone over there had that rarest of things in a spaceborne battle: a heavy sniper rifle. On top of that, they were good with it.

"Here they come," Simon said, swinging her shotgun out around the truck and emptying its magazine in a single long burst.

As Brad rose to fire, he saw one of his mercenaries take a pistol bullet through the helmet and flop back onto the bridge.

There was no time for careful targeting, so Brad emulated the Security lieutenant, unloading his shotgun into the foes ranged against them before letting it fall on its strap. He followed up with shots from his pistols.

He stepped to the left to get a better angle, and a rifle bullet cracked through the space where his head had just been.

Brad ducked back under cover, checked his forces, and cursed. Three of Simon's troopers and two of his own were down, dead or wounded.

"Someone kill that damn sniper," he shouted as he rose and finished emptying his pistols at the rapidly approaching pirate platoon. Perhaps a third of the pirates were down, but the rest were still coming, laying down suppressive fire as they advanced.

These people had to be more of those damned commandos his people had fought on the automated JoveCorp freighter. They were far too well trained to be just pirates.

As he ducked back to reload, Saburo stepped in front of the truck. The wiry officer had grabbed the grenade launcher from his dead trooper. Brad watched in horror as the man carefully took aim at the bridge on which the sniper knelt and opened fire.

A full belt of twelve grenades ripped into the air. They began to arc downward before they escaped the gravity field of the main bridge. Their path from that point was as straight as anyone could've hoped.

Most of the grenades slammed into the target span. The deadly fragments were more than enough to kill even an armored man, and they set up a visible vibration in the metal bridge.

Then the armor-piercing grenade, tacked onto the end of the belt almost as an afterthought, slammed into the bridge and ripped it in half. If the pirate sniper had still been alive, he would've been doomed as the two halves whiplashed across the empty space of the column to mangle themselves against the walls.

Against the cacophony of the bridge's destruction, Brad's eyes jerked back to Saburo just in time to see him collapse sideways, blood spurting from his leg.

Brad launched himself toward his officer and friend, but a burst of flechettes from the pirate platoon slammed into Saburo's armored chest and sent him tumbling off the span and into zero g. He spun away, blood spreading around him in a cloud of droplets as he tumbled.

––––––

Trista yanked Brad back behind the truck. "He's gone, sir. Stay down or we'll lose you, too."

Before he could even process what had just happened, Simon shouted and his heart went cold.

"Blades!"

He pulled away from Trista, jammed his empty pistols into their holsters, and drew his mono-blade.

The distinctive hiss of monofilaments activating echoed through the column as the pirates charged in. Brad stepped in front of the truck to meet them.

Two pirates lunged at him. He parried both with a single swing of his blade, slicing one's arm off. He twisted the blade back around, cutting through his friend's stomach on his backswing.

A bullet smashed through the first pirate's visor and he crumpled. Brad glanced back to find Lieutenant Simon already looking for fresh targets.

Brad traded blows with another pirate for a few moments and then beheaded him. He looked for more targets of his own but found only bodies. The second skirmish was over.

Counting Saburo, he'd lost two more of his mercenaries and two of Simon's troopers. They wouldn't survive another attack like that.

"Son of a bitch," he said softly. The pirates had never faltered. They'd pressed home like real soldiers. Definitely commandos.

He deactivated his blade and holstered it. As he was reloading his pistols, he activated his link to Raine.

"Raine, this is Madrid."

"Raine here," the Chief replied breathlessly. "Go."

"Gamma is secure for the moment, but we've taken heavy casualties. I'm not sure we can still hold."

"Doesn't matter. We've blown the bridge in Alpha to smithereens with explosives, but they wiped out the team holding Beta. Our people fried the doors, but they're bringing up a cutter. All the enemy forces are converging there."

"Understood," Brad said in a flat voice. "We're withdrawing. Madrid out."

He turned to the Security lieutenant. "Get everyone off the bridge and prepare to fall back to Central. The pirates have Column Beta."

The woman didn't waste time cursing, motioning for the survivors to help the wounded back out of the column.

"What are you planning to do?" Marshal asked.

"I'm going to secure the bridge," Brad said, drawing his mono-blade again.

"Crude but effective," the pilot said. "Don't dawdle."

Brad approached the side of the bridge. With a single slash of his blade, he severed the rail, which also killed the power to the gravity plates farther out. He began hacking at the bridge, shearing chunks out of it with every blow.

He'd only made it two thirds of the way across when a rifle bullet cracked by his head. A quick glance over as he dodged confirmed he had another rifle-armed sniper on the wreckage of the bridge connecting to the main span.

Brad threw himself down just as a second bullet cracked through where his torso had been. The impact, combined with the now-fluctuating artificial gravity, began to twist the last shreds of the bridge.

Without waiting to see if it held, Brad scrambled to his feet and ran. He was barely moving before the sniper shot a bullet literally in front of his eyes.

The bridge groaned behind him. The stress of the twisted metal had grown too great for it to hold.

As he reached the hatch exiting the column, two of his mercenaries grabbed him. Bare moments after they had him clear, the convulsions of the massive span down the center of the column ripped the lesser structure entirely out of the column wall behind him.

"Well," Simon said into the silence that followed. "That was impressive, Commodore. I doubt they'll be using this hatch, but let's get it sealed and get to Central. We still have the finale to look forward to."

Brad leaned back against the wall and deactivated his blade. How high was the bill going to be? He'd lost Michelle, Saburo, and three other mercenaries who had served with him for years. Trista, Marshal, and three troopers were all he had left. Would any of them live to see the end of this fight?

He prayed so because he wanted vengeance. The pirates would pay in blood for what they'd taken.

CHAPTER ELEVEN

MAYBE TEN SECONDS after his dramatic exit from the structural column, Brad's com chirped. More good news, he was sure.

"Madrid."

"I need you in corridor eighteen, section J," Raine said. "Simon knows where it is. Make it fast!"

Brad turned to the lieutenant as soon as the chief disconnected. "Raine wants us at corridor eighteen, section J."

She nodded. "That's the one corridor they have to go through to get to Central from Column Beta."

"Lead the way," he instructed quietly.

They found Raine blocking off the corridor. He was directing people to place barricades and to get behind them. When Brad and Lieutenant Simon arrived, he turned to them.

"Is Gamma secure?"

The image of the twisting and snapping bridge flashed through his mind. "I'd say so, yes."

"Good. Like I said, we've secured Alpha, but they have Beta. I've put teams in place to slow them down, but I've lost contact with almost everyone. The few people still responding have been kicked out of the way.

"I hate that, but they've bought us time to set this up." He gestured at the barricade crossing the corridor. "The Cadre is going to be here soon. I need your people to reinforce mine."

His mercenaries combined with Lieutenant Simon's people only brought a bit more than a dozen people to the party. This was going to be grim.

Well, they'd do what they had to.

He turned to his people and opened his mouth to tell Saburo to take care of it but stopped. Saburo was gone. The man was never going to pass on an order again.

"I'll take care of it," Marshal said quietly.

With a sharp nod, Brad turned back to Raine. "How long do we have?"

Raine shrugged. "They're using jammers to screw with our communications and scanners. I can guess where they are from the blank spots, but that's a fairly large area. Ten minutes. Fifteen max."

A shout from the corridor interrupted his response. A quick glance behind him showed that time had run out. A single pirate—likely a scout—had rounded the corner. Brad and Raine were on the wrong side of the barricade.

Brad almost grabbed at his auto-shotgun from where it hung on its harness, but he already knew it was too late. The pirate had his own shotgun raised.

So, instead, he ducked and turned, trusting the security people to take out the scout.

A blast of flechettes mostly slammed into the barricade, but he didn't come out unscathed. Several of the darts ricocheted off his armor, and at least one penetrated his side protection. It stung like hell.

The thundering discharge of several shotguns boomed over his head, dropping the pirate and partially deafening him. A glance confirmed that had eliminated the immediate threat.

He yanked a battle patch from his pouch and slapped it onto his side, covering the hole. As the plastic molded itself to his armor, sealing the dangerous holes in his vacuum-proofing, jets of specially designed foam sealed his wound.

Brad took stock of the situation and felt the bottom drop out of his stomach. Raine hadn't dodged fast enough.

Dozens of holes marked the man's armor where a straight-on burst of flechettes had cut into him. Blood was pouring from the wounds.

He lunged across the corridor to the man's side just as he sank to his knees. Brad eased him to the deck.

"My people...help them...please," the dying man rasped.

"I will."

Raine grabbed Brad's arm weakly. "Hold the line." And then he died.

"Dammit," Brad muttered.

The sound of running footsteps and shouts got him to his feet and over the barricade. He rolled to his feet, weapon ready, just in time to see the first pirate squad trot around the corner.

"Open fire!" he shouted.

This time, not only did the people behind the barricade open fire, so did the light flechette cannon they'd set up to cover the corridor. It spat hundreds of the lethal darts down the corridor in one long burst and ripped the pirates to pieces.

Before anyone could relax, the rest of whatever platoon the squad had been part of came around the corner, firing as they moved. Flechettes ricocheted off the barricades and the cannon cut loose again.

Brad and the rest fired too, keeping behind cover as well as possible. The dumb bastards charged right into their withering fire.

He finished his magazine and reloaded but didn't need to fire again. The pirates were all down, none closer than fifteen meters.

Unfortunately, the attack had taken its toll on the defenders. The two troopers manning the cannon were down and others had taken their places. A total of nine security personnel were dead or seriously wounded.

The Vikings' armor was heavier and they were more experienced, but they hadn't made it through intact either. He was still down to only four of his people: himself, Marshal, Trista, and one trooper.

Altogether, Brad had a total of thirty people manning the barricade. Five others were caring for the wounded as best they could.

The number of casualties was not a good sign, considering how many pirates remained unaccounted for. Brad prayed they kept fighting dumb.

———

Twenty minutes passed before the pirates came again. This time, they brought assault shields—little more than sheets of metal on wheels— but still quite effective at providing cover in environments like the corridors of ships and stations.

The pirates couldn't move very quickly. If they tried, they left themselves vulnerable to having grenades rolled under the shields. That's exactly what happened to a number of them by the time they'd advanced halfway down the corridor.

His people's superior cover was giving them the advantage—each shield only covered five or six pirates, and there were a couple of shields that were stopped because they simply didn't have the troops to keep pushing them forward anymore. Unfortunately, the enemy had superior numbers.

It was less than an hour until the pirates would have to choose between running or committing to a do-or-die scenario. He hoped they could keep them back long enough to force the decision. At this point, he wasn't sure.

His thoughts were interrupted by Simon crawling up to him.

"We got half a dozen people from one of the other defensive positions," the security officer told him. "They have grenade launchers."

"That'll help. Are they on our frequency?"

"They are now."

Brad activated his com. "Grenadiers, this is Commodore Madrid. On my command, I want a massed volley straight down the buggers' throats—start with armor-piercing rounds to break as many of the shields as you can, and then put as many frag grenades among them as you can. Clear?"

Affirmatives came back.

"Everyone else, be ready to charge as soon as I give the order. Grenadiers, fire!"

For a moment, all he could hear were explosions. Then the screams began to overwhelm the blasts.

"Grenadiers, cease fire. Everyone else, up and at them!"

He rolled over the top of the barricade and started shooting anything that moved as he ran forward.

An amazing number of pirates were still up. It looked as if forty pirates were coming toward him, abandoning their worthless shields. They had to know the only path to survival was overrunning the barricade.

Brad forced himself to remain calm, picking off single targets as the pirates closed. Just as he fired his last shotgun shell, he saw a pirate with a grenade launcher come racing around the corner behind the enemy.

He drew his pistol and fired at the man but killed him moments too late.

A trio of grenades fell behind the barricade. The team servicing the flechette cannon never even had time to scream.

He reversed course and literally ran into Marshal as they both raced to get the crew-served weapon back into the fight. Without its controlled bursts, the pirates would quickly kill them all.

"Feed me!" Brad snapped, oblivious to anything beyond the need for that cannon.

That's when another pirate company came around the far corner and raced to overrun the defenders. Far too many for them to stop without the cannon's heavy firepower.

Marshal jacked a belt of flechettes into the gun. "Go!"

Brad sighted on the largest concentration of pirates and pulled the trigger. He tracked the heavy weapon back and forth across the corridor, carefully not shooting where his people were. With the shields out of commission, it was worse than a slaughter.

He stayed down, focusing on the holo-sights as every pirate that could tried to kill him. The gun shields around the barrel were reasonably effective, but there were a lot of bullets flying around.

Doing his best to ignore the occasional flechette that zipped past his face, he put a burst into the last group of pirates. They broke and ran, allowing the surviving security people to shoot several in the backs.

Brad pulled the trigger to add to their fire, but the cannon remained silent. He looked back to see what was holding Marshal up.

The pilot was sprawled on the deck, his head a gory mess. He'd probably died before he even realized it.

Incandescent fury and grief welled up inside him. Michelle was dead. Saburo was dead. And now Marshal was dead too. Someone was going to pay.

He stepped away from the gun and calmly checked the time in his helmet display. In no more than twenty minutes, the pirates would have to run for their ships or take Central to reactivate the gun platforms.

Of the mercenaries, only he and Trista remained standing. Security had fifteen effectives left, most of them walking wounded. Holding wasn't an option. The next assault would roll right over them.

That made his decision simple, really.

Brad stepped over to Lieutenant Simon. The woman's left arm was covered in blood, but she didn't seem to be letting that slow her in organizing her people.

"It's crunch time," he said over the high-pitched ringing in his ears. "Tell Central they'll need to blow the gun platform controls if the pirates get past us."

The corner of her mouth twitched. "I did that ten minutes ago, Commodore. Good news. They found our traitor. She was trying to hack into the weapons platform controls remotely, but we've got a serious nerd that counter-hacked her. If we survive, she might be able to give us a few answers about what the Cadre intended."

Answers would be good, but only if any of them lived to hear them.

"Let's hope so. Are you the chief now?"

She raised her good shoulder. "That's up to management. I'm the senior surviving officer, but they'll be asking a lot of pointed questions about how we let someone infiltrate us like this. I might be looking for a job by the time this is all over."

"If the Vikings survive, you'll have a place to land," he said. "You've got a good head on your shoulders when the flechettes start flying."

"Talk about a double-edged sword," she said in a dry tone. "I'd have a job, but people would be shooting at me like this all the time."

"Hardly," Brad said with a humorless chuckle. "This is worse than anything we've ever faced without lots of other mercenaries and Fleet helping us. Make it through this fight, and you'll have passed the most arduous entrance exam ever."

He looked out over the sea of dead bodies in the corridor. "I'm going to need you to put on your chief's hat and take over."

The woman frowned. "Why? What are you going to…"

Her voice trailed off as Brad stepped through the gap between the gun shield and the barricade.

He unslung his shotgun and handed it to her. Silence reigned over the com circuits behind him as he calmly made his way forward, his hands empty.

The pirates were gathering for a final rush just around the corner. He could hear someone barking orders.

He stopped short of visual contact and activated the speaker in his helmet. "My name is Brad Madrid. Who among you is man enough to face me blade to blade? I challenge your leader to a duel to the death. Right here, right now."

He smiled coldly behind his faceplate. There was no way the pirate leading this part of the attack could refuse a challenge phrased like that. His men would never follow his orders again if he did.

A figure in a black armored vac-suit stepped around the corner, mono-blade coming to life. He took two steps forward and stopped, bowing slightly toward Brad.

"How could I possibly refuse such a thoughtful invitation, Mr. Madrid? Well, well. Jack is going to be quite angry that he missed you."

The cold, gravelly voice was one Brad still heard in his nightmares. It was the Terror. The man who'd taken Shari, his uncle, his friends, and now Michelle.

The time for vengeance was at hand.

<hr>

CHAPTER TWELVE

"I GUESSED that Mader was your man," Brad said conversationally as a number of pirates stepped out cautiously to watch the duel. "Thanks for the confirmation. It must've really pissed you off when I blew his cover. And when I cut the throats of your slaver allies."

The Terror chuckled. "Jack has his purposes, even when not embedded in the Governor's office. Losing that placement was very annoying, but I have people in a lot of places. Which is how your name came to my ears in the first place.

"I don't mind telling you this because you won't survive to tell anyone else. And, as much as I'd like to chat, I'm in a bit of a hurry. It's time for you to die."

"I couldn't have said it better myself," Brad said as he drew his mono-blade and activated it. "You killed someone very important to me when you blew up that diver on the way in. I'll have your head for it."

The Terror stepped in, his blade flashing around in a glittering arc. Brad easily interposed his own blade between the strike and himself. Using the rebound of the weapons, he spun away from the Terror and then lunged in an attack of his own.

The Cadre leader deflected his attack and counterattacked with the blinding speed that Brad remembered from the engineering compartment on *Mandrake's Heart*.

The speed of the blow might have taken Brad Mantruso's head, but Brad Madrid had put in countless hours of practice in anticipation of this moment. Which didn't mean this fight was easy, but it gave him a chance.

The wound in his side wasn't helping, though. It slowed his responses and he found himself unconsciously favoring it. A weakness the Terror exploited.

The Terror drove Brad back one slow step at a time. He was holding his own right up until the moment that he stumbled over one of the bodies on the deck.

That brought the pirate chieftain in fast, his blade slashing at Brad as he scrambled back and rolled for his life. The strike swept through where his chest had been just a moment before. That he managed to get back to his feet was a testament to his skill.

As much as it galled him, he had to admit that the Terror was still a better bladesman than him. But skill didn't always carry the day. Brad parried again, twisting his blade back in to launch an attack of his own.

This forced the pirate warlord to retreat just one step.

Brad pressed his advantage, not giving the man even a moment to recover. Three times he lunged at the Terror, and three times the bastard managed to avoid or parry the blow. On the third strike, the pirate parried from the inside, using the rebound of the blades to send Brad's weapon swinging out, leaving Brad exposed.

He tried to follow up, but Brad used an advanced technique he'd been working on with Marshal and Saburo to interpose his own blade and execute a lightning-fast riposte.

He almost took the man's head, but the pirate ducked at the very last moment, losing only the top edge of his armored vac-suit helmet.

"What's wrong?" Brad asked in a mocking tone, allowing his hatred of the man who'd destroyed his first life full reign. "Getting slow in your old age?"

The Terror snarled and advanced, his blade lashing out in a series of brutally vicious attacks.

Brad parried each attack as it came and then stepped inside the

Terror's guard and smashed the hilt of his blade into the pirate's face-plate. Before he could bring the filament into play, the Terror's armored knee hammered into his injured side.

His vac-suit armor absorbed most of the blow, but intense pain made him stagger back. The Terror advanced, trying to take advantage of the stumble with a quick slash. Brad parried it and used the rebound to push himself still farther away.

For a moment, the two combatants separated, each regaining their breath. Then Brad raised his left hand and made a come-hither gesture.

"What's holding you back?" he taunted. "Checking your watch? Do you have somewhere you need to be?"

The warlord snarled and lunged in, his blade striking out in a text-book-perfect lethal strike.

Brad managed to interpose his blade, deflecting the attack, but nothing could have stopped that strike entirely. Searing pain ripped through his left arm as the pirate's blade took his arm off just below the elbow.

The intense agony drove him to his knees. The Terror stepped forward and brought his blade hurtling down in a death blow meant to take Brad's head.

Somehow, Brad managed to bring his blade up to parry the strike, but the Terror struck again and again.

Then, at the moment of his potential death, Brad saw an opening. The pirate's imminent victory had robbed him of some of his caution as he tried to end the fight now.

Brad smashed his blade into the side of the Terror's just enough to deflect the next strike into the floor, leaving the man momentarily off balance just a little.

For one instant, the Terror was overextended, his entire body open.

Before the Terror could recover, Brad struck with all his remaining strength and skill.

It still wasn't enough to kill the bastard. The Terror flinched aside at the last moment and got his blade back in just enough to stop Brad from taking the top of his head off.

That didn't mean he emerged unscathed, however. Brad's almost-lethal blow sliced through the Terror's helmet and deeply scored his jaw, cheek, and right eye in a glittering flash of light and blood.

With a scream, the Terror staggered back even as Brad struggled to his feet. The strike had come at the right angle to shear the faceplate off the man's helmet, and Brad could see that half the nerves and bones in his enemy's face were gone. Blood ran from his ruined eye socket.

Brad longed to pursue him and end this, but the loss of blood from his severed arm was making him dizzy. If he didn't stop it, he'd die before he got the vengeance he craved.

He managed to get a patch out and covered his stump. Even so, he wavered on his feet, just on the razor's edge of collapse.

The surprise upset had broken the will of some of the pirates. Some were beginning to slip away, no doubt headed back for their ships. Before the Terror could recover enough to come at him, the mood had shifted and his men were in retreat.

For a long moment, Brad and the Terror faced one other across the body-strewn corridor. Both grievously wounded, but each with his blade at ready.

"This isn't over," The Terror said. "We swore a fight to the death, you and I. I'll come for you or make you come to me. This will not go unanswered."

Before Brad could respond, the pirate warlord shut down his blade and turned. Two of his men made to help him and were struck for their impudence. Moments later, all the pirates were gone. To Brad's astonishment, none of the surviving security forces had shot at the pirates as they retreated.

The attack on Blackhawk was over.

Brad tried to turn and walk back to the barricade, but his vision wavered. The corridor seemed to lose its orientation, and he dropped his blade from nerveless fingers. Simon raced toward him, but the world went dark before she reached his side.

———

He came back to consciousness with a groan. He reached across his body with his right hand and found his left hand there but strangely unfeeling. Had he dreamed losing it?

"You're awake?" Shelly asked, her worried face popping into view over his.

"How long?" he asked, his throat dry and scratchy. "Where am I? What happened?"

"You're aboard *Heart*. The medical center on Blackhawk is swamped. The doctor said he had far too many critically wounded to give you the attention you deserved, but he talked a nurse through reattaching your arm.

"He said it's quite possibly the worst limb reattachment that could be deemed successful by some measure. The nerves are still severed, but the blood vessels are connected. That will keep it alive.

"Unfortunately, you'll need a lot better facility than he has here to regenerate the nerves and correct some of the deficiencies in the reattachment. Something better than on the Fleet ships, too. A first-class facility."

Brad nodded and shaded his eyes with his good hand. "I need a stim."

"No, you don't. You should rest."

"Stim, Shelly," he said coldly. "Now."

She hesitated for another second, then sighed theatrically before turning to the cabinets and extracting a packet. She handed him the pill and a glass of water. "I still don't think this is a good idea."

"Neither do I, but it's necessary."

He downed the pill and stood. Too quickly, as it turned out, and Shelly had to grab him.

"Everlit, sir, you're only going to do more harm this way."

"I need to get to the bridge." He hooked his good arm around her shoulders to support himself and gestured toward the hatch. "Now."

Shelly sighed again and helped him walk forward.

Upon reaching the bridge, Brad slid thankfully off her arm into his command chair. "How far away are the pirate ships?"

"Most are an hour away and accelerating," Shelly said. "They'll get clear before Fleet can catch them."

She smiled a bit coldly. "But they didn't get away clean. Blackhawk got their weapons platforms back online while the pirates were still barely within range. That cost them another two dozen ships."

That was something, but it would never make up for the losses he and his people had suffered today.

"Did Trista make it?" he asked quietly. "She was the last trooper standing out of our squad."

Jason nodded. "Didn't get a scratch. She's on her way now. Someone named Simon from station security pulled her away, or she'd have already been back aboard. What happened over there?"

"I dueled the Terror and almost lost."

"I heard a little. You hurt him bad."

"He lost an eye and part of his face. I suspect I'll have a nice bounty on my head before too much longer."

Shelly opened her mouth to say something, but her console chimed. "Trista is back aboard. She says she's on her way up."

When he heard the sound of footsteps in the corridor a minute later, he turned to ask her how she was and froze.

Trista stood in the hatchway, but she wasn't alone. With his arm around her shoulders stood Saburo.

The mercenary officer smiled wryly. "If only you could see your face, Commodore. It's most unbecoming of a flag officer to gape."

"I saw you die," Brad said, feeling a bit numb.

"No," he said, gesturing at his bandaged thigh. "You saw me gravely wounded. I managed to grab onto a wall in the support column and pull myself to safety. Thankfully, I escaped before you destroyed the bridge and sent debris all through the area."

"I thought I'd lost you, too," Brad said hoarsely.

"We all lost someone," Saburo said softly. "Or something. Did your skill with the blade come up a little...short?"

In spite of himself, Brad chuckled. "It's still too soon. At least I have the chance of getting some use back. You should see the other guy."

Shelly's console chimed again. She checked it and gave it a double take. "Incoming call, sir. For you by name."

"Lieutenant Simon?" he asked.

"No, sir," she said. "It's from one of the pirate ships."

He grunted. "Why can't they stop themselves from gloating about escaping or heaping threats of retribution on us? Put them on."

The main screen switched from a view of Blackhawk Station to the bridge of a ship. Sitting in the command seat was the Terror. He'd allowed someone to bandage his face, but the scar Brad had inflicted was going to be epic. The man's remaining eye radiated hot rage.

"Isn't it a bit soon to start bragging?" Brad asked with a sarcastic smile. "Can't you see that I've got my hands full?"

He raised his bandaged limb, hoping the man thought it was in better shape than it really was.

"You think you're clever," the pirate warlord snarled. "But I can wipe that smile off your face."

He grinned like a shark. "I've been going over every moment of our encounter. Every word you said. You mentioned the diver ship that attacked us. How you'd lost someone important to you."

"And that's what you want to gloat about?" Brad asked coldly. "I haven't begun to make you pay for what you've taken from me."

"There you go, making assumptions," the pirate said. "You seem to have a bad habit of doing that. You see, not everyone from the diver died when we blew its engines.

"I had a ship stop to pick up any survivors. I wanted to make them suffer for what they'd done to me. That's borne unexpected fruit."

He reached off to the side and dragged Michelle into view. Her face was deeply bruised and her arm was in a sling, but she was alive. Someone had tied her up and gagged her. Her eyes were filled with terror.

Brad stood as quickly as he could, matching fear filling him. Was the bastard about to murder his lover right in front of his eyes? He didn't know if he could stand losing her twice.

"Now, I'm sure your mind is filled with the possibilities of what I will do to this pretty thing," the Terror drawled slowly, obviously savoring every word. "Your lover, perhaps? You have excellent taste, if so.

"Put that fear aside. You see, I have no intention of harming her right now. She's the bait for my trap. If you want to see her leave my company in one piece, you'll need to find me within the next six months."

"What?" Brad asked, unsure of what was happening.

"We have unfinished business, you and I. The duel was to the death and I will not allow you to simply walk away. Yet I refuse to make your work easy. You have six months to find my base—something no one has managed to do with years of searching!—and present yourself to finish our fight.

"That should allow us both an opportunity to recover. I won't want to be called unsporting. Believe it or not, the Cadre has a code that dictates how we deal with duels. I mean to see it done right."

Brad shook his head, trying to clear his mind. "I don't believe you. You won't wait. You'll send your thugs after me."

The pirate laughed. "Of course I will! If you can't keep yourself alive, that's your problem. If you don't stand before me in six months with your blade in hand, I'll cut off something she values and send it to your office on Io.

"And I'll keep doing that every few weeks until there's nothing left of her. She'll die by inches, and you won't be able to do anything but run like a coward. Just remember that every moment of peace you enjoy from this moment forward is at your lover's expense."

The screen blanked, leaving him gaping. Michelle was alive, but he had to do the impossible to save her.

So be it. He wouldn't let the Terror take one more person from him while he had breath left in his body.

CHAPTER THIRTEEN

As much as he wanted to take off after the Terror, Brad knew that was a fool's errand. Even the Fleet cruisers and their escorts weren't going to be able to bring them to battle.

Even if he did catch them, he had no ground forces worthy of the name to board with. Saburo wasn't fit to fight and neither was he. That left Trista as their boarding team.

No, that wasn't going to work. There was nothing he could do but grit his teeth and prepare for the next meeting with the Terror.

And there would be one. Of that there was no doubt. He'd find the Cadre base before Michelle's time ran out or die trying.

The Fleet ships eventually broke off their useless pursuit and headed for Blackhawk. When they did, Brad finally allowed Shelly to bully him back to the sickbay. Though he wouldn't admit it, he was hollow inside. Physically and emotionally.

Then the stim wore off and he found out exactly how right Shelly had been. Taking it had been a serious lapse in judgement.

Three hours later, when he almost felt human again, Lieutenant Simon came by to check up on him. She looked around the sickbay curiously as he sat up blearily on the bed.

"It's bigger than I expected," she said. "I always figured compartments on a ship would be smaller."

"This *is* pretty small," he said as he swung his legs over the side of the bed. "What's wrong?"

"Thankfully, nothing. I've been placed in provisional command of what's left of Blackhawk Security. Based on some of the looks I've seen from management, that probably won't last, but they don't have a lot of options right now. None of the other officers survived.

"Commodore Wilson of the Seventh Cruiser Battle Group wants to meet with us on his ship as soon as he gets here. That's maybe half an hour from now. I figured I should give you the warning and help you get there. Unless you want to tell him you can't make it."

She looked pointedly at his arm. "I talked to the doctor. He told me what he did. It was a raw deal, considering everything you did for us, but the choice was literally your arm or someone's life. He regrets having to make that choice but wouldn't do anything differently if he had a chance to do it over."

"And he shouldn't have done anything else. Life is more important than limbs. I have more of a chance than if he hadn't done what he could.

"You told me you had a prisoner right before the duel. Who is she and what does she know?"

"First, let me say that I've never seen anything like that duel. I'm a gun girl myself. I've never understood the fetish some people have with mono-blades. They give me the creeps.

"Your fight with that bastard was amazing. I've reviewed my helmet-cam video in slow motion and you both were so skilled. Masters of the blade. The fight is going to be the talk of the system before long."

He hadn't considered the possibility anyone had recorded it. "I'd like a copy of that. It might prove useful when I'm ready to start reviewing what happened. Any chance we can keep that close to the vest?"

Her lips quirked into a smile. "Mine? Sure. Unfortunately, I wasn't the only one watching. I'm sure that someone has sent a copy off station by now. That cat is out of the bag for sure."

Brad grunted. Maybe that wasn't terrible. Word was going to get out that he had a hard-on for the Terror. Some notoriety might open a few doors during the process of finding the Cadre base and rescuing Michelle.

"What can you tell me about your prisoner? Was she Cadre? Could we turn her and get details on Cadre operations?"

"I doubt it. Sadly, she's one of ours. A Cadre contact provided her with a big payday to betray us."

The woman's words dashed Brad's hope that the mole knew where the Cadre's base was. Well, maybe she knew something else that would lead him to the Terror. Only time would tell.

Brad stood and found his footing more stable than earlier. The stim had been exactly the wrong thing for him to take. Lesson learned.

Shelly had found him a sling for his dead arm, so his hand wasn't flopping around anymore when he moved. That was good. He wanted to make the best impression he could with Commodore Wilson. The man could be a boon to Brad if he played his cards right.

"I suppose we'd best be off, then," he said.

He picked up his weapons belt from the shelf and realized he was going to have a lot of reconfiguring to do with only one functioning arm.

"Let me see if I can help with that," Simon said. "We have two working arms between us. I had to have someone help me change clothes, which was mortifying. I'll recover enough to use my arm soon, though. I can hardly imagine having to work with one hand for months."

"Or forever," Brad said fatalistically. "The nerves might be beyond regeneration."

The female security officer gave him a level stare. "Let me be so bold as to give you some advice, Commodore. Never focus on the lemons life hands you. Make lemonade."

He laughed in spite of himself. "I'm not precisely sure what that has to do with my particular situation, but I get your general meaning. Also, I think we can dispense with my rank. We've fought together. Call me Brad."

She smiled a little. "Lisa. Come on. We have just enough time to make it over to the dock where the Commodore's shuttle will dock."

When they stepped into the corridor, Brad found he hadn't been alone. Trista Doary was standing guard outside sickbay in light armor with a full loadout of weapons.

"Trista," he said, somewhat bemused. "Shouldn't you be getting some rest?"

The short woman shook her head. "I can rest when we have more people. Someone needs to keep an eye out for pirates we missed."

He felt his eyebrows rise. "I thought they all ran off. Did we miss some?" The last question was directed at Lisa Simon.

The tall security chief shrugged. "Maybe. We won't know until we search the station completely. Fleet is sending Marines to help with that, but it's going to take time to be sure. Even then, I suppose it's possible that we still have people aboard that the Cadre planted.

"She's right to be cautious, though. Word arrived that the Terror has already put a price on your head. Ten million credits might just convince any number of people to come looking for you. Even here on your own ship.

"I put four people I trust implicitly on guard duty at the Blackhawk side of the airlock, but even one of them might be tempted. Hence the larger number of guards."

She was right, Brad decided. They only had one combat-capable fighter on hand. If someone came after him, he probably wouldn't be able to effectively defend himself. He'd have to take steps to fix that deficiency as soon as possible.

"I suppose we'd best be on our way," he said with a sigh. "Fleet Commodores don't like to be kept waiting."

"No commodore does," Trista said with a smile. "I should know."

———

Sadly, Brad found himself slowing by the time they made it to the shuttle dock. The fight had really taken it out on him. He hoped the Terror felt worse.

Two Confederation Marines in full battle rattle stood guard at the shuttle hatch, but they were obviously expecting them. As a sign of how unsettled things were, the men didn't even demand their weapons.

Inside, a Fleet lieutenant commander stood waiting. He was tall, heavily muscled, and wearing his blond hair in a buzz cut. He extended his hand to Brad and then Simon.

"Commodore Madrid, Chief Simon. My name is Lieutenant Commander Evan Pallas. Allow me to extend Commodore Wilson's compliments and escort you back to *Goliath*. In deference to the unusual circumstances, he's chosen to waive the requirement that you surrender your weapons, but please do us the courtesy of keeping them where they belong."

"Right now, I doubt I could best a pair of Junior Mars Scouts," Brad admitted. "Thank you, though."

The flight to the Fleet cruiser was mercifully brief. No one was waiting for them, but Pallas saw them directly to his commanding officer's office.

Commodore Wilson was a short man of Asian descent. His appearance was completely at odds with his surname. Brad wondered what his story was.

"Commodore Madrid, Chief Simon, please sit. I apologize for asking you to come meet me, particularly when you've both been injured. If I might ask, could your subordinate wait in the outer office? My officer will see to her needs."

"Certainly, Commodore," Brad said. "Trista, please wait outside."

The mercenary inclined her head, exited, and closed the hatch behind her without a word.

Once everyone was settled, Wilson took the lead. "I'm sure you both are aware of how close Blackhawk Station came to capture. If it had—particularly with its weapons intact—my battle group would not have been able to dislodge the Cadre forces.

"That said, there's no way Fleet would've allowed this to stand. As formidable as your weapons platforms are, Chief Simon, we would've retaken the station. Eventually. That begs the question, why did they attack at all? What were they really after?"

The security officer shrugged. "They didn't exactly hand out their itinerary. I'm in the dark about what they hoped to accomplish. Based on the amount of force they brought and the fact that the Terror was here in person, it must've been important."

Brad nodded his agreement. "There's very little here to interest the Cadre, but I have a possibility. We encountered some people near Jupiter that could conceivably be connected to the attack."

He gave them the short version of the fight with the commandos on the automated freighter.

"That is intriguing," the Fleet officer said with a frown, "but I'm not sure I follow. What's the connection, precisely?"

"He3," Brad said. "Or, more specifically, the ability to refine it. If they'd destroyed the JoveCorp refinery in that attack, it would have been an inconvenience to Fleet. If they took out SaturCorp's refinery too, that would've been a crippling blow."

"That's concerning," the commodore admitted, "but I'm not sure I agree about the connection. Yes, Fleet is one of the major consumers of He3 for our large ships, but even eliminating Jupiter and Saturn as sources, we can get what we need elsewhere.

"We don't advertise, but I know Fleet has a strategic reserve somewhere. What would the Cadre hope to gain from something like this, other than pissing us off even more?"

"I'm not sure," Brad said with a shrug. "As you said, this is only a hypothesis based on partial information. All I know for sure is that the Cadre sure seems interested in He3."

"If they wanted to destroy our refining capacity, why didn't they destroy Blackhawk Station on the way out?" Simon asked. "They had us dead to rights if they wanted. Everdark, why board us at all? There must be something else."

"Do you have a clear understanding of what they did while they were aboard?" Brad asked. "I assure you: the Cadre might be subtle but their pirate minions aren't. If they had other objectives, you'd know."

"The data is still coming in. They caused widespread damage and killed far too many people for us to be able to easily sort things out. It will take days to see things clearly. Maybe weeks."

Commodore Wilson rubbed his chin thoughtfully. "I'm inclined to believe they had a different mission in mind. The sheer number of ships involved in the attack and the trained attack forces mean something too."

"This was a high-priority mission," Brad agreed. "I've never understood how they support themselves. How do they support so many people? How do they get them in the first place? Where does the loot go?"

"All excellent questions," Commodore Wilson said with a sour face. "Ones that Fleet Intelligence and the Commonwealth Investigative Agency have been unable to answer since the Cadre started operations."

The man sighed. "I'm afraid we're going to remain clueless today, as well."

He turned to Simon. "I'm given to understand you captured someone in their employ."

The lieutenant nodded. "She was one of our security people, dammit. They gave her great gobs of money to hack our systems. Successfully, I might add. That's a black mark that we won't be erasing anytime soon.

"We've been questioning her since we captured her. She's terrified now. Too bad her greed got the better of her common sense. She also claims she had no idea what they would do when they got here."

"Anyone that even pretends to listen to the news knows how the Cadre operates," Brad said dismissively. "She's lying. Either to you or to herself."

"Probably both. We might be able to trace where they paid her from, but I have my doubts. The Cadre covers its tracks when it comes to their finances. Just like the rest."

"I'll want her," Wilson said grimly. "I hope she likes being hot. The mines on Mercury will be her eventual destination."

"You can have her," Wilson said. "I'm concerned about her safety. Her actions killed a lot of her former comrades. Accidents happen."

"Then we'd best expedite her transfer. I'll have Commander Pallas accompany you back to Blackhawk with a brace of Marines right now."

He returned his gaze to Brad. "You, on the other hand, have an appointment with my chief medical officer. He's coming back for additional supplies to assist on Blackhawk, and I want him to take a look at your arm.

"I saw that fight, by the way. Someone on Blackhawk sent it on wide beam. Not just to us but to Io. It'll be everywhere before you leave Saturn, I'm afraid. Might I say your skill is only equaled by your foolishness? Challenging the Terror to a duel was a risky, ill-advised thing to do."

"I didn't have a lot of choice," Brad said with a halfhearted shrug. "If we didn't hold them, I'd still have died. And after all he's taken from me, I *will* kill him."

The Fleet officer nodded. "You lost a lot of your fighting force today. And that woman from the diver."

"How did you know that?" Brad asked with a frown.

"The transmissions were in the clear. We heard both sides. I saw her and how you reacted to the Terror having her. He's put you in a terrible predicament."

Brad smiled coldly. "He has to come into the range of my blade to take my head. I'll bet on myself when that time comes."

"I'll be rooting for you, Commodore Madrid. I think we all will be."

CHAPTER FOURTEEN

It only took a few minutes for *Goliath*'s doctor to declare that Brad's injury was beyond his help. Perhaps beyond anyone's help. Not exactly what Brad wanted to hear, but not too surprising, either.

Brad and Trista caught a ride back to Blackhawk on the doctor's shuttle. He was sorely tempted to return to *Heart* and rest, but the anger and restlessness inside him demanded he keep working on what had brought the Terror to this outpost.

The four Blackhawk Security troopers were waiting for them when they landed. Someone on *Goliath* must've called ahead to let them know they were coming.

Amusingly, Trista stayed close by his side, watching the security guards while they watched everyone else.

The group passed Commander Pallas and his prisoner on the way to Security Central. The cowed woman in shackles seemed to need her Marine guards more to protect her from the people hurling threats and insults than to keep her from doing anything nefarious.

The officer nodded and they were gone.

"It's hard to believe that little thing made all this possible," Trista said. "She doesn't look any more dangerous than a child."

"Danger comes in many forms," Brad said with a shake of his head.

"So does evil. That woman killed people she knew just as surely as if she'd put a gun to their heads. All for money."

"What are we going to do now, boss? Head back to Io?"

"Very shortly, yes. As sad as it is for me to say, we need to recruit new people. Not just for the new ship but for *Heart*. It looks as if you and Saburo will be training up entirely new squads."

"With our reputation, that shouldn't be a problem," she said, scanning around them, probably to be sure the station guards didn't miss anything. "The Vikings will attract a lot of interest from the top talent."

That was true. Placement in a platinum-rated mercenary company ensured the best in contracts, pay, and equipment. On the downside, he'd painted a target on his people's backs. The Terror's bounty would bring scum out of the woodwork.

"We'll manage," he said. "I've had Shelly collecting resumes from people interested in joining because of the new ship. Sara Kernsky, the Mercenary Guild factor on Ganymede, has been sending them our way too. Sara's got a good eye, so I'd imagine we'll be back up to full strength within a few days of docking.

"That means you get to organize your new squad from the ground up. Any ideas on how you'll do that?"

She raised one shoulder in a shrug. "Pretty much like Saburo did. It's a good structure and I know it like the back of my hand. You should be asking how he'll organize the new ship. He'll have four times as many people under his command."

That was true, too. The jump from eight troops to thirty was going to require some changes to the loose structure Saburo had favored before. And it would mean changes to what Trista did, too.

"Your people are going to have to interface seamlessly with his," he warned. "To the point of plugging your squad in for one of his. Whatever structure he comes up with, you need to mimic it enough to be a part of the whole in combined operations."

She considered that for a moment and then nodded. "I'll talk with him on the way back to Io. I'm sure he'll have a plan by the time we get there."

"One other thing you both need to keep in mind," he warned. "As this fiasco proved, we never know when we'll meet our end. You need to be ready to fill his shoes if something goes bad. And one of your people needs to be able to do the same for you."

Trista sighed. "I know. We'll manage. Until now, that wasn't a problem. You know the same is true for you. You almost died today. Who steps in if you go? Marshal died first, so your designated replacement is gone. If you'd lost, the Vikings would've been headless."

The reminder of his dead friend, and Michelle's uncertain fate, soured his mood even further, but Trista was right. Having an executive officer was only a good start. He needed to fully populate the chain of command.

"Good point. I'll have my own homework to do while recuperating."

When they arrived at Central, their guards stepped into a break room with Trista, while the young man Brad had dealt with the first time showed him in to see Simon without any of the attitude he'd previously shown. He looked haunted now.

Chief Simon was sitting at her desk, looking at something on her console. She glanced up at his entrance. "Good timing. I think I found something. Park it while I get us some coffee."

"No need," Brad said as he sat with more than a hint of relief. "I'm just happy to be off my feet. This has been one shitstorm of a day."

"I'm getting some for myself," she said. "It's on the burner back here, so it's no trouble making two. Chief Raine had a stash of the good stuff."

The last came with a sad expression.

"He'd have wanted you to enjoy it," Brad observed. "Particularly today. What happens to him? Did he have any family?"

She shook her head as she poured some excellent-smelling coffee into two chipped mugs. He held up two fingers when she gestured to the sugar and shook his head at the creamer.

"He was a bachelor," she said as she handed him his coffee. "We'll have a ceremony in the next few days and send him out to float in the ring. That was his preference. Personally, I'd have let them drop me into the atmosphere to burn up."

The coffee tasted even better than it smelled. He'd have to find out what kind it was and get some for *Heart*. And the new ship, of course.

"What did you find?" he asked after a moment.

"The pirates came onto the station at several points. Almost all of them moved to secure critical infrastructure like Security Central, Central Power, and life support. But not all.

"One group seems to have gone rogue. They headed straight for Ringbolt Associates. SaturCorp is the major company here on Blackhawk Station, but not the only one. Ringbolt is the only other big one, though."

"What do they do?" he asked, savoring another sip of coffee.

"In general, they provide cutting-edge technology. Their staff has some of the brightest engineers and scientists when it comes to the extraction and refining of materials from gas giants."

Her face soured. "Had, I should say. We're still sorting out the damage, but it certainly looks as if the pirates killed everyone in the offices and workshops. Of course, with the general chaos we're experiencing, that might not be completely true. I have people looking for survivors as we speak."

Brad considered that. How could it play into his theory? Or was it simply a distraction? Rogue pirates looting to fill their pockets?

"What shape are the offices in now?" he eventually asked.

"Rough," she admitted. "It's hard to tell if they took anything or simply wrecked the place."

"Did they wreck any other section of the station?"

"Not like that."

Brad nodded thoughtfully. "That certainly sounds like an intentional act, then. Any word on what Ringbolt Associates might have been working on? I assume they supplied SaturCorp."

"They did, but not exclusively. They also worked with our biggest rival, JoveCorp. And a number of smaller outfits looking to break into the business, of course."

"Is that difficult? Breaking into the gas extraction and refining business."

Simon shrugged. "It must be. No one else has managed to turn a profit yet. New groups try every few years, but they go out of business because they have no infrastructure and their pockets are too shallow."

A tap at the door drew their attention. A dark-skinned man in a security uniform inclined his head as he leaned in. "Sorry for the interruption, but we found someone from Ringbolt Associates in the medical center. Svetlana Garrow. Some kind of research scientist."

"What's her condition?" Simon asked.

"Physically, she's fine. She was off shift when the attack happened, and we found her helping to move the wounded from elsewhere in the station. Emotionally, she's a wreck. She just found out everyone she's worked with for years is dead."

Brad rose to his feet, setting the mug on the edge of the desk. "I think we'd best go talk to her."

———

The medical center was worse than Brad had expected. Even with all the help from the Fleet cruisers, the medical teams were still overwhelmed.

Injured people overflowed the working areas and filled the surrounding corridors. It only took a glance to tell that some of the people desperately awaiting care wouldn't make it.

Their wounds sickened him. They'd been shot, cut, and burned. The injuries seemed to show the pirates vying to outdo one another in cruelty. The Cadre had so much to pay for.

They found Svetlana Garrow moving an injured woman to the line of stretchers awaiting surgery. The tall, swarthy woman was crying. From her stricken expression, she hadn't adjusted well to the news that all her friends and coworkers were dead. Of course not.

He made a mental note that to spend more time with his people, especially Saburo and Trista. The two combat specialists hadn't shown this level of grief, but it had to be buried inside them. He just hadn't seen it because he'd been suffering with his own grief.

"Miss Garrow?" Simon asked gently. "We need you to come with us."

The woman blinked at the security officer, seeing their group for the first time. "I'm busy," she said harshly. "I told your people what I know. Leave me alone so that I can help someone. Anyone."

"You're not helping them like this," Brad said softly. "Your pain is affecting them. Come away with us for now."

It was obvious to him that the people near her were interpreting her anguish as an indicator of their own prognosis. She was terrifying people who were already in dire straits.

Simon lightly took the other woman's arm, pulled her out into the corridor and away from the medical center. Garrow didn't resist. In fact, her removal from the medical center seemed to break her. She cried with great, gasping sobs and had to be led to a nearby room.

The security chief sat the woman down and found tissues for her. She glanced at Brad and then at the door, so he took the hint and stepped outside.

"Trista?" he asked, focusing his attention on his officer. "How are you feeling?"

Her face was ashen and filled with rage.

"Like I want to kill someone," she ground out, wiping away a tear. "I feel just as bad as that woman. Just as lost. Only, I have an outlet for my pain through violence."

He nodded. "I think I need to find someone for us all to talk to. We'd been lucky until now. We'd never lost a person. Today, the universe took its due by taking almost everyone on the combat team and our executive officer. Not one of us is going to be okay for a while."

"I don't want to be babied, sir. I can manage."

He shook his head, disagreeing sharply with her assessment. "Before I became a mercenary, I lost everyone I cared about. I know how badly that rage can twist you into a person you wouldn't recognize. I almost gave it power over me before I figured out how to make it serve my ends.

"I'm not going to give you some kind of pap about making it go away. The pain never goes away. It only lessens with time. And getting a grip on how to focus your vengeance will make your life worth living again. Trust me on that."

Her eyes widened. "That's why you named our ship *Heart of Vengeance*? Because the Cadre took everything from you?"

"I don't advertise it, but with a Cadre bounty on my head, I suppose it's not much of a secret anymore. Yes. Back when I had a different name, the Terror killed my family and the woman I loved. I swore to make him pay."

"And now he has Captain Hunt and he's killed so many of our people," she said sadly. "Maybe you need to talk to someone, too."

"I will," Brad promised. To himself as much as to Trista. It was too easy a mistake to make. "I've learned my lesson. Still, that previous loss taught me what I needed to do to keep the rage from eating me up. Rather, it did once I talked to someone that could help me. We'll get someone to help us through this so we can enjoy our revenge when it's done."

The young security officer that had been managing Central's office hurried around the corner with a box in his arms. He brightened at seeing the group in the corridor and lengthened his stride.

"Commodore Madrid," he said with a smile. "I'm glad I found you. A Fleet officer brought this for you from Commodore Wilson."

Brad couldn't imagine what it could be, but he'd best take a look.

That's when he saw the man peering around the same corner the troop had just turned. His furtiveness set off alarm bells inside Brad's hindbrain.

"Stop!" Brad shouted and began backpedaling. "Everyone back!"

Trista spun him around and interposed her body between him and the man just as the world ended.

CHAPTER FIFTEEN

BRAD OPENED his eyes to a dimly lit room with a white ceiling. It wasn't one he was familiar with, but he recognized the theme. He was quite familiar with infirmaries of various kinds by this point. It wasn't the medical center on Blackhawk, *Goliath*, or *Heart of Vengeance*, though.

He struggled for a long moment to remember how he'd gotten there. Then the explosion came back to him.

Trista.

Brad fumbled a bit but managed to find the call button with his good hand. A nurse—a strapping young man with long black hair and a hooked nose—appeared.

"You're awake," the man needlessly observed. "You're safe."

"Trista Doary," Brad said in a rusty-sounding voice. "She was with me. Is she okay?"

"She's alive and receiving treatment," the man said, his voice pitched into a soothing lower tone. "Let me summon the doctor so she can answer your questions."

Brad wanted to shake the answers he desperately needed from the man, but he knew arguing would get him nowhere. Medical types were all the same. They never wanted to tread on their peers' toes.

A few minutes later, footsteps sounded in the corridor as someone approached at a brisk pace. The footfalls turned out to belong to an attractive auburn-haired woman shrouded in a white lab coat.

Brad grabbed hold of the bed's rail with his good hand and pulled himself into a partially upright position so he could see her better.

"Good evening, Commodore Madrid," she said as she checked a computer readout next to the bed. "Let me tilt the bed up a bit so that you don't have to spend your limited strength looking at me. How do you feel?"

"Like I should be dead." His throat felt like a pounce of cats had used it as a litter box.

"You were never *quite* in danger of that, but I can understand the feeling," she said sympathetically. "You've had a lot of trauma between the original severance of the arm, the gunshot, the effects of those horrid patches, a wide-spectrum stimulant that some mental defective gave you, and the blast damage.

"That last is what convinced Blackhawk Station's chief medical officer to place you in a medically induced coma until you were in a position to receive appropriate treatment. An excellent call to follow up on the earlier shortcomings."

"So, I'm not on Blackhawk?"

"Obviously not. You've been unconscious for six days and your crew has brought you to Serenade Station in the leading Jovian trojan cluster. I'm Dr. Gina Duvall."

Brad had heard of Serenade Station from…somewhere. He couldn't remember where off the top of his head.

It functioned as the central hub of the Jupiter-leading trojan cluster —the asteroids that led Jupiter through its orbit. It had a metals refinery, an industrial site, a minor shipyard, and the only medical center in the cluster.

And not just any medical facility. One of the most cutting-edge research schools in the Sol system. Some of the best physicians in the system came from there. As he remembered, the medical school was founded by brilliant idealists that had actually managed to create what they'd intended when they'd set out from the Inner System. He was in better hands than he deserved.

"Thank you. Since you don't know my background, I have a

request to make. May I have your word that everything about me will be held as confidential?"

"You needn't ask, since that is always how we operate here, but you have my word."

"The Cadre put a rather large bounty on my head. I would like my presence kept to as few people as possible, and I must insist that my files be locked down."

She nodded. "Commander Finley appraised me of that, and I assure you that no one but I has even heard your name or the name of your ship. Everything that can be done to obscure your presence has been done. We are *very* discreet."

"Excellent. The other thing I need to tell you is that you won't find my genetic code in the Commonwealth gene base, and that the only medical records you'll get are the ones my people probably brought you.

"I'd like to keep it that way and I insist that no copies of my DNA be kept on file. Once I'm gone, I don't want anyone to know I was ever here."

"I know someone that might be able to help with that paranoia," she said dryly.

When he failed to respond, she sobered and nodded. "Very well. It will be as you wish."

"Thank you. I suppose I should find out what treatment options are even possible with my injuries."

"Everything except your arm is readily treatable. It presents something of a challenge, to put it mildly. If I hadn't heard the story of what had happened to the station, I'd have been looking for whoever did the reattachment surgery to have their license revoked.

"As it is, I'm sure the nurse did the very best she could. Frankly, the fact that she succeeded as well as she did with something less than minimal supervision is an astounding feat. You should've lost that arm."

The Fleet medical officer had said something similar.

"I don't fault the nurse or the doctors," he agreed. "I was lucky and she was more skilled than I had any right to expect."

"Indeed. I've sent her an invitation to apply for instruction here. I feel she has more to offer her patients, and we might just be able to help her do so.

"That said, the nerves in your lower left arm are dead past the gross incision. Regenerating them is possible, but it will not be easy or quick. It will also be time-consuming. I wouldn't expect to be going anywhere for the foreseeable future, Commodore."

Brad slowly settled back against the bed. "When do we start?"

"Not today. We need to do a preliminary workups and exams. Tomorrow, I'll start regenerating the gunshot. Perhaps the day after that, we can have enough information to begin that conversation."

She fixed him with a steely gaze that any combat commander would instantly recognize as demanding obedience. "You just woke up, Commodore. You need to relax before I can start fixing you. And you'll need to convince your heavily armed crew that you're going to be just fine in our care."

"My crew?"

Duvall snorted and lifted her wrist-comp, touching a series of keys. "Major Saburo, your commodore is awake."

A moment later, the door to the infirmary slid open and Saburo limped in. He wasn't dressed in the Vikings' standard uniform but rather a set of black fatigues.

He was indeed heavily armed. He had an auto-shotgun slung over his shoulder and wore his blade and pistol on his hips.

"It is good to see you awake again, Commodore," he said. "I'm glad you're all right."

"*All right* is stretching it, Major," Duvall retorted. "But he *is* alive."

"Why aren't you in bed?" Brad asked as he looked over at Dr. Duvall. "He was shot in the hip."

"I examined the wound," she said with a shrug. "It was well treated and healing as well as can be expected since he won't stay off it. I prescribed bed rest, but he declined."

Saburo's eyes briefly flitted to the doctor. "The Cadre came far too close to getting you for my peace of mind, Commodore," Saburo said. "I was the best suited to provide protection."

His man was keeping the fact they were short of fighting personnel between them, speaking between the lines.

"Trista Doary," Brad said sharply, attempting to sit up and wincing as pain shot through him. "She was hurt. What's her condition?"

Duvall put a hand on his arm. "She came through the explosion with some minor injuries, but her armor protected her vitals. Her previously broken arm is now spectacularly broken, but that is the extent of her serious injuries.

"I'll be writing a paper about her treatment. And yours, I might add, with all identifying information scrubbed. And before you argue, that *is* within the bounds of my word. No one will ever know it references you, nor will they know anything about you. The treatment for your injuries, however, might help someone else in a similar situation in the future."

He started to say something but she held up her hand. "And we are done for the day. The Major and I will retire so that you can rest. You're going to send him back to your ship, correct?"

Her tone made that less of a question and more of an order.

Brad chuckled. "I can't make him abandon his duty, so you might as well hang it up, Doctor. What I will do is get him to stash the auto-shotgun in a small case. I'm afraid that's the best you're going to get."

She sighed. "I suppose I'll have to accept that. Could you possibly get him to stop glaring at my staff as if they're assassins intent on slitting your throat?"

"I'll try, but no promises."

"I don't glare," Saburo said as he glared at the doctor.

"This is going to be a trying recovery," Duvall said mostly to herself.

———

It was the next day before Dr. Duvall let Brad's officers in to see him. By then, she'd already put him through the beginnings of his treatment: dealing with the bullet wound in his side.

When she grudgingly admitted Jason and Shelly, Brad's midsection was still covered by the arch of the regeneration unit. He greeted them with a smile he knew was wan, but it was the best he could muster.

"You worried the Dark out of us," Jason said quietly as the pair pulled up chairs next to his bed. "Don't do that again, sir. I'm not sure I'm quite ready for being the man in charge, thank you."

Even though Brad had told Jason that he wasn't quite ready for independent command, that didn't mean he couldn't manage when the chips were down. That was what being an executive officer was all about.

"You've learned a lot in the last week, I'd wager," Brad disagreed. "Me, too. As I'm sure Shelly is about to tell me."

His communications officer—no, his pilot, he thought with a pang —glared at him right on cue, but he held up a hand, wincing as he did.

"Please, I don't need the well-deserved lecture," he told her. "I made some bad calls. I'll listen more closely in the future."

Her eyes softened. "How are you feeling?"

"Battered, with a few holes and a bum hand. On the positive side, I'm alive."

By the look in her eyes, Shelly wanted to say more but heroically restrained herself. "How do you like my hometown?"

That was where he'd heard of Serenade Station. Shelly had been born and raised there.

He smiled a little. "I haven't seen anything outside the clinic, but it seems very well equipped."

"Yes, indeed," Dr. Duvall said from the foot of the bed. "And some of that expensive equipment is telling me you've been talking too long. I need you to relax or you're going to screw up the regen."

"I've also met a very good—if somewhat aggressive—doctor," Brad added.

"You haven't begun to see *aggressive*, Commodore," Duvall said, a small smile hovering around her lips to take some of the sting out of her words.

"At least let them tell me everything is okay," he cajoled. "I can't relax if I'm worried about my people and my ship."

"We're as good as can be," Jason assured him. "I've kept the ship out of sight and a bit away from the station. I called the Guild on Ganymede and hired a ship to come keep us company in case we get some unexpected visitors. That contract stipulated some extra officers to help us man *Heart* and a combat team to relieve Saburo of guard duty. They arrived right before I headed down, and we have a team outside the door."

Duvall scowled. "In combat armor and ready to repel a boarding action. I'm not pleased."

"They *are* ready to repel a boarding action," Jason agreed evenly. "And to get Commodore Madrid out of here if one comes calling. That's not negotiable.

"It's a team from Heimdall's Raiders. People personally vouched for by Captain Branson."

Brad nodded. Heimdall's Raiders was a solid-gold company—if one could forgive the pun—that the Vikings had fought beside three years earlier. He expected Captain Branson to make the jump to platinum soon—it had been a surprise to him that the Vikings had made it first. His own bump had allowed him to add his recommendation to the pile, and he suspected it wouldn't be much longer before the Raiders traded up insignia.

He couldn't think of a stronger defender to have guarding his back at a time like this.

"An excellent choice," he said, making sure his tone carried his approval. "Well done."

"And the new trooper is doing fine, too," Shelly said. "She's keeping an eye on Trista now that we have the spare manpower. I think they *like* one another."

Brad blinked. "New trooper?"

"Lisa Simon," she said, her brow furrowed. "Blackhawk fired her after the explosion that hurt you killed five of their security people. I think they were looking for an excuse to clean house," she added somewhat angrily.

"Ah," Brad said, remembering his offer to the former security officer. "I did extend an employment proposal. I just didn't realize it would be so immediately useful for her."

Well, Simon was steady under fire and smart. She'd fit right into their organization. And, if she and Trista really were interested in one another, that could help them both recover from the Blackhawk trauma.

Jason and Shelly stood as he was considering that.

"We should let you rest," Shelly said as she swooped in to place a soft kiss on his forehead. "Get better soon."

Jason nodded to support his lover's directive. "Indeed. *Heart* won't be right until you're back on her bridge, sir."

"You'll do fine," Brad assured them. "And no matchmaking, Shelly!"

"As touching as this is," Duvall interrupted, "your time is now *very* much up. Everyone but the patient must go."

Brad ignored her for a moment and met the eyes of both his officers in turn. "Take care of my ship and my people."

Jason nodded and gestured for Shelly to precede him out. "We'll visit as much as Dr. Duvall allows."

Duvall snorted as the pair finally began to walk toward the door. "More than I'll allow, I'd wager. Shoo!"

After they'd left, Brad lay back and tried to sleep. Anguish at the fear Michelle had to be suffering kept sleep at bay for a long time. Rest would be hard until he finally rescued her and put an end to the Cadre forever.

CHAPTER SIXTEEN

BEYOND THE THICK transparisteel of the observation dome, the stars glittered and Jupiter's multicolored sphere hovered in the lower left corner. In the last month, Brad had come to enjoy the view quite a bit.

About a tenth of the "stars" were actually asteroids in the trojan cluster. A couple of slowly drifting sparks of light marked freighters making their slow, leisurely way toward or away from Serenade Station.

He was alone in the observation dome just outside the clinic. Well, as alone as one could get with armed guards in the corridor outside. Saburo had been very insistent before he left for Io with *Heart* that Brad never wander too far from his minders.

After all, there were ten million reasons why someone might try to kill him.

It was early in the station's morning cycle, so no one was likely to come there except him. All too often these days, he wasn't able to sleep. Or he awoke hours before his scheduled treatments and therapy sessions, like today.

It had to drive the mercenaries guarding him nuts.

His mind wouldn't stop worrying about how to find the Cadre base and save Michelle. He needed to act, but he couldn't unless he developed some lead to follow. One he wasn't going to find here.

Of course, without finishing his recovery, he'd have a very difficult time dealing with the Terror. Oh, he could probably kill him any number of ways, but that wasn't how it was destined to play out and he knew it. This would end with the blade, just like it had started.

Brad liked being in the observation dome. The stars soothed his mind and allowed him to relax. It was also one of the few places he could get away from Dr. Duvall for a while.

Of course, being outside the clinic was a risk. Enemies were much more likely to strike when he was away from the clinic's protection. Spacers—even pirates—treaded carefully around doctors. They were few and far between out there, and one never knew when one might be in desperate need of their assistance.

While physicians weren't really a protected class in the truest sense of the word, spacer traditions were strong. Just look at the pirates and their refusal to arm themselves with heavier weapons.

Doctors in space were neutral parties and treated anyone who needed their help. Except in certain rare cases where someone crossed them and the unlucky bastard found himself shunned.

Someone like the Terror could probably force a doctor to help him, but when even the slightest mistake might cost someone their life, did anyone really want to piss off a doctor? The general consensus was no. A few salutary examples made certain that everyone respected the healers.

Brad carefully positioned his left hand on the chair arm and leaned back to watch the stars overhead. After a month of regeneration treatments, basic tasks were once again within the realm of possibility.

He could dress himself, even handle objects. Fine motor control was proving more challenging, though. His ambidexterity was a thing of the past. His off hand—for now he had one—was less useful than other people's and he knew it.

Nerves were notorious for not responding as well to regen as other tissues. Duvall had completed the gross work and would soon start the intensive business of stimulating the reconnected nerves in a way that would hopefully restore his normal dexterity.

Having to take time to do this when he should be looking for Michelle was maddening, though. At least he wasn't completely idle on that front.

Jason had gotten word four days before from Io through the secret communications channel he'd arranged with the Vikings' home office. The new destroyer was ready. That was why Brad was without any of his usual companions.

He'd sent *Heart* back home so that his people could do their final interviews. Well, everyone except Trista Doary and Lisa Simon.

Sarah had managed the face-to-face meetings with Hiroshi Kawa and interviewed prospective crewmembers. Everything that could be done without them was done.

Jason, Simon, and Saburo would do the final interviews after they arrived sometime tomorrow. Oh, they'd send him their choices to be sure he agreed, but he'd accept their recommendations.

He'd named the new ship *Oath of Vengeance*. She was their promise of retribution to the Cadre. He could hardly wait to take her out.

The door slid open behind him and Brad sighed. One of Duvall's apprentices had come to bring him in for the day's treatments. It always happened around this time, and they knew where to find him.

When the door slid closed again but no one spoke, the hairs on the back of his neck tingled.

Even woefully out of practice, he managed to get out of the chair just before a shotgun blast blew the backrest apart.

He caught a glimpse of his attacker. The man was dressed in a white smock from the clinic, but Brad didn't know him. The Cadre bounty hunters had found him.

Brad landed hard, using his less-useful left arm to absorb the impact as he dropped behind a slowly spinning replica of the Sol planetary system. The flechettes from the next shot tore into it moments later.

He had no idea how the man had gotten past the mercenaries guarding the door, but he knew instinctively that he wasn't going to get back up in time to matter. He'd have to save himself.

Brad drew his pistol—professional paranoia had its benefits!—and dove out from behind the now rapidly spinning worlds. As he did, another blast smashed into the Earth, shattering it and sending debris across the room.

Firing as he rolled, Brad put shot after shot into the intruder. The man folded over and collapsed, his weapon clattering to the floor.

Wary, Brad stood, searching for other threats. There was danger in opening the door. If there was someone else out there, he'd invite another attack.

He edged forward and grabbed the auto-shotgun. Once he'd holstered his pistol, he walked to the door, hit the switch, and stepped out, sweeping the corridor with his appropriated weapon.

The two mercenaries who'd been guarding him were down and unconscious. They had no obvious injuries. One of them was missing his shotgun, though.

Brad didn't know what had taken them out, but he could imagine the sequence of events. The attacker—apparently solo—had come unarmed. He'd probably observed Brad's habits for at least several days.

When he got close enough to the mercenaries, he incapacitated them and armed himself. If Brad hadn't been quite as suspicious, he'd have died today.

Based on the assassin's clothing, there was probably a medical student somewhere in a similar condition to the mercenaries too. He raised his wrist-comp to his lips and called Lisa Simon. He'd let her tell the Raiders' detachment leader that there'd been an attack.

This was certainly going to spice up the day.

Lisa Simon walked into Brad's room and tossed a data pad onto the table. "That's Serenity Security's report on the body. He's an unknown. They're not even sure how he got onto the station yet."

"The Terror's found me," Brad said flatly.

"One hunter did," she argued. "That doesn't mean he told the Terror."

"We can't count on that. They might be heading here in force right now. Even if the attack doesn't get onto system-wide news—which it likely won't, since these people are rather insular—there's almost certainly at least one Cadre agent on Serenade. He'll know."

"What difference will it make?" Simon asked. "Stay inside the clinic and we'll guard the outside. How are they going to get in and not screw themselves with doctors everywhere?"

Brad shook his head, resting his injured hand on his nanite vat. "I honestly don't know, but I'm sure it might involve killing people here. Patients. Visitors. Doctors. Who knows? We can't stay. How are the two mercs?"

"Fully recovered," she said. "Duvall isn't sure what the assassin used, but it knocked them right out. They found a medical student in the same condition. There was an aerosol can in the dead man's pocket. They're analyzing it."

She gestured at the vat. "What's that?"

"Something to keep myself occupied," he said with a shrug. "Saburo once told me that unconventional weapons win fights through surprise. I'm seeing if I can't do my part to do exactly that."

"Sounds like the sort of crap he'd come up with," she said with a snort. "That man is a character."

"Surprises do work," Brad disagreed softly. "You just have to engineer them ahead of time."

The former security officer shook her head. "Engineer whatever 'unconventional weapons' you want. I'll just focus on shooting any bad guys that show up."

"Tell the Raiders that we'll be pulling out. Have them recall their ship as soon as it gets *Heart* docked at the Io Yards. Serenade is no longer safe for us."

The woman didn't approve, but she nodded. "That gives us four days, give or take. Your treatment isn't complete. Make sure you get the name of another place we can go to while you finish recovering."

He nodded, but not in agreement. Simply to acknowledge what she'd said. The time for arguing would come later.

Once she'd left, Brad returned his focus to the vat. He'd spent hours like this in his youth, producing everything from bullets, to spare parts, to the art that had once decorated the bridge on *Mandrake's Heart*.

They'd recovered that last item and it now filled the wall in his quarters on *Heart*. He'd move it to *Oath* when the time came. It was a reminder of what had happened and why the Terror needed to die.

As complex as the art was, only one thing he'd made rivaled the complexity of what he was making now. That had been his mono-blade. Its coils, power generators, and lethal monomolecular filaments had taken intense concentration and focus.

Even his blade was simple when compared to this new device. The blade only had one filament and power source. This device had six filaments, each coiled into a container identical to the one in his mono-blade—though much shorter than his weapon's fifty-six-centimeter blade—and two power supplies.

The filaments, their containers, and the power sources were done now, after nearly twenty hours of work. All that remained was fitting it to himself. He focused on that as the nanites scurried to his will.

He opened the vat, removed the device, and turned it over, allowing the gray goop of the nanites—drawn by a low-power transmitter in the vat—to fall back inside before he sealed it.

The device looked like a decorative armlet. He slowly attached it to his left arm, carefully fitting it in behind his wrist-comp. It was invisible to the casual eye. Perfect.

Brad pressed the symbol he'd marked on the band. With a half-heard hum, hiss, and click, the armlet split in half. One half, propelled by the filaments charging—and hence repelling themselves and extending out perfectly straight—shot up his arm, while the other half stayed at the wrist.

Six softly glowing strands of light fanned along his left forearm. Charged monofilaments, capable of repelling any other monofilament in the same way as a mono-blade now protected him. His own personal shield.

One with a deadly edge of its own. Thankfully, these short strands wouldn't deform enough to be a threat to his arm, though he'd have to be *very* careful how he moved it around. It would be embarrassing to cut one's own head off in combat.

He regarded the glowing monofilaments and a cold smile spread over his face. The next time he and the Terror dueled, he'd end him.

CHAPTER SEVENTEEN

"I⊤ isn'⊤ possible to stop your treatment at this point," Dr. Duvall said firmly. "It will have a profoundly negative impact on your prognosis."

"So will getting shot," Brad retorted. "And not just for myself. Consider what might have happened to your associate. Or to you, if you'd been unlucky enough to come looking for me yourself."

She considered him a long moment and then nodded. "True, but that doesn't change the reality of your situation. If we interrupt the regeneration process, I'm not talking about it taking longer or even simply starting the therapy over. Your nerves will set in at the current level of use forever."

That was…less than optimal, he conceded. He could use his hand for very simple things, but he wouldn't want to try fighting with it.

"How much longer are you envisioning the treatment taking?" he asked. "Bottom line, minimum time."

"Two weeks minimum," she said briskly. "Potentially as many as four."

Brad shook his head. "I can't risk that kind of time. If this guy had someone waiting elsewhere in the Jovian system, they could be here in just a few days. Anything longer than a week is just begging to have an attack. There must be another option."

Duvall sighed. "I can't imagine what it might be, but you've said we have a few days before there could possibly be a response. Let me ponder what's possible while we continue treating you for now."

"I said that it was *conceivable* they could take a few days to respond," he said. "If they have additional people here or in the near vicinity, they could act sooner. I'd rather not take chances with other people's lives."

He looked at his wrist-comp. "Let's do today's session, and then you can start researching options. The Raiders' ship can be here in four days. That's how long you have to figure this out before I leave."

———

Brad sighed as he finished a set of exercises with his left arm. It felt as if he was a four-year-old. A clumsy one at that.

Dr. Duvall gave him an encouraging nod. "Not bad, but that's enough for today. We'll take you through another regen session in the morning, and then we'll try these exercises again."

"And you'll have those options for me?" he asked, reminding her of his impending departure.

Her expression soured. "I've already asked some of my best people to look into it, but I don't hold out much hope, Commodore. This is very delicate work, the regeneration of nerves."

"Do what you can, Doctor. In the end, the decision is mine. I'll make it and I'll deal with the consequences."

At her brusque nod, he quietly left the treatment room.

His Raider guards fell in around him and they moved as a group toward the main atrium area of the clinic. After the earlier attack, they were in combat armor. He hoped that level of precaution didn't become necessary.

Brad spotted one of Duvall's apprentices—there were four of them —guiding a group of men who appeared to have been injured in an accident. Bandages swathed all three men's heads and other parts of their bodies.

The apprentice spotted Brad and waved at him. He acknowledged her gesture with a nod and changed direction toward her. His help was probably more of a hindrance, but it gave him something to do to alleviate the boredom.

The trio of patients noticed her wave and turned to see him. At the simultaneity of their turn, Brad's heart froze. They had the look of predators searching for prey.

"Look out!" he shouted as the men reached into their bandages.

The apprentice—oblivious to what was happening—stepped between him and the assassins. Her look of confused alarm was forever etched into Brad's memory as the man directly behind her cut her down with a burst from his submachine gun.

Brad dove behind a nearby fountain as the assassins and his guards exchanged fire. One of the killers dropped, but so did the two Raiders. The assassin's surprise had been total.

Bullets shattered the stone of the fountain as the remaining killers and the two mercenaries struggled to end the conflict. One of the mercenaries was screaming into his com for backup while the other fired short, controlled bursts at the enemy.

Gathering his wits, Brad drew his pistol and leaned out far enough to fire at the man who'd casually murdered the assistant. The assassins were both under cover, and his fire was ineffective.

"The response team is on the way," the mercenary that had been calling for help said, hunching lower. "We're exposed out here. Zach and I can cover you while you get back into the corridor, but you have to get moving when we say."

The fountain was in the middle of an open area, so that plan seemed more like wishful thinking.

"That's not really an option," Brad said. "They'd just gun us down while we ran. How long until support gets here?"

Brad stuck his bad hand up and fired several shots to keep the assassins from getting too froggy. He couldn't see any targets, so he made sure and shot high. He didn't want to hurt a bystander.

The assassins seemed unconcerned about collateral damage, though. From the hoarse screams coming from several directions, a number of people had already been hit.

"Sixty seconds," the man said. "We weren't expecting them to already be inside the clinic."

He wished he could blame the Raiders, but Brad hadn't expected the bounty hunters to arrive so quickly, either. The first one must've been part of their team. This was the less subtle option.

"We don't have a minute," he told the mercenary. "We need better cover or they're going to outflank us."

The man he was speaking to grunted and collapsed. Brad couldn't see a wound, but that hardly mattered. The mercenary's open eyes told the tale. He was dead.

"Screw this," the remaining mercenary—Zach—said as he gathered his feet under him. "Raiders!"

The mercenary popped up and began firing as he raced toward where the assassins were hiding.

Momentarily stunned at the suicidal charge, Brad was late getting up to fire at the killers. That seemed fine, as they were late in shooting Zach down.

Brad managed to drop one of the attackers before Zack skidded and fell onto his back. He got a shot lined up on the final assassin just as the man turned his attention back his way.

Several of the assassin's shots threw bits of stone into Brad's face, but that didn't stop Brad from putting two shots into the shooter's chest.

Once the last man was down, Brad cautiously scanned the room for other threats. All three assassins were on the ground, seemingly out of action. All four mercenaries from Heimdall's Raiders were down too.

Brad slowly stood and stepped away from the fountain. The walls, plants, and decorations showed the spall marks where fire from the automatic weapons had hit them. Violence had ravaged this place of healing.

His eye fell on the crumpled corpse of Duvall's assistant—Beth Redfield, that had been her name. He'd known her somewhat. She'd struck him as rather naive and, well, young. She'd been eager to get her license and help people.

She hadn't deserved to be killed in a battle that didn't involve her— that should *never* have involved her.

That's when the Raiders' response team arrived, weapons up and looking for threats. Dr. Duvall was running right behind them with her medical kit.

Brad didn't have the chance to say a single word before two mercenaries virtually carried him away under the cover of their comrades.

––––––––

"Six people dead," Duvall thundered. "Including a very dear girl that would never have harmed anyone."

She and Brad were in her office. It was late in the local night, and the medical staff had been slaving away to save as many people as they could. In some cases, they managed the impossible.

Sergeant Zach Salyer—the suicidal mercenary—had pulled through. His three companions had not.

"I told you how dangerous it was for me to be here," Brad said sadly. "Do you believe me now?"

"I believed you then," the woman said waspishly. "And I'm not blaming you. Not much, anyway. You made a moral decision, and immoral men want to kill you for it."

"That does nothing to bring Beth Redfield back."

The doctor slumped in her chair. "No, it doesn't. But I want to be very clear about this. You are not at fault here. Neither I nor my colleagues blame you for the death of our associate.

"That is not true for the Cadre or the Terror," she continued grimly. "I've sent word to Ganymede and Io. Our people have been neutral up to this point, but the Cadre crossed a line when they invaded this clinic and killed one of us."

Brad raised an eyebrow. "Forgive me, Doctor, but the Terror and his people will force you to work if required. They can use any number of punishments to make certain of your compliance."

She smiled coldly. "Give us the credit of our convictions. He might be able to do so, but he can't force us all. Say he orders one of us to treat a badly injured man. I would personally comply.

"That sprained wrist? Well, I think not. Will he force me and make me unwilling to save the next man? No."

"You don't know him like I do, Doctor," Brad said with a shake of the head. "He will kill people to compel you. 'Fix my wrist or I shoot that innocent person in the head.' He'd do it, too."

"Well, what do you want me to do?" she shouted, throwing her hands up. "I have to do *something*."

He felt bad for her. She was in a mental space he was very familiar with after all these years.

"You do the best you can," he said quietly. "Your people have been neutral until now. That lowers people's defenses. Perhaps someone overheard something or knows something that would lead to the Cadre base. You don't have a means to make the Terror pay. I do."

That made her sit back and think. "You think that's true? I would hope that if someone knew where a group of killers like the Cadre were hiding, they'd have said something long before now."

"Probably," he admitted. "That doesn't mean someone didn't pick up a clue that will add together with something else we know to point right at them. Every little bit helps. Eventually, we'll find them."

Duvall slumped in her chair. "I suppose you're right. Serenade Security found the ship they came here on, by the way. They're confident there were no others in their group, but they've locked the clinic down tight. No one else will get in like that."

"There's an old saying about horses and barns. And even that won't be true when word gets back to the Cadre where I am. They attacked Blackhawk Station. They'd do the same here. I'm going to have to move along as soon as practical."

She shook her head. "I still haven't found anything that would help preserve the regeneration treatment in your arm. The harsh fact is that you will cripple yourself if you leave before the work is complete."

"It no longer matters what you or I want. We could have a ship here in a matter of days and we have no way to stop them. The Raiders' ship hasn't gotten back from escorting *Heart of Vengeance* to Io."

In hindsight, having them escort his ship had been a mistake. He'd have been much better off with it here to backstop him. The Raiders' detachment commander had called their ship and they were on the way back, leaving *Heart* to make the last leg without escort.

He hoped that wasn't *another* mistake.

"So, you can't leave in any case," Duvall guessed shrewdly. "When will they get back here?"

"Two days," he admitted. "You've got two days to come up with something, because I will not be here on day three. Even if it cripples me."

"I'll gather the best minds at my disposal and come up with an option. Now, go get some rest. You've already set the regeneration back with your hard landings."

Her tone implied he should've been more graceful. It was amusing how people like her could make everyone else feel about a centimeter tall when they wanted to.

He rose to his feet. "Get some sleep of your own, Doctor. You won't do your patients much good if you collapse from exhaustion."

With that, he stepped out of her office and found his new shadows waiting for him. Trista Doary—one arm in a large cast—and her new best friend Lisa Simon fell in beside him.

The six remaining Raiders spread out to the front and rear as he headed for his quarters. Today had been hard. He'd sleep tonight, if he could.

If not, he'd refine his plan to find the Terror and his base. He was done passively waiting while Michelle suffered. And the Cadre would murder no more people hunting for him.

CHAPTER EIGHTEEN

BRAD REGARDED HIS CONSOLE BALEFULLY. Half out of paranoia and half out of boredom, he'd set himself the task of reviewing incoming ships, hoping to gain some measure of warning before another attack came.

Of course, he had no clue what that attack would look like, and the last two days had frustrated him greatly. His presumption was that something odd would show up, but that had all been hypothetical. Until now.

The ship that had caught his attention was a courier, one of the high-speed ships that were two-thirds engine and carried hardcopy dispatches, samples, and small groups of people all across the Sol system.

They were rare and those small groups of people could easily include attack squads. One traveling to a small refining station in the middle of nowhere was unusual—and trouble of one sort or another.

This ship was registered to StelCorp, which did no business at Serenade. Or in Jupiter's leading trojan cluster at all, for that matter.

He reached for his communicator, but the console chimed before his hand touched it.

Brad accepted the call. "Madrid."

"Commodore, this is Major Lemansk, Serenade Security. I have a communication from a StelCorp courier approaching Serenade. The woman asked for the senior security officer present, and once she had me, she asked for you by name. I have her on the line now."

Lemansk was the second-in-command of Serenade Security. Like his boss, he'd been informed of Brad's identity—mainly so that he could help cover up Brad's presence.

"Did she identify herself?"

"No." Lemansk allowed that single word to sink into the air. "She said to tell you, however, that you owe her some kind of gambling debt."

For a moment, Brad was incredulous, but then snorted. "Put her through."

The security officer's image vanished. A moment later, the visage of a tall, hawk-featured woman appeared.

Brad relaxed at once. "Agent Falcone. And here I thought I was well hidden. I don't recall a gambling debt."

"No one expects the Spanish Inquisition," she said with a straight face. "You're a difficult man to find, Madrid. We need to talk."

"I think you know where to find me," he said dryly.

"Actually, I need you to come to my ship. Privacy is of the utmost importance."

While anyone else could've been part of a Cadre trap, Brad had worked closely with Kate Falcone before. She'd never be involved with anything like that.

"I'll be along in short order. I have mercenary guards, but I think I can convince them to stay outside the ship."

"That would be best. I'm told we'll be attached in fifteen minutes."

"See you then."

Brad ended the call, sent a note to Major Lemansk via his wrist-comp asking where the ship was docking, and stepped out of his quarters. The four heavily armed mercenaries from Heimdall's Raiders seamlessly bracketed him as he headed for the docks.

Fifteen minutes later, he was at the correct boarding tube and waiting for the lights to change. The red warning had already switched to yellow. Once the connection was solid, it would become green.

Thirty seconds later, the tube indicated it was safe, and he pressed the call button.

"Yes?" Falcone asked, voice only.

"You ordered a pizza? Pepperoni with extra cheese?"

"That's just cruel. The food on these things leaves a little to be desired. Come in. Alone."

He turned to the mercenaries. "I know this woman and trust her. Wait here."

They didn't look very comfortable with having him out of their sight but obeyed.

Brad stepped into the boarding tube and was at the ship in a few steps. The airlock slid open as he approached. Waiting inside were Kate Falcone and a dark-skinned man in a plain white uniform.

She looked Brad up and down. "You're in remarkably good shape for someone who went blade to blade with the Terror."

He felt the corner of his mouth quirk up. "Things didn't work out as well as they might have, but I'm still here. It's good to see you again, Kate."

"I feel the same. This is Captain Abdel Mahdi of *Lion Courant*. He works for StelCorp but is also associated with the Agency."

The man smiled, showing a mouthful of shockingly white teeth in his dark face. "Welcome aboard *Lion*, Commodore. Your presence honors us. If you would come this way, I have what passes for a wardroom ready for your meeting."

"Who else is here?" Brad asked Falcone as they walked.

Her eyes twinkled. "What? And ruin the surprise?"

Brad shook his head and followed Captain Mahdi. The man opened a narrow hatch and allowed Kate and Brad inside, but remained in the corridor once the hatch was sealed.

The wardroom was smaller than his closet back on Io. It could seat four people if they were friendly. Only one of the seats was occupied. It held Senator William Barnes, who rose to his feet and extended his hand.

Surprised, Brad took it. "Senator. It's good to see you, but you could've called. How is Josephine?"

"She's fine, thanks to you," the older man said. "I have far too many people around to be certain anything I say is unmonitored. When Agent Falcone stopped at Io Yards looking for you, I made arrangements to secretly join her."

That must've been quite the trick. Commonwealth senators didn't just vanish without a trace.

"I can see that look in your eye, Commodore," Barnes said with a ghost of a smile. "Everyone thinks I'm at the Io Yards. Only my most trusted guards are aware that the suite they're guarding is empty.

"I slipped away in the dead of night, disguised as hotel staff. Even my aides think I'm in working seclusion for the week. No interruptions at all."

"This must be very important."

"Exceptionally so," the senator agreed. "And it fits into what I suspect Agent Falcone wants to talk with you about, though she's been admirably close-mouthed. Have a seat. We have a lot to discuss." He smiled a bit more widely. "Mr. Mantruso."

———

For a long moment, Brad said nothing. Then he shook his head. "You will excuse me if I wonder just where you heard that name and why you think it applies to me."

Barnes gestured to the table. "Please, both of you sit."

A glance at Falcone told Brad she was as surprised as he was by the revelation, but she only shrugged and sat.

Brad settled in beside her and made a gesture for Barnes to continue.

The senator shrugged. "It's simple, really. I hired you to find my daughter based on your sterling reputation, but your history only goes back so far. I took steps to uncover your identity so I could be sure that I have the right man on retainer for the continuing mission of locating the people behind my daughter's kidnapping."

"I'd appreciate knowing how you found out. I'd rather not have any one else repeat it."

"You have little to fear on that front, Commodore. I have a contact in the Commonwealth Investigative Agency. A highly placed one that is quite discreet. I am uncertain of the methods he used, but he managed to get me a summary of your history in very short order."

That caused Brad to shoot Falcone a sour look. "I guess I shouldn't be surprised."

"Don't look at me," she said firmly. "I only told my boss. He and the Senator go way back, though. I can't say he wouldn't have told him. If so, he and I are going to have words."

Barnes cleared his throat. "That is indeed where I got the data. He and I were once roommates at university. He won't have told anyone else."

"I see," Brad said with a sigh. "There is no real point in denying it, is there?"

"Not really. All it really did was confirm what I already suspected. I like to know men's motives. Yours are more complex than most but very understandable."

"What's complex about them?" Brad asked, his voice deadly soft. "I want the Terror dead."

"That's completely understandable, based on what I've learned about you. As a matter of fact, I feel exactly the same way. And that was even before I found out he was behind Josephine's kidnapping."

Somehow, the news didn't surprise Brad in the least. The timing of the kidnappers' arrival at Blackhawk and the Terror's attack had suggested a connection.

The Senator's expression had gone from purposeful to grim. "The Terror and his crew have caused me great problems in the past in addition to those he has inflicted on the Commonwealth. Personally, I can survive what he's done to my business, but he's hurt and killed my people, which I will *never* forgive. And now he has touched my family."

The man focused on Brad. "We both want him dead. We just have to find him. I might be able to assist in that."

"I'm listening," Brad said. "The Terror is already my blood enemy but not one I can easily locate. I also have a pressing reason to find him sooner rather than later."

"The Commonwealth has conspicuously failed in trying to find the Cadre," Barnes said. "So conspicuously, in fact, that I decided to covertly help them with the process. The Cadre seemingly strikes with impunity in the Jupiter system, so I made certain that I had a means to track both a ship that would interest them and the cargo it carried.

"One of mine, of course. The crew surrendered and was allowed to board escape pods. A blessing, that. About a third of them vanish, never to be seen again."

Falcone's interest seemed to sharpen. "Exactly how do you hope to track something like that? The ship will have disappeared and they'll make certain to disable all the transmitters. Even the ones you think you've hidden."

Senator Barnes showed his teeth in a ferocious grin. "That's true, but I gave them additional hidden transmitters to find. My people devised something that doesn't trigger their alarms.

"When the engines are firing, a concealed port opens every five hours or so and takes a passive scan of the star field. It determines where the ship is and, based on what potential obstacles are around it, uses a narrow-beam transmitter to squirt that data to ships I've tasked with collecting the information."

Brad gave him an uncertain look. "That sounds like something Fleet would've already tried. Or the Agency."

"Indeed they have," Barnes agreed. "Which is why all the cargo and ships the Cadre seizes go through a number of steps to be certain that only the patsies get caught.

"Admittedly, the ship and cargo were quickly separated, but one of my people managed to determine where the goods were going. Mars. The ship is on its way out into the Fringe. We'll continue shadowing it at a great distance to find out who receives it."

Brad leaned back in his seat and considered that. "Mars is different from the Outer System. Do you know if the cargo is going to the planet itself or just to orbit for transshipment?"

"That remains yet to be seen. My people were able to determine that the cargo was removed in deep space and loaded aboard another ship. Once that ship arrives at Mars, other people will be watching for it. They can use low-powered transmitters to confirm it's there and where it goes after it arrives."

"All of this has been done before," Falcone said. "The Cadre always figures it out somehow. What makes you think your undercover operation will succeed where more professionally run ones have failed?"

The senator smiled coldly. "Don't mistake *private* for *unprofessional*. I hired the very best people to design these systems. I then found people I *knew* I could trust beyond any doubt at all to run the operation.

"They have no idea why they're doing this or even who the targets are, though I presume they have their suspicions. They certainly have no idea how wide an impact their work will have."

"That's one more lead than I had when I walked on board this ship," Brad said. "I'll help, of course. You might not have heard, but the Cadre, or perhaps some unaligned bounty hunters, attacked me here. Innocent people died.

"As soon as the ship I've chartered from Heimdall's Raiders gets here, I'm free to travel. I'll need to go back to Io and get my new ship, but I have enough financial cushion to spend the time to track down these leads."

"You haven't heard what I have for you yet," Falcone said. "Not to interrupt, but it may bear on this. Lieutenant Commander Greer got word to me about the commandos you encountered, as you requested. I dug into their backgrounds and found a few places where they intersect. One of them is Mars."

"I suspected that might be the case," Barnes said, rubbing his chin. "Commander Greer is a resource I've used for a long time to get data from and to Fleet quietly. She saw your arrival at the Io Yards as being connected to the unusually trained pirates. She mentioned you'd come from Mars."

Falcone scowled. "Too many people I know are telling you things I'd rather keep quiet, Senator."

If that bothered him, it didn't show. "I can make it up to you. I'm certain that the Agency has people on Mars, but the Cadre has to have ears everywhere to get away with what they do. That alarms me more than I can tell you.

"I can get you onto the main orbital or even the planetary surface without anyone else being the wiser. I can also provide you with alternate means of getting equipment and information. Even some things that the Commonwealth would frown upon. The smaller the chance for someone to betray you to the Cadre, the better, I think."

He turned his attention back to Brad. "As I said when we spoke previously, I will continue our financial arrangements while you go after the people behind my daughter's kidnapping. That means I have prepared a contract just like the one you signed last time. Double pay until you kill the Terror, starting now and running until the bastard is dead."

Brad grinned. "I think we have a deal, Senator."

CHAPTER NINETEEN

"I REALLY THINK you should consider pulling out before the mercenary ship gets here," Falcone said. "You need to vanish off the Cadre's scanners for a while."

Brad was doing his evening therapy. It involved dropping lots of objects that normal people could easily manipulate.

He raised an eyebrow at her. "It's my ride back to Io so I can get together with my crew on the new ship."

"It's just like when we broke into Fabian Breen's house on Ganymede. You didn't need a ship full of people for that. You can't use it running down leads on MOSO or on Mars itself, either. You only need their firepower when you find your prey.

"Besides, if you leave without it or them, the Cadre bounty hunters have no way of finding you. Poof! You've just vanished. They'll be watching the Io Yards, your offices, your crew, and your ships as closely as they can. Turn up there and they'll have you.

"Which brings me to the final argument. *Heart of Vengeance* is back at Io. The Cadre informants will have noted the Raiders' ship escorting it, even though they turned back before *Heart* docked. What makes you think they won't ambush your new ship just to kill you?"

He set the small rings he'd been manipulating on the table and gave her his full attention. "So, you think I should just pack up and leave with you on *Lion*? We'd head straight for Mars? What about the Senator?"

"Not exactly," she said with a shake of her head. "We'll still head back to the Io Yards but come in from a more roundabout direction. The Senator would leave the ship and we'd continue on our way without raising any red flags."

"And what should I do with Trista and Lisa Simon? For that matter, what do I do about the kill teams they're going to send to this station?"

The Commonwealth agent shrugged. "The station is beyond your control. The bad people will be coming whether you're here or not. Announcing that you've left will just shift the attacks to another location. As for your people, we'll bring them along."

"That little ship doesn't have much in the way of bunk space," he said doubtfully.

Falcone smirked. "My impression is that they'll only need one. It'll be crowded with all of us, but that will ease once we've dropped our distinguished guest off at the Io Yards."

"Exactly how much spare cubage does your ship have?" Dr. Duvall said as she walked up. "I have excellent hearing, in case you're wondering."

"Dr. Gina Duvall," Brad said, "meet Agent Kate Falcone of the Commonwealth Investigative Agency. Why do you ask? Is this part of pausing my treatment?"

The physician shook her head. "No. I've already told you that isn't going to work. If you prematurely terminate the regeneration treatments, the nerves of your arm will be locked into their current response levels for the rest of your life."

Falcone picked up the rings Brad had clumsily dropped and stared at the other woman. "You mean he'll be like this all the time?"

"Precisely," Duvall said with an aggrieved tone. "I've told him this repeatedly, but he refuses to listen to common sense. He must continue to have daily regeneration treatments for a minimum of two weeks more. Four weeks is a more likely span of time, but six weeks is not beyond the realm of believability."

"And I've told you why I can't stay. In two weeks, we'll have more bounty hunters killing innocent people. In four weeks, we'll have Cadre ships firing on the station. Light only knows what will happen in six."

"You can't cripple yourself," Falcone said. "Once you catch up with the Terror, you'll finish that fight you started on Blackhawk. He'll kill you."

"Maybe," Brad admitted. "Maybe not. I almost took the top of his head off. He lost an eye. We'll both have our off sides."

"Or you could go the novel route of doing what makes the most sense," Duvall said. "Allow me to continue treatments. That's my plan."

Brad shook his head. "We just went through why I can't stay here."

"Indeed. Which is why I will be accompanying you on this escape, at least until your regeneration is complete. Hence my need to know how much cubage that ship has. The regeneration equipment is not as compact as one might wish. I'll need something on the order of four meters by three in a contiguous space."

Falcone overrode him before he objected. "We'll find a way to fit you and your equipment, Doctor. The Commonwealth is in your debt."

"Don't you think you should at least ask the other passenger?" Brad asked wryly. "He might object to being stacked into the wardroom like a log."

"You think you're being funny," Falcone said with a snort. "That's exactly where I intend to put the regeneration equipment. The crew uses two small cabins for a total of four people. That leaves the two remaining cabins for the other passenger, myself, Dr. Duvall, you, and your two mercenaries.

"The other passenger will be off in three days, but we'll still be putting five people into two cabins. Four of them women."

She gave Brad a steady look. "I sense that one of us is not like the others. I'll wager the captain can fit you in with his crew. Hot-bunking is rough, but you're a big boy."

"It's not as if I haven't done it before," he grumbled. "Not that I enjoyed it then, either."

He gave the doctor his full attention. "I don't get it. Why would you even suggest going along for what will end up being months away from home, even if everything goes right? I get being dedicated to your patients, but this seems to go far beyond that."

"It does," she agreed. "I have other patients I'll need to pass on to my colleagues, teaching assignments my students will need to get from said colleagues, and the conditions will undoubtedly be arduous. So be it.

"You asked how doctors such as myself could strike back at the Cadre? By making you fit to kill the man responsible for killing one of us," she said coldly. "In doing this, I act in the stead of all of us."

Brad considered that and slowly nodded. "That is something I can understand. I wish you didn't have to make such a hard choice, considering how much good you'd have done right here, but I won't decline your offer."

"I wasn't worried that you would," she said serenely. "If you'd declined, I'd have spoken to the unnamed—but undoubtedly impor-tant—passenger you've both ever so carefully failed to name for the last hour. I'd wager he wouldn't hesitate in welcoming me aboard."

———

"Welcome aboard, Dr. Duvall," Senator Barnes said warmly. "Once Agent Falcone informed me about the situation regarding Commodore Madrid's recovery and your selfless offer, I would've moved into the engine room to make space for you and your equipment."

She shot Brad a smug look. He wondered if it was natural or it was part of all doctors' training.

"That won't be necessary," Brad assured him. "I'll hot-bunk with the crew. The ladies will sort themselves out."

Putting four of them in one tiny cabin was going to be rough for the next few days, but he wasn't feeling too bad about it. Not really.

"I'll speak with the captain and we'll all hot-bunk, as you call it," the senator said. "Where will the regeneration equipment go?"

"Into the wardroom," Duvall said. "I verified everything fits. Barely. Commodore Madrid will actually be partly in the corridor during sessions, but we can make it work."

"How long will it take you to get everything moved aboard?" Falcone asked. "I'd like to be on our way before we get any unexpected visitors. This ship isn't armed, and isn't the stealthiest thing in space, either."

"Two hours, I believe. Unless you believe I need to move it in a manner unlikely to arouse suspicion. That will take longer."

Brad shook his head. "In this case, I think being open is the best plan. In fact, let them know where I've gone. Make sure the word spreads far and wide."

Falcone blinked in surprise. "We still need to drop the senator back at the Io Yards. If everyone knows you've boarded this ship, we don't dare dock there."

"Don't worry," he said with a grin. "It's all part of my mad plan. I should've thought of this earlier. The senator will have a different ride back to the Io Yard. One that will be just as unlikely to arouse suspicion as this ship would've been."

Senator Barnes raised an eyebrow. "I can't wait to hear how this will work."

"Have you ever considered becoming a mercenary, Senator? Because I'm about to call the guards in. One of them is about your size, so you'll be able to wear his armor. He can borrow a crew uniform and go ashore with some of the real crewmen. No one will know, since his helmet hid his face and they haven't left the ship.

"When the Raiders arrive in a few days, they can get you back to the Io Yards easily enough. I'll leave messages I want hand-delivered to my people there. While they do that, they can get you off the ship and back to your hotel with no one the wiser."

Falcone considered that for a moment before smiling. "That works," she admitted. "No one would suspect a thing. And with you making a big show of leaving Serenity Station, the Cadre would have no reason to even be looking at the mercenary ship."

Barnes grinned. "I wanted to be one as a boy. Mother wouldn't hear of it, of course. Do I get a weapon?"

"Of course," Brad assured the man. "Maybe not any ammunition, but you'll need the weapons to blend in. Welcome to the Mercenary

Guild, Senator. Do us proud and let's hope you don't have to earn that combat bonus the hard way."

———

The doctor was as good as her word and they were on their way in just over two hours. Brad made a point of being seen entering and exiting *Lion* several times as part of helping her people load the gear.

Or perhaps *hindering them* was more accurate.

In any case, it made for a good show, and Senator Barnes didn't get a second glance as he stiffly marched off the ship about halfway through the process. If anyone looked less like a mercenary than the wealthy politician, Brad couldn't imagine how.

Someone would get word to the Cadre, and that would spare Serenity. That was all that truly mattered.

Lion's bridge was far too small to have visitors, but he, Falcone, and his two mercenaries jammed themselves into the tiny cabin the ladies would all share, and observed the departure via the small screen. Dr. Duvall was in the wardroom, putting everything back together.

They'd been discussing what to do once they made the turn for Mars for almost an hour when a chime sounded and Captain Mahdi's voice came over the speakers. "We have company."

Brad would've said they all crowded around the screen, but they were *already* crowded together like thieves planning their next crime.

He flipped the display to show the ship's scanner readings. Indeed, there was a vessel racing in from the Fringe. It was at a terrible angle to intercept them under the best of circumstances, but someone was trying heroically to do so.

The courier showed them the error in their thinking by piling on the acceleration. Brad watched the projected courses alter and allowed himself to feel a bit jealous of this ship's ability to leave the enemy in their stardust.

The enemy was going to be able to hound them for hours but never come close to being inside realistic weapons range.

That didn't mean they wouldn't try, of course. Small markers spat out of the enemy icon as they fired mass-driver rounds at them in wild abandon.

Lion adroitly began altering course, and it very rapidly became obvious that none of the shots would even come close. They'd handily escape unless other ships were out there trying to bracket them.

And they wouldn't know that unless that plan actually worked.

Brad shut off the screen and turned back to Falcone. "Let's focus on things we can control. We've got about a week to get our plan in order. It would be faster if we didn't have to convince everyone we were going to the Belt, but I suppose that can't be helped.

"I'd like to game out as many contingencies as possible. I asked Trista and Lisa to join us because Trista needs to learn how to plan at this level and Lisa was a senior station security officer and can contribute possibilities for MOSO that we might not have thought of."

The agent nodded and settled in. "We won't know exactly where we're going at Mars until we get there, but I think MOSO is the most likely cargo destination for transshipment. We'll plan on that and improvise as needed. I think we should start with…"

CHAPTER TWENTY

A WEEK LATER, Brad sat in the cramped cabin with the rest of the ship's passengers and watched MOSO growing larger on their small screen. Their little side trip to the asteroid belt had been uneventful.

Considering the amount of trouble the Cadre had caused for him, that was surprising. He'd expected to run into several bounty hunters or pirate ships looking to collect those ten million credits.

"Someone is going to be keeping watch on the approaching ships," Falcone said. "Our best bet is going to be squawking a different transponder code than the one they expect and docking at one of the smaller substations."

Brad raised an eyebrow. "Does this ship happen to have more than one transponder code?"

She grinned at him. "As a matter of fact, it does. That's one of the perks of working with the Commonwealth Investigative Agency. At this very moment, anyone observing us believes that we are a small freight carrier that was last seen leaving Venus three weeks ago."

"And what if that ship shows up here?" Trista asked.

"It won't. You see, that ship doesn't really exist. I put out a tight-beam call to some of the folks I know at the Venus Control Center, and they inserted false data into the record for us. Yet another perk of working with the Commonwealth Investigative Agency."

Dr. Duvall looked skeptical. "While this is all suitably spy-like, I'm not certain how that's going to assist us in finding your wandering cargo. Of course, I'm only a simple doctor, so these convoluted plans seem a little silly to me."

Lisa Simon smiled. "Actually, Doctor, going to the smaller side station is going to assist us in finding the cargo. Or at least maintain our anonymity while we try.

"Everyone who comes into Mars orbit tries to get onto MOSO. It has all the best shops, all the best brokers, and all the juiciest little bits of illegal goods that a criminal would want. The smaller side stations don't get nearly the same attention as the big boy.

"Of course, that means the smugglers love them and lavish bribes on the controllers here. They're already trained to look away if they see something odd. I assume you made sure to pay them to look the other way, Kate?"

Falcone nodded. "Absolutely. Once we're into the system, we can move between stations without drawing undue attention. We won't be listed as new arrivals, either. I included the creative editing of the logs about us, too.

"We'll be established individuals with presence in Mars orbit. Of course, I have yet other of our associates that will make certain nothing about us stands out in our electronic footprint. Just in case we need solid credentials."

Brad shook his head. This was a lot different from what he was used to. Mercenaries never got to change things around and blend in.

Captain Mahdi deftly guided the small courier ship through the relatively heavy traffic of Mars orbit to a small substation about a thousand kilometers away from MOSO. It was roughly the same size as Blackhawk Station but had significantly more ships—both visitors and short-range craft—moving things around.

Brad wasn't listening in on the communication between *Lion* and the station, but everything seemed to go well. Captain Mahdi let them know they'd been assigned a dock. Of course, getting to it took them almost an hour because nothing was allowed to move very fast near the station.

Once the ship was docked, they all assembled near the lock. All were dressed in civilian clothes, which thankfully Brad had. He'd been in disguise on Serenity Station, so none of his people wore their customary uniforms.

That had a downside, though. None of them were carrying anything larger than a pistol. As he knew from his last trip, MOSO Security was tough. They'd never tolerate having someone with heavy weapons—which is what they considered rifles and submachine guns —just walking around.

Welcome to the Inner System.

Dr. Duvall would stay with the ship for now. Brad's treatment had been going well, and his arm had shown marked improvement, but he wasn't out of the woods yet. No matter what their eventual disguise ended up being, he would need to return to *Lion* every day.

Inconvenient but necessary.

———

"So, where are we going first?" he asked Falcone as they stepped onto the station proper.

She was dressed in a rather colorful tunic with dark leggings. To add more flair, she added large gold earrings that dangled almost to her shoulders. They chimed as she walked.

"To meet an old friend," she said, not bothering to speak softly like he was doing. "He doesn't live here, but he does a lot of work in Mars orbit. He made a side trip specifically to see if he could help us out."

Brad took her hint and stopped trying to be furtive. As long as he kept anything he said general enough, he should be fine.

The two of them walked through the station as if they didn't have a care in the world. It was hard not to stare at everyone around them, looking for Cadre assassins, yet none of the people going about their business seemed to pay them any mind.

Even though he suspected Falcone had never been on this station before, she moved with an easy confidence that indicated that she knew where she was going. It even hinted at familiarity, so no one would assume they were visitors now that they were away from the docks.

Her destination proved to be a small café set into the side of a working-class neighborhood plaza. It was the type of place where locals went to have lunch without paying tourist prices. It was cozy.

Seeing as they weren't arriving during the normal dining periods, the café was only about a quarter full. As soon as they stepped inside, the scent of something frying in the back made his mouth water.

"I'm told that the po' boy sandwiches are really good," Falcone said as she waved at a young man sitting in a booth. "We'll order some for all three of us and talk while we eat. I'm starving."

Once she gestured for him to sit to the inside, Brad slid into the booth. The young man they were meeting had faintly reddish hair and pale skin with freckles. He also had a winning smile.

"Kate! It's so good to see you again. How long has it been? Six months?"

"More like six years," she said dryly. "Randy Cartwright, meet Brad. Randy used to work with me back when I was stationed at Luna."

Brad extended his hand across the table and the young man shook it firmly. "I'd say she's told me so much about you," Brad said, "but she hasn't mentioned you at all."

"Some of us aren't much for talking about past assignments," Randy said with a laugh. "Or old friends."

A waiter showed up and took their order. Randy continued as soon as the man had left.

"I've been doing a little checking around since I got your message, Kate. It turns out that something matching your needs is available. Unfortunately, it's been shipped down to the surface. You'll have to go and check it out yourself."

She raised an eyebrow. "That's surprising. I figured I'd be able to get what I wanted here in orbit."

"Not this time. The cargo went down to Olympus Mons three days ago. The good news is, as far as I can tell, it's still there. I'll give you the name of the broker who has it in his warehouse. You'll have to negotiate with him about obtaining it."

He slid a small data chip across the table. Falcone pocketed it without even glancing around to see who was watching. Brad admired her cool demeanor.

"So, if we want to get down to the surface without any unseemly delays at customs, do you have any recommendations?" she asked.

"It just so happens that I have a lead on a small flyer heading down today. It's a company job, so you'll have to work your passage. Customs won't even look at you.

"Once you've completed your work, I should be able to arrange for you to get back up here without any issues."

She glanced at Brad. "There is one potential complication. My friend here needs to get back to our ship within the next eighteen hours. I won't bore you with the reasons, but this is a nonnegotiable deadline."

The young man considered that. "Depending on how difficult it is to acquire your cargo, that could prove challenging. However, if I drop a little extra into my payment to my friends below, they should be able to accommodate your needs. When are you thinking of heading down?"

"After lunch."

He pursed his lips. "I think I can make that work, but you're going to owe me."

She grinned, showing him her white teeth. "Are we talking credits or dinner?"

He smirked. "Dinner, of course. And, if you have time, perhaps a little dancing. I know a place over on MOSO that's absolutely divine."

"We might be able to work something out, but no promises. This is a fairly delicate mission and I have to be cautious about making promises I can't keep."

"We'd also like to keep a fairly low profile," Brad added. "I've got some old friends looking for me that I'd rather not know I was here."

"So I gathered," Randy said with a small smile. "Don't worry about that. Discretion is both of my middle names."

Brad laughed. "How peculiar. It seems that Kate has the same middle names as you do."

"I blame our mentor. He had peculiar ideas about how we should see the world."

He glanced at his wrist-comp. "I'd best make a few calls. If you'll have them wrap my sandwich, I'll drop back by and pick it up when I'm done. I'll send Kate the dock number."

He gave Falcone a steady look. "Be careful. The neighborhood you'll be wandering around isn't widely known for its low crime stats."

"We will," she assured him. "Any other advice?"

"Don't dawdle," he said as he stood. "The longer you're there, the better the chance that someone will question your presence. If you want your business to remain private, you'll hurry things along. Good luck."

———

Once Randy had left, the server delivered their sandwiches, and the two of them spoke in low tones as they ate.

"Do we know exactly what kind of neighborhood we're talking about?" he asked.

She shrugged. "Not really, but I can imagine. People fencing stolen goods aren't likely to live and work in decent neighborhoods. We're probably talking about one of the slum areas on the surface of Olympus Mons, the city."

"Have you ever been there?"

"I passed through about five years ago. I wasn't in the city long, but it's not a place one forgets. I'm talking about Olympus Mons, the volcano. *Impressive* doesn't begin to cover it."

"I seem to remember reading that it was big."

"Sure. If by the word you mean *monstrously huge*. The lava bed around the volcano is so heavy that it deforms the planet's crust downward about two kilometers at the edges. It's six hundred kilometers wide and twenty-five kilometers tall. Someone at the highest elevation can't see the edge of the lava flow, because it's over the horizon.

"The nested calderas at the center of the volcano are where they located the city. There are six calderas that cover an area about sixty kilometers by eighty. The atmospheric pressure on the shield is twelve percent of Martian standard, which is itself is less than one percent of Earth's."

"I see," he said slowly. "If it's so high up, even the caldera is probably cold compared to the rest of Mars. It doesn't seem like a very hospitable place to put a major city."

"You could say the same thing about the entirety of Mars," she said with a laugh. "Yet the planet has the second-largest number of humans in the system. Admittedly, there are far fewer than on Earth, but a lot more than one might think.

"Martians tend to build deep. They like domes and underground chambers. That way, everything can remain pressurized and warm. If someone has to go out onto the surface, they tend to keep their business short.

"There are lots of mass-transit tubes under the surface. Walkways, too. Honestly, the surface of the city isn't where you'll find the cream of society, which is why I suspect that's where we're going to be skulking about."

Brad took a bite of his catfish po' boy. It was good. Really good.

They didn't have a lot of time to waste appreciating the meal, but he enjoyed it anyway. After all, if things followed true to form, the next several days would probably be unpleasant and dangerous.

At best, they'd be breaking into a criminal enterprise, trying to locate where stolen goods were going, who was being paid for them, and what supplies might be going in the other direction.

At worst, the Cadre would find them and there'd be a fight. Here in the Inner System, the criminals would have the heavy weapons while he and his friends were limited to pistols and blades. If that happened, Brad wouldn't be enjoying many more meals like the one before him now.

They stretched the meal out to a leisurely twenty minutes, and then headed out as soon as she received the dock number. It was time to go down to Mars.

CHAPTER TWENTY-ONE

BRAD DISCOVERED that Randy's idea of working their way down to Mars meant cargo loading. He had no objection to hard work, but portions of the process were somewhat challenging with his reduced dexterity.

Thankfully, Falcone took up the slack. She worked tirelessly at his side, proving that she had more than a passing familiarity with freight.

Once they had the small craft loaded, the pilot told him to strap down near the cargo while he inspected the load.

He grinned at them once he finished. "I sure hope you secured the cargo well. If not, it might shift when we hit atmosphere. That could end up being a mite…heavy."

"As in *we'd be squished*," Brad said with amusement. "No worries. It's right and tight."

"As you well know," Falcone added. "You're just trying to scare the newbies."

"Everyone needs hobbies," the pilot admitted as he headed toward the cockpit. "Depending on how full the traffic pattern is, we should be on the surface in about ninety minutes."

There must've been more traffic above Olympus Mons than the

pilot had expected, because it was almost two hours before they touched down.

Brad and Falcone made short work of unloading the cargo and seeing it loaded into the transports. The spaceport was inside a massive dome nestled against the wall of the caldera—or so Falcone told him—so the area was fully pressurized.

Once the trucks were on their way, Falcone led him away from the loading zone. They walked through common areas used by employees from a number of different cargo companies, dodging powered lifts moving crates most of the way.

Only once they were clear of the landing area did she slow down and consult her wrist-comp.

"Here's where things get complicated," she said. "There are several methods of accessing the warehouse we want. If we go through the pressurized zone belowground, there'll be more people to hide among, but that will also be how they'd expect anyone to come at them.

"Or we can go onto the surface and attempt to access the building from that direction. That means less people but also increases the possibility of booby traps to an almost certainty."

He considered the options for a moment. "When you say *booby trap*, exactly how deadly are we talking?"

"Potentially very deadly but probably low-key. They wouldn't want to get the kind of attention something like explosives would get. As you might imagine, Olympus Mons City, takes decompression risks *very* seriously. And unless you want to sound like a tourist, just refer to it as 'the city.'"

"So, we're talking about something in the nature of guns, monofilament, or electrical discharges. That sort of thing. The question I have is, how much of a rush are we in? I'd rather do the job right rather than do it fast."

She gave him an odd look. "I'm surprised to hear you say that. Doesn't the Cadre have your girlfriend?"

"You're well informed. They do, but I'm not going to rescue her if I'm dead. I've got to balance my desire to rush ahead with enough caution to make sure I reach the finish line."

"I'd expect nothing less from you," she said with a nod. "I got the information from Trista, by the way. Not as gossip but as background information."

"That's okay, I suppose. I know she doesn't talk out of school.

"No matter what we do, this job is going to take longer than eighteen hours. Why don't we plan on scoping the place out and finding ourselves a local room where we can hide? That way, I can head back up tomorrow for my next treatment once we've been here half a day.

"If things look promising, we can come back tomorrow with a much better idea of how we're going to break in and who we will be dealing with. And speaking of dealing with, exactly who owns this import/export business? Someone associated with the Cadre, I assume, but that leaves a lot to the imagination."

She dug into her pocket and produced the data chip that her friend had given her. "We'll find out as soon as I get some privacy to read this. Perhaps we should begin by finding a local room that won't draw any undue attention. I use the comp there to go over the data, and that might give us a better angle of attack on the problem."

With that in mind, the two of them found a lift.

He eyed the number of buttons on the panel. "Twenty-two floors? Just how deep does the city, go?"

"A lot deeper than twenty-two levels," she assured him. "Though the city does seem to be getting somewhat restrictive on going down any farther. If you believe the conspiracy theories, they'd found chambers deep in the volcano with strange runes carved all over the walls."

Brad raised an eyebrow. "Seriously?"

"I did say conspiracy theories," she said with a grin. "Don't believe everything you read on SysNet. Anyway, the depth is all dependent on the section of the city you're in. Someone is always digging deeper below the best parts of the city, and the wealthiest citizens are relocating as they do.

"If you're poor, you live just below the surface. If you're rich, you never see the surface. Or the poor."

He shook his head slightly. "I can't see wealthy families continually moving just because there's a new opening down below. Surely, there are still some rich people living higher up."

"Not so that you'd notice. The status that comes with wealth here also requires that you keep up appearances. Admittedly, you won't find people moving every five years. Not even every fifteen years.

"But there is no way in Everlight you're going to find a wealthy family that hasn't relocated in the last thirty. Which means, by the way, that the city has hundreds of old family estates that are now being used by the merchant class. That way, they can live just like the people they want to become, sneering at the poor people they're leaving behind."

"Some things never change," he agreed. "I'd be willing to bet that the criminal element is also moving into those old homes. They like to put on as many airs as merchants. Maybe more."

She nodded her agreement and pressed a button about halfway down the panel. "I don't know precisely where we're going to find lodging, but if we stick to the middle of the city, we should be relatively safe."

Finding what amounted to a budget hotel wasn't difficult. In fact, advertising screens along every major thoroughfare made certain that a number of possibilities were presented to them. He imagined the city had a lot of visitors.

Half an hour later, they had checked into a nondescript hotel. The clerk at the front desk had barely glanced at them before taking their reservation for the next three days. The fact that they had no luggage didn't faze him at all.

The room they'd gotten was about as plain as one could ask for. It held a double bed, a small desk, and built-in closets and dressers, and had a small enclosed heating unit for food. The bathroom was also nothing to write home about.

Falcone sat at the desk and pulled out the chip, plugging it into her wrist-comp to sort through the data "This is going to take me a little bit. Why don't you go to the deli across the street and get us something? And dessert. I want something sweet."

"Good idea. That po' boy was a long time ago. Be right back."

———

"This is Paul Chandra," Falcone told him an hour later, after they'd eaten. "Randy's file says that he's a high-level fence for various organizations based here in the city. There is no known connection between him and the Cadre, but if he has the cargo, he's their fence, too."

The man's image showed him to be a dark skinned, dark haired man, likely of Indian descent. He was a relatively handsome fellow, but his eyes were cold and hard. This was a man you didn't trifle with.

The image had been taken on a crowded street. The subject was surrounded by large beefy men who were probably his bodyguards.

"So, we're planning to break into his warehouse and see if we can locate any records about the Cadre?" he asked. "I think the odds of him having anything written down about the Terror are pretty low. And why would he keep them in the warehouse? Surely, he does business somewhere less…industrial."

"Probably," she admitted. "But it's not as if we have a choice. The warehouse is more accessible than his home. Not easy, but we're more likely to get in and out safely.

"If we're going to locate where the Cadre has your girlfriend, we need a lead on their base. Someone supplies them. If we don't directly find the Cadre, we can at least get the names of individuals who may have closer dealings with the Terror."

"Do we have plans for the warehouse? Is it reachable from the surface?"

She nodded. "I'm certain the plans are out of date and that they don't completely reflect what we're going to find inside, but it's better than nothing.

"It's not reachable from the surface, but it's not exactly underfoot, either. I think the best course of action will be to find a location that overlooks the main entrance to the warehouse and see who goes in and out. Once we have a better idea of the traffic levels and the players, we'll be able to more comprehensively plan a course of action."

Brad brought up a map of the city. It was geared toward tourists, but at least it had most of the levels marked and many of the major corridors and thoroughfares.

He double-checked the address for the warehouse and entered it. "That's not exactly close by, and you're right about it not being underfoot. We're going to have to be very careful that we don't let him or any of his people spot us."

She checked the time. "It's early afternoon, local time. I suggest we make a trip in that direction and drive past it. So long as we don't linger, we can make enough of an examination to know what we're dealing with and find a good spot to covertly observe the warehouse.

"Then we can return here and get some sleep. We'll head back up to the station in the morning, you can get your regeneration treatment, and then we'll head back down here and see if we can plant some cameras to watch everything for us."

"You're not planning on observing it in person?" he asked with a raised eyebrow. "That hardly seems spy-like."

She laughed. "That's an amateur move. They'll be watching for anyone who doesn't belong. We want to find a good location to plant cameras, and then we'll swing back by and pick up the video they record at a later point in time.

"We don't dare leave them transmitting, because it's a certainty that they'll be looking for strange signals. If we play this low-key, they won't even become aware of our presence. Trust me. That's the way we want it."

***

They rented an older corridor car and had it take them to the general area around the warehouse.

"We'll go just south of the warehouse and rent another car," Falcone said. "Then we'll make a trip across the district to an area tourists frequent. If someone sees us, a check of the corridor-car logs will show our origin and destination. That way, we won't raise any suspicion."

"And if they check to see where we're staying? Our hotel is quite a ways off."

She smiled. "That's why we will be renting another room. Don't worry. The Commonwealth will cover this one."

It was eerie how similar their second hotel room was to the first. It was almost as if they had been designed and built by the same person, one with no taste in wall art.

They left their corridor car at the new hotel and rented a second one. This one was slightly newer but of a similar style.

By the time they reached the warehouse district, traffic was picking up because many workers were getting off and heading home. Most didn't have their own transportation and instead relied upon public transportation.

Most of that was handled via trains running through dedicated tubes in a vacuum. He imagined the 3-D map showing all the routes looked like a tangle of yarn. They had to be built when a level was constructed, and moving them at a later point in time would be virtually impossible.

As the city grew, what had once been popular transit lines most likely needed to be abandoned every once in a while because the population had relocated. And perhaps there were areas of the city that needed this type of mass transit that couldn't get it.

"There it is, on the left," Falcone said as they approached the warehouse. "There's an eatery just up the street that'll make a great stakeout location. We can drop in for dinner, I'll slip off to the floor above and plant a camera, and then we'll be off."

That sounded so simple in theory. He was certain it was going to be a nail-biter when they tried to actually pull it off.

They were even with the warehouse when the front door opened and a group of men walked out. Brad had just one glance at them before the corridor car moved past, but he recognized Paul Chandra in the center of the group. And he wasn't the only person Brad recognized.

Standing right beside the Martian crime lord was Jack Mader.

CHAPTER TWENTY-TWO

"Was that who I thought it was?" Falcone asked incredulously.

"If you thought you saw Jack Mader, then you're right," Brad said, fighting the urge to look over his shoulder. "I suppose that means we can confirm Chandra's connection to the Cadre. What do we do now?"

She sat silently for a minute. "I'm not sure this changes anything. We still need the same information as before. I suppose Mader's presence means we have a better opportunity to get good data, though."

That was the understatement of the year. While Brad couldn't precisely place Jack Mader in the Cadre organization, he was definitely a senior man. One with a very large price on his head, too. Anything that needed his personal attention in a heavily policed place like Mars had to be important.

"Maybe the cargo they seized from the Senator was more important than we believed," he ventured.

"Why would Barnes lie?"

"I'm not sure he did. It may just be the cargo that he chose to lure them. In any case, we need to get inside that warehouse as soon as possible. Perhaps sooner than we'd planned."

"Why don't we try to snatch Mader?" she countered. "If anyone knows where the Cadre base is, it would be him."

By this time, the corridor car had left the warehouse district and was back in an area of the city with a more varied population.

"To get our hands on him, we'd have to call in extra support," Brad said, shaking his head. "We know the Cadre has eyes and ears everywhere. We'd blow this entire operation."

"What about Randy? We can trust him."

"Just because he wouldn't personally betray us doesn't mean that the resources he taps won't, if they get wind of where we're working or who we're interested in. I'd much rather miss the chance to capture Mader than tip him off that we're here."

The corridor car pulled into a parking lot adjacent to a mall, and they climbed out. The collection of businesses was much like similar areas on any inhabited body in the solar system. Places that proclaimed the simplicity of shopping many stores all gathered for your convenience.

At exorbitant prices, of course.

Their plans called for them to spend the next hour window-shopping. If something sparked their interest, they'd buy it. Then they'd have dinner at one of the trendy little restaurants that served the tourist community. Also for much higher prices than any of the locals would pay.

They couldn't exactly talk about breaking into a warehouse or capturing Cadre pirates with so many ears walking past, so the conversation turned to inane matters. That gave him time to think.

Why was Mader there? Was he making the right call by keeping his hands off the man who probably knew where the Cadre base was? He'd much rather snatch the bastard and beat the truth out of him, but the risks were too high.

Even if they succeeded, it would tip the Cadre off that something was going on. The very last thing he wanted was to put Michelle at risk.

Besides, other than the single sighting they'd had, tracking someone like Mader down would be almost impossible. He wouldn't be staying at the warehouse. In fact, he wouldn't be anywhere Olympus Mons security could find him.

No. As much as Brad would love to get his hands on the bastard, he had to stick with the plan. Though it might not be a bad idea to accelerate the timetable. They might benefit from having a camera on the warehouse tonight.

They finally settled into a somewhat upscale café. Once they'd ordered appetizers and drinks, Falcone smiled at him over the rim of her glass.

"You're thinking about him, aren't you? Mader. Second-guessing yourself."

"Should we really be talking about him like this?"

She gave him an elaborate shrug. "Look at all the people around us. What do you think they see? How much do you think they hear?"

"To them, were just another couple out for a night on the town. Even the closest table can't hear what you're saying with all these conversations going on. We're safe enough."

"I want him," Brad said bluntly. "More than you could possibly imagine. I'm just not sure grabbing him won't set off a sequence of events that we can't control. For us to get what we need, everything has to go perfectly.

"They can't suspect that we're tracing the cargo. They can't know we're watching their people. Worst of all, they can't wonder who took Jack Mader."

"You're probably right," she sighed, "but I'm not willing to give up on the possibility quite yet. The first step to any plan we make involves planting listening devices and cameras inside the warehouse.

"You're right that we're not going to find any files that say, *Cadre base here*. The data we need is going to come when someone mentions a name or location. That's going to lead us to someone we *can* snatch and make talk."

Her wrist-comp chimed, and they both stared at it for a moment before she answered. "Hello?"

"Kate," Randy said, a note of relief in his voice. "I'm glad I caught you. We have something of a situation."

The other man's voice was calm but tense. With all the noise in the café, Brad could only barely hear him.

"What kind of situation?" Falcone asked.

"One of my confidential informants called to tell me that Chandra is searching for you."

———

"What happened?" she asked tensely.

"I'm still not completely sure. All I can say for certain is that we have a leak. A very highly placed one."

Brad leaned forward. "Who even knew we were here?"

"By name? No one. But I had to bring in several people to help track the cargo. I thought I could trust everyone involved, but someone told Chandra. And that same someone must've told them I was sending you down to the planet."

"It won't be easy to find us. I picked our hotel at random."

"I'm sure you did. The problem is that they know how you got onto the planet. If they have access to the security apparatus in Olympus Mons, they could've traced you."

Brad's gut clenched. Followed to its logical conclusion, that meant that it was only a matter of time before Chandra found them at their new hotel. Or in this café.

He turned in his seat and scanned the other diners. No one seemed overly interested, but did that really mean anything?

"I'm going dark," Falcone said. "Find your leak."

She ended the call, took off her wrist-comp, and disabled it. "I think you'd best do the same. We can't trust that they don't have people in Olympus Mons Security."

"What do we do now?" he asked as he disabled his comp.

"Pay our bill and walk away. We'll find some other place to spend the evening. And don't make the mistake of thinking we're going to let this change our plans. We're still breaking into the warehouse."

He felt both of his eyebrows rise. "Seriously? They have to be on the lookout for us now."

"I have a plan."

Falcone flagged the waiter down and paid their bill in hard currency. That made the man's eyes widen slightly, but they were tourists. There was no accounting for taste.

She led them out of the café and into the crowd of people still swarming the mall. They dodged across the walkway and into one of the service corridors as a man walked out. It was clearly marked AUTHORIZED PERSONNEL ONLY, but that didn't slow her down.

He wasn't certain how, but she managed to figure her way through the service corridors until she arrived at a central supply point. They passed several individuals who gave them odd looks, but she held out a clip-on badge and just kept walking.

Only when they arrived at her apparent destination did he get a good look at it. It was an employee badge. The one belonging to the guy who'd opened the door, allowing them into the service corridors. He hadn't even seen her take it.

The parking area held a large number of bicycles. Brad supposed they made more sense for people living nearby than corridor cars, those that just didn't take the public transit cars.

Falcone headed for the area reserved for the few corridor cars. In fact, she headed for the most expensive-looking vehicle and pulled out a small pack of tools.

"You know security is watching us right now," he said as he looked at the camera in the corner.

"Not a chance," she said, not even pausing as she worked on the door. "They have far too many public areas to monitor. That's just recording in case there's a crime."

"Like this one?"

"Exactly like this one," she confirmed, popping the door open. "Get in."

Since he really didn't have any other options, he got in. She activated the car's internal controls just as adroitly as she'd broken in. The entire process of stealing the vehicle took less than a minute.

"You've done this before," he observed.

"More than a few times," she admitted. "It's a mandatory part of the curriculum at the academy. Even Kevin Blake passed that part of the final without getting caught."

"From your tone, I'll assume this Kevin didn't graduate at the top of the class."

"The exact opposite, as you probably guessed. He works in headquarters now, making the rest of us miserable. Dammed bean counter thinks he knows everything about field work because he's technically qualified to be a field agent. I wouldn't trust him to rescue a cat from a tree."

Based on the cats Brad was familiar with, he couldn't imagine them ever needing rescue. Not that he had much experience with trees in space.

The corridor car arrived at the security checkpoint situated at the mall perimeter. It barely paused as it headed past the guard in the clear booth. Falcone waved at the man cheerily as they sped by.

Brad imagined the man was going to be making some very awkward explanations soon.

"Okay, now that we're clear, what do we do? I'd really rather Olympus Mons Security didn't apprehend us."

She leaned back in her seat and gave him her full attention as the corridor car headed for whatever destination she'd programmed into it.

"Even if they do, I have a get-out-of-jail-free card. This is Commonwealth business. I want at least a few kilometers between us and the mall before we get out of the car, just in case Chandra's people managed to trace our rental.

"After we get out, we'll take the slideway back to the warehouse district. We're not going to wait until dark to make our move, either. That's when they'd expect us."

"How sure are we that they are even looking for us in this part of the city? They might not have even found the first hotel room yet."

"We can't count on that," she said with a shake of her head. "While paranoia is generally bad, it makes perfect sense when you know they really *are* out to get you.

"If a mole in Randy's organization did leak our presence—which it sounds as if they did—then we have to assume that Chandra's people have already accessed port records and seen what we look like.

"It's a very short step from that to using the facial-recognition software security uses to locate us in the hotel records. You can be sure that he has people in security on his payroll for things like that."

Brad hadn't been aware that their images were saved during hotel check-in, but this *was* the Inner System. It shouldn't have been so surprising.

The mall probably had similar security functions. Most public areas likely did, now that he thought about it. They'd have to stay away from places that security might have a camera watching.

"Can we evade Chandra and security long enough to get where we need to go? Aren't the slideways monitored?"

She smiled. "Sure, but I picked a destination to help us with that. There are some disguises we can manage that mess with facial recognition. That's yet another aspect of our training. We'll be fine once we get out of this car and get some new clothes and other props.

He opened his mouth to ask her exactly how that worked, but the corridor car suddenly changed direction and sped up. The locks in the doors clicked.

"I'd say this means someone called security after all," he said as she cursed. "I certainly hope your get-out-of-jail-free card is effective. And that Chandra's people don't find us first."

CHAPTER TWENTY-THREE

"How likely is security to send someone out for us?" he asked.

"They'll direct the car to the nearest security substation."

"Then we're getting out of here."

He opened his jacket and drew his pistol. He used the bottom of the grip to smash the window. It was surprisingly tough and took several strikes before it cracked, then several more before it came apart.

"We're going a little fast to jump out," she observed.

"I hope they taught you how to tuck and roll in the academy," he said as he grabbed the door. "We're not out of the populated areas, so I can't see them racing us through intersections. While I doubt we'll stop, we'll almost certainly slow down. There's no traffic on this side of the car, so use it."

Traffic control there in Olympus Mons City wasn't exactly an obvious sort of thing. The corridor cars didn't need signals, and the pedestrian traffic directions were facing so that he couldn't see them.

Brad holstered his pistol, climbed out of the car, and hung onto the window, earning more than a few stares and even a few shouts. He expected the car to slow as it approached the intersection, but it accelerated.

He jumped anyway and slammed into the ground as if he'd run

into a wall, rolling into the intersection. His bad arm hurt like hell, even though he'd tucked it in for protection. Then a corridor car coming in from the side almost ran over him, swerving only at the very last moment.

Unsure from what direction the next threat might come from, Brad scuttled to the side of the road as quickly as he could. A good idea, since a car from the other direction only barely missed him as obstacle avoidance systems belatedly recognized his presence.

Several of the pedestrians grabbed him, pulling him up before any other vehicles came along to run him down.

A man stared at him in amazement. "Did you just jump out of a moving car?"

Brad clearly heard the unspoken *you idiot* added to the end.

"There was a malfunction." That sounded lame, even to him.

"I'd better call security," the man said, obviously unconvinced.

Falcone walked calmly across the street, seemingly not bothered by her landing. "I'm security," she said sternly. "Thank you for apprehending this petty thief. I'll take him from here."

Brad wasn't certain whose look was less believing, his or the pedestrian.

"Really?" the man asked. "Who are you people?"

She presented her identification. This time, it was an official looking badge and holographic ID card. It looked real, even if she only held it out for a moment.

Without waiting for a response, she tucked the badge away and grabbed Brad by the arm. The good one, thankfully.

"Thank you, citizen," she said. "I have another vehicle meeting us."

Though Brad wasn't certain the explanation would satisfy the pedestrian, the man wasn't actively trying to stop them as they walked away.

It only took them a minute to get out of sight. Falcone released him and they sprinted away from the area.

He had no idea where they were going and he didn't care, so long as it wasn't into the arms of Olympus Mons Security or Chandra's goons.

Her path seemed random, but she slowed after a few streets and ducked into a side corridor. There, she slowed to a walk.

"Are you okay?" she asked. "That was a pretty rough landing."

"I've had better," he conceded. "It looks as if you managed yours fine."

He hoped his jealousy came through.

It must've, because she laughed. "You could say that. Once you jumped, the shove to the car made it slow down because it thought it had hit something. I didn't even have to roll."

"Figures," he muttered. "Do you think security will be able to catch up with us? Will the guy call it in? And what was that ID?"

"It's my Agency ID. He didn't see it clearly enough to know anything other than it was authentic-looking. As for him calling it in, I have no idea. We'll find out if we start hearing a lot of sirens."

They walked in silence for the next twenty minutes. No sirens. The man must've decided not to get involved.

Security would be annoyed when the corridor car made its way to them without the thieves they expected. By then, someone would have video of them stealing the car. Their pictures would be out before long, if they weren't being distributed already.

"We've got to get off the street," she said. "There's a neighborhood bar over there. Let's duck inside and let things cool off for a while. We'll have to adjust my plan now. No helping it."

He trusted her, but he wasn't sure the two of them needed to be planning a solo assault on the warehouse now. Chandra was expecting them, and now security was hunting them too. This had gone bad fast.

The bar turned out to be cozy and dark. Just the sort of watering hole where people didn't want to be bothered. Perfect.

A large screen on one wall had most of the patrons watching some kind of sporting event that looked less organized than a brawl but possibly more violent.

Falcone headed for the bar. Brad started after her but saw a couple of men in one of the booths, wearing enlisted Fleet uniforms. That gave him an idea. One Falcone probably wouldn't like, but that was too bad.

He diverted to the table and cleared his throat. "Excuse me, gentlemen, but are you assigned to *Eternal*?"

Eternal was the Fleet battleship in permanent orbit around Mars. It acted as the central point of the Fleet presence around Mars. Brad had been aboard her once and knew some of her officers.

The two men looked up, obviously surprised at the interruption to their private conversation. One of them started to say something, but the other man held up his hand.

"Can we help you, sir?"

"Yes. I need to contact Commodore Angel Bailey. Discreetly."

The man laughed. "As if I'm calling the Commodore when some guy in a bar asks me to. I'll give you the main number and you can call her yourself."

"This is official Commonwealth business," Falcone said, presenting her ID. This time, she held it so the man could read it. "Fleet's assistance would be greatly appreciated."

The look she shot Brad wasn't exactly appreciative, but they needed the help.

The man read her ID and then studied her face. "This is outlandish, but that looks real. Real enough for me to call my lieutenant. You can try to convince him to call the commodore."

The man brought up his wrist-comp, called someone, and apologized for disturbing them. He then briefly explained that he had some civilians with badges asking to talk to their CO.

"He wants to talk to you," the man said after a moment, extending his wrist-comp toward Brad.

The image on the screen was of a slightly older man in civilian clothes. He frowned at Brad.

"My name is Lieutenant Ibrahim Al Jabari. I understand you're looking for help. Who are you and why don't you call *Eternal*'s main contact number?"

"I'm Commodore Brad Madrid," Brad said. "Your CO knows me. I can't afford the wrong people figuring out where I am, so I'm doing this through you. My associate is with the Commonwealth Investigative Agency."

The man looked as if he wanted to tell Brad to stop bothering him but examined Falcone's ID when she presented it. After a long moment, he sighed.

"I'll call her, but it's on your head if you're screwing with us."

The image vanished from the wrist-comp. Sixty seconds later, it signaled an incoming call. The man wearing it leapt to his feet when he answered.

"Commodore!"

"Pass the man the comp." Brad recognized Commodore Angel Bailey's voice.

The Fleet man almost threw his wrist-comp at him.

"Commodore, it's good to see you again," Brad said once he could see her.

"It really is you," she said, sounding more than a bit surprised. "Is your companion really an officer of the Commonwealth Investigative Agency?"

"She is and we need your help."

"In regards to what?" she asked, sounding more than bit wary.

"The same sort of thing as last time. Only with that bigger organization we talked about."

The last mission he'd worked with the woman on had involved the slavers. She would know the larger group was the Cadre.

"You have my undivided attention," she said with a cold smile. "Can you come to my office?"

"Actually, we can't. I don't want to get into details, but we've annoyed Olympus Mons Security, and action is going to be here on the surface. I'll pass the wrist-comp back to its owner and he can tell you where we are.

"I need your very discreet assistance in the form of some people that can assist us with getting into a secure area under the control of that group. They're aware we're in the city and know what we look like. They probably want to do unfortunate things to us."

"I see," Bailey said dryly. "And having met you, I can sympathize. It'll take me a few hours to get some people together."

He nodded. "That works. We suspect everyone at this point, so if you could keep this quiet—even from the people coming—that might help."

Bailey nodded. "I'll take care of it."

———

Two hours later, they were in the back room at the bar. The two enlisted men were at a small table in the corner, keeping to themselves. Commodore Bailey had just arrived, alone, dressed in civilian clothes.

Bailey shook Brad's hand firmly. "I have to confess I never expected to see you again, Madrid. Are we really after the Cadre?"

"We are. Commodore Angel Bailey, this is Agent Kate Falcone. She's assisting me in this matter."

Falcone raised an eyebrow. "I'd have said he was helping me, but that's substantially accurate. I was here last time, Commodore, but we never met."

"As I told you on the com," Bailey said, getting to the point, "I'm at your disposal. What are you looking for assistance with?"

Brad gestured to a table on the far side of the room from the enlisted men who were watching the commodore with poorly concealed dread.

Once they were seated, he told Bailey everything from Blackhawk Station to the present. She listened without comment until he got to them stealing the car. At that point, she laughed before motioning for him to continue.

"Actually, that's about the end," he admitted. "We got out of the car and made it here. The bottom line is that we have to get into the warehouse and they'll be waiting for us."

"Are you going after that Mader fellow?"

He shrugged. "I originally thought it was a bad idea, but circumstances have changed. If I can get him, I'll make him talk. The problem is getting in without them destroying all the evidence. If we call security, Chandra's people will know. They'll purge the data and Mader will vanish."

She nodded. "I can provide the manpower and skill to get inside the warehouse, but the odds of getting into a firefight are pretty high. What happens when it all goes to crap?"

"This has become a make-or-break mission. We need to get Mader or Chandra, I think. No one lower in the organization will know where the base is."

It was a terrible risk. If Mader got away, the odds were exceptionally good that bad things would happen to Michelle. The Terror would know that Brad was coming then, for certain. He'd lay a trap and the base's defenses would be on high alert.

"I figured that would be the case," Bailey said. "Just based on your general comments, I took the liberty of gathering some men and equipment. I can't move a lot of people without raising suspicions, but I have two platoons of Marines quietly filtering down here. We can get equipment now that I know what the mission is.

"I've taken the precaution of stripping them of coms. Only the senior officer has one, and he's under constant watch by two other men I trust implicitly. There will be no untoward messages."

Fleet Marines were tough. The criminals might have better weapons than Brad, but the Commonwealth military could deal with them.

Bailey turned to Falcone. "I need to understand what your authority is in this matter, Agent. The use of Marines on Mars like this is going to raise havoc. Is my ass covered?"

Falcone smiled coldly. "It is. Give me your com code and I'll send my orders and authorizations to you."

Moments later, the Fleet officer was reading. She started nodding a few moments later.

"I can work with this. Still, I think it might be best if we have a little local cover. I've made arrangements."

She made a call from her wrist-comp and smirked. Moments later, the door opened and two people walked in. One was Captain Weldon Shelby, *Eternal*'s chief engineer. The other was Detective Margaret Huddleston, Mars Security.

"Well, well, well," the security officer said, her eyes cool as she took Brad in. "I saw an order for your arrest a few hours ago, Mr. Madrid. This is going to be an unexpected pleasure."

CHAPTER TWENTY-FOUR

"Detective Huddleston," Brad said as he stood. "This is a surprise."

"I'm sure it is," she said dryly. "And it's Detective Lieutenant Huddleston of Mars Security, not MOSO Security now. Goodness, but you've been a busy man."

She walked slowly around the table and looked him over with cool eyes. "Criminal trespass of private property, grand theft of a very pricy corridor car, destruction of said private property, unlawful representation as a Commonwealth official, and fleeing arrest.

"I'd wager you were carrying illegal weapons during the commission of your crimes, too. All of that adds up to a lot of time in custody."

"I never said I was a Commonwealth official and had no illegal weapons," he said primly. "Besides, I can explain."

"I can't wait to hear you try to tap-dance your way clear of charges when this all sorts itself out. Your face is known to us now. Good luck getting off Mars without having to answer for your heinous crimes."

The woman smiled a little. "That being said, Commodore Bailey said this meeting had to do with the Cadre when she abducted me—a somewhat more serious crime, I feel the need to point out. Being the generous sort of person that I am, I've decided to give you all the chance to explain yourselves before I start arresting people."

"Since I'm forcing you to do all sorts of things you shouldn't be doing," he said with a smile, "can I coerce you into accepting a drink?"

"I couldn't possibly keep you from forcing a glass of wine on me," she said as she took a seat beside Falcone. "Who might you be?"

"The purported false Commonwealth official," Falcone said, extending her hand. "Which I actually am, by the way."

Huddleston took Falcone's ID and examined it closely. "Not the security badge the witness claims someone showed him, but I suppose eyewitness testimony is questionable for a reason."

She handed Falcone her badge back and took the glass of wine Brad had poured for her. He had no idea how expensive the bottle was, but it would be worth it in the long run. At the other women's gestures, he poured two more. Captain Shelby grabbed two cold beers, one for himself and one for Brad.

Now that they were fixed for alcohol, Brad went through the explanations again. The detective listened closely, interrupting to ask clarifying questions as he went. Once he finished his story, she took him back through it and made him repeat sections in greater detail.

Only once she was seemingly satisfied did she lean back in her seat, frowning. "This is both good and bad. I'm pleased that I won't have to put the pair of you in prison for your crimes, though the Commonwealth Investigative Agency will be paying restitution for the damages.

"On the other side of the balance sheet, finding out that Chandra is more than a local crime lord raises many uncomfortable questions for Mars Security. It also explains his remarkable success in preventing us from arresting him and dismantling his organization."

Brad nodded, sipping his beer. "If his group is like any other Cadre organization, he'll have paid informants and even active subordinates in security. Which, by the way, is probably why Commodore Bailey shanghaied you rather than asking for your assistance."

The Fleet officer nodded. "Exactly. I have no idea who I can trust, so I'm keeping all the data as compartmentalized as possible. If word gets out, Mader vanishes and so does Chandra. We need them to get a lead on the Cadre base."

"I hate to be the bearer of bad news," Huddleston said, "but it's unlikely that Chandra knows where the base is. Basic information security says you only tell the people who have to know. He doesn't need to know."

"Perhaps not," Falcone said, "but he knows something that will lead us in the right direction. He fences materials they send to him and almost certainly sends shipments back. Those will pass through middlemen, but if we can get their names, that will give us one more stepping-stone toward the Cadre base."

"Not if the Terror hears about his capture," Brad said glumly. "He's more than willing to kill every middleman that could lead us to him. We need to keep the details of this operation as close to the vest as possible."

Shelby shook his head. "That's not going to work. No matter how quiet we are, word will get out that we've raided Chandra. The Terror would almost have to take steps."

"Then we need to use misdirection," Brad said as he thought furiously. "Convince him we didn't get anything."

"It's all too likely you won't get anything," Huddleston said flatly. "The cargo you followed here might have led you to his warehouse, but that won't be where you catch Chandra or Mader. Neither of them will go near the place now. That means your planned assault will almost certainly come up empty-handed."

"Where will he be?" Falcone asked.

"Chandra has a rather large home in one of the better neighborhoods. What we call the third tier. It belonged to one of the founding families a decade ago, but they moved deeper when he made them an offer they literally couldn't refuse."

Brad nodded. "Falcone was telling me about that kind of thing. That means he's in an area with restricted access that he probably keeps well-guarded. An assault into a residential neighborhood has far too much risk of hurting or killing innocent people."

"Perhaps not as much as you think," Bailey disagreed. "I've been to some parties in places like that as part of my official duties. The wealthy snobs don't really like having neighbors at all. They design their homes so that they don't have to worry about running into them.

"That means we might be able to manage a breach into part of the housing complex that is safe for the use of heavy weapons. We'd also end up behind their defensive perimeter. Remember, criminals aren't trained fighters like my Marines. They don't think about defending places the same way. Of course, that changes if there are Cadre goons on top of the usual suspects."

"There may be something to that," Huddleston admitted, "but I think he'll be ready to defend himself with lawyers, not guns. What weapons he has will be to delay security while he makes his getaway.

"Speaking of which, he'll have an escape tunnel to get him clear. One that will lead to an area where he can board a shuttle and get up into orbit. It wouldn't surprise me if he has a fast ship waiting there to get him clear of Mars in a hurry. Mader, too."

"Is there anything we can do about that?" Brad asked Bailey.

"I'll lock down all orbital traffic as soon as we kick this off. If someone decides to make a run for it, they'll find out how fast my picket ships can run them down. Mars Traffic Control will raise all kinds of trouble, but I can make it stick long enough."

"Is it possible to get the plans to Chandra's home?" Falcone asked. "I realize they won't be completely accurate, but we have to have something to start with."

Huddleston nodded. "I can do that without raising any eyebrows. It'll take about an hour, though."

Brad smiled. "That's okay. I need about that long to get a diversion up and running."

"What kind of diversion?" Falcone asked, an eyebrow edging up.

"The kind that everyone sees coming but doesn't recognize it for what it is. I want you to get your friend Randy on the com for me. He's going to play a big part in this."

———

Brad walked to the other side of the room once Falcone had Randy on the com for him. "Have you found your leak?"

"Not yet," the CIA agent said through tight lips. "Whoever it was, they're deep. I didn't trust many people with information on this project. Now I don't trust any of them."

"I'm taking a risk trusting you, too," Brad said bluntly. "Falcone says you're a good man, but you could be in the Cadre's pockets. Can you think of a good reason I shouldn't cut you loose?"

"Not really. I could protest my innocence until the end of time, but that proves nothing. In my defense, I will offer that the odds of them catching you would've been a lot higher if I was on the take. They could've had people waiting to take you into custody the moment you touched down."

Brad had already considered that. It didn't prove anything, of course, but it *was* evidence in the man's favor.

"We don't really have a lot of choices. Like you say, if you're on the take, we're screwed. I need you to get us men and equipment to get into the warehouse quietly. That's still the most likely area where computers containing Cadre data are sitting. Unless they can be accessed remotely."

"They won't be connected, but I'll verify that and get word to you if I'm wrong," the agent said. "What kind of timeframe are you looking at? I need to work around my usual people, and that'll take longer."

"Do they know you suspect a leak?"

"I doubt it. I've kept things low-key."

"Then don't worry about hiding it. Make noises like you're having doubts about someone outside your organization, and get the same people you used last time working on helping us slip into the warehouse."

Randy opened his mouth to object but stopped, his eyes narrowing. "You're not going after the warehouse."

"We're not *only* going after the warehouse. It remains a target, but you've just become the diversion."

The other man nodded slowly. "You've found other people to help you. Who?"

"I'm keeping that to myself, just in case I'm wrong about you."

That made the other man smile a little. "Smart. Well, I'll leave that part to you. What about your people here in orbit?"

"They can stay there. Did you warn them that our cover was blown, so that they could keep their guard on higher alert?"

"I did. Someone named Trista told me not to teach my grandmother to suck eggs, whatever that means."

It meant that he'd really spoken to Trista, for one thing. She occasionally came up with the oddest sayings.

"Are you going to have an alternate means to get back up here tomorrow?" Randy asked. "I remember you said that part of the schedule was nonnegotiable."

"This is going to be settled one way or another before I have to worry about that. I want you to have the people down here and ready for an infiltration mission a few hours before local dawn. Let that information slip and then try to backtrack on it. That'll make them sure the timetable is accurate."

"You've done this before," the other man said in an admiring tone. "I'll make it happen. Should I be expecting all hell to break loose?"

"I would, in your shoes. This might be the perfect time to find your mole, when everything starts going to the Dark."

"I'll do that. Good luck." The other man ended the call.

Brad walked back to the common table and handed Falcone her wrist-comp back. "It's all set. Randy is going to arrange everything so that we have forces to infiltrate the warehouse."

That brought a slow smile to her face. "And that he'll make sure gets leaked about from a source that Chandra trusts. Very nice. That'll draw defensive forces from Chandra's home."

She gestured toward the table. "We've been going over the plans and have spotted a few potential avenues of access and some possible escape routes. Two platoons of Marines isn't going to allow us to keep them from running, but we might be able to ambush them when they do."

"I've got an idea about that," Huddleston said, looking up from her comp. "I've organized a manhunt for the two of you."

Brad blinked. "And that helps us how?"

"It gives us access to mobile manpower. I'm going to gather them together for a group planning session about the same time you're making the push into Chandra's home.

"I've conveniently chosen the closest security station to his place, by the way. When you signal the intrusion has started, I'll make certain that someone reports you in that area and get our people out in force. We'll make sure no one manages to slip away."

Falcone sighed. "I don't like this. There are far too many people running around that have no idea what's really going on. The potential for the Marines and security forces to shoot at one another is too high."

"We've taken that into account," Bailey said, not bothering to look up from the part of the map she was examining. "The Marines have strict rules of engagement, and Lieutenant Huddleston will make certain that no one gets too close to Chandra's place."

"And if things start coming apart, I'll tell them what's really happening," the security officer said. "It's going to piss my bosses off, but they'll be happy we've taken Chandra off the table."

"When are we planning on moving into staging positions?" Falcone asked.

"Two hours," Brad said decisively. "I want to give them time to move people to the warehouse. We launch the attack on his home in no more than four hours.

"One way or another, I want Mader and Chandra alive," he said grimly. "They'll get us to the Cadre base. Someone I deeply care about is depending on me and I'm tired of waiting. From this moment forward, I'm taking the offensive."

CHAPTER TWENTY-FIVE

"How do we get in?" Brad asked as they rode toward Chandra's home in the back of a windowless delivery van. Falcone sat beside him and Bailey sat across from them.

"The place is dug into solid stone," Falcone said. "Its walls are thick, too. Rich people don't like the idea of people getting to them easily."

If the task sounded daunting to Bailey, it didn't show on her expression.

"Marines have done this kind of thing before. While they can be subtle, this isn't one of those times. They'll slap shaped charges on the walls in four separate locations and blow them all at once. Then they'll go in shooting anyone that has a weapon."

"Not that I'm objecting," Brad said, "but aren't you worried about collateral damage? He has a family, right? Serving staff that aren't criminals?"

"It's not likely those people will be shooting at Fleet Marines holding automatic weapons," she said bluntly. "If my people have any doubts, they'll use less than lethal force, if possible. I'm sure that won't satisfy Mars Security, but they didn't solve this problem with their methods, so we'll do the best we can."

The van slowed and made a sweeping turn to the left. It came to a halt a few moments later and the back door popped open.

Four Fleet Marines in full combat gear gave them a look before stepping back.

Bailey climbed out first and motioned for them to join her.

A Marine officer in combat armor walked out of a side room and saluted the commodore. "Welcome to forward base gamma, Commodore. We've got eyes around the target and teams in position to plant the breaching charges when we get the word to proceed."

Bailey introduced the man as Major Damien Rico, *Eternal*'s senior Marine officer. "The major is a seasoned combat officer and I trust him implicitly, Commodore Madrid, but this is your operation. I'd like the two of you to work together to make sure we've covered all the bases."

"Thank you, Commodore," Brad said. "If you don't mind, Major?"

The man inclined his head and gestured for Brad to precede him into the side room.

"I actually do mind," Rico said bluntly. "You might have combat experience, 'Commodore,' but you're not a combat officer. Platinum mercenary or not."

Brad restrained his first choice of words and counted to five silently.

"I'm not going to tell you how to conduct this breach, Major," he allowed. "Not directly. What I will do is make sure that nothing in the plan represents an obstacle to getting the information we need."

He took one step forward and looked up into the Marine's face. "That said, I wouldn't go out of your way to piss me off. I might only be a mercenary, but I've fought the Terror blade to blade. That fight is still unresolved and I'm not going to allow some puffed-up Marine officer's ego to screw it up."

The other man's lip twitched and a glimmer of humor made its way into his eyes. "I see we have a middle ground. I can work with that. This way, Commodore."

Inside the small side room, they had an old-fashioned paper map unrolled onto the table. A dozen officers and senior enlisted Marines stood around it, discussing something in soft voices. They all looked up as their commanding officer and Brad walked in.

"Listen up," Rico said. "This is Commodore Madrid and he needs to hear the operation plan from start to finish. Tomas, take us through it one more time."

A slender woman with the rank tabs of a Marine lieutenant nodded. "Rachel Tomas, sir. We have four entry points selected as primary, and two additional ones in reserve."

She pointed them out in sequence. "We chose these four because of the areas behind the walls inside and how easy they were to get to on our side. We'd rather not come in right on top of the enemy. Surprise works both ways."

Brad nodded. "Understood. Please continue."

She ran him through a breaching plan that Saburo would've approved of. Nothing seemed to have been left to chance. Still, the enemy had a knack for turning the best-laid plans on their heads.

He made a few suggestions but nothing substantial. His ego didn't require he change a perfectly adequate plan simply because he hadn't thought of it.

"How long until you're ready to move?" he asked when the last details had been worked out.

"I'd like to put my people in place about an hour from now," Rico said. "It'll be the middle of the night, so we can make reasonable guesses about where the targets are going to be."

"I'm going with you. I'll need armor and weapons."

The Marine officer's eyes narrowed. "I don't think so. Our mandate is to make the assault, not shepherd a civilian through the fight. No matter how experienced he may be."

"Make no mistake, Major, I *will* be coming along." He paused to let that sink in. "The targets of this mission are my ultimate responsibility. And, if I were you, I'd plan for armor fitted for a woman, too. My partner is not going to hang back."

A rap at the door interrupted the man's response. It was Falcone. "We have a situation. Lieutenant Huddleston is on her way."

The Marine officer looked at Falcone for a long moment and then nodded to Brad. "I'll see what I can do."

Brad followed Falcone back out. "Do we know what's gone wrong?"

"No clue," she said. "Huddleston called Commodore Bailey and said she had a hot delivery that couldn't wait. Her ETA is five minutes. She should have just enough time to drop it off before she has to run to her big briefing."

He turned to Bailey. "And she didn't tell you what it was?"

The Fleet officer shrugged. "Just that she had to get it to us before the attack. Everyone, clear the room. She might not be alone and I don't want anyone tipping off her companions. That goes for you, too, Madrid."

Brad and Falcone hid out in the Marine planning room, but they planted a video camera out front so that they could see what was so important.

A security van pulled into the room and Huddleston stepped out of the passenger side. She didn't say a word, only banged on the side of the vehicle.

The rear doors of the van popped open and two armored figures stepped out. They had weapons in their hands, and the Marines behind Brad surged forward.

"Stand down," Brad said. "Those are my officers."

Trista and Lisa had arrived. Somehow.

Brad waited to see if the security lieutenant said anything, but she only climbed back into her van and drove away. Once she was clear, he stepped out.

"How in Darkness did you two get down here? Better yet, how did you find Huddleston?"

Trista took her helmet off with her uninjured arm. "It wasn't as hard as you might think. A Fleet captain dropped by the ship and identified you both by name. He was in the company database as someone we could trust, so when he said you needed us, I assumed it was on the level.

"The detective was waiting for us when the Fleet shuttle landed. She had us get armored up and brought us right over. Did I make a mistake?"

"No," Brad said with a shake of his head. "I actually do need you but wasn't sure how to make it work. I don't suppose you brought my armor and weapons, did you?"

Lisa hefted a duffle bag. "Right here, sir."

Brad turned to Rico. "Looks like you only need one set of armor and weapons."

———

It took almost an hour to get Falcone into armor and armed in a way that satisfied Rico. That put them closer to the planned assault time than Brad liked, but they didn't have far to go.

By this time, the diversionary mission should be gearing up, though Randy wouldn't allow it to proceed. It should have all of Chandra's attention and hopefully more than a few of his thugs set to repel it.

The breach point that Brad was going through was situated near a storage room in a sublevel of the residence. The reinforced wall was covered with explosive charges, and the Marines were back in an old transit tube that had been discontinued and sealed over a few decades before.

It wasn't connected to the area where they were breaching. Or it hadn't been before someone had dug through a stretch of Mars. If word of this got out, Brad wondered how many wealthy families would start doing something about unexplored access points.

"Five minutes," Rico said. "My people go in first. We'll head up the stairs and isolate the main entrance. The other teams will try to box the targets into the primary hall. I don't want any of you to engage unless you feel as if you have no choice. Is that clear?"

He was looking at Brad when he said that.

"I hear you," Brad said, not really promising anything.

The man sighed. "Once this kicks off, everything will happen all at once. If you get separated, I want you to hunker down. Under no circumstances do I want any blue-on-blue fire. My people will *probably* recognize you, but accidents happen."

"How long do you think it will take you to secure the whole residence?" Falcone asked.

The officer shrugged. "That really depends on how organized the resistance is. If they're understaffed and not heavily armed, we'll roll them in less than fifteen minutes. If someone sets up a hard point, we'll blow it and them to Darkness.

"If they have anything more than basic rifles and shotguns, it might take as much as half an hour. If they break and run, it'll take longer to mop them up."

Lieutenant Tomas stepped over to them. "All breach teams report ready, sir. We can kick this off whenever you like."

"Everyone proceed to their primary assault positions," Rico said. "Breach in sixty seconds. All teams sound off."

Brad couldn't hear the teams calling their readiness reports, so he focused on his people.

"Trista, I want you to watch my back. With that busted arm, you need to stick to pistols. Lisa, trail after Falcone. Try to keep her from getting in over her head."

Falcone scowled at him. "Did you seriously just warn me about getting carried away? After that duel with the Terror?"

He grinned. "Helmets on, ladies. We're about to get busy."

Brad and his people were stacked behind the assault team. As soon as the breaching charge went off, they'd race forward and he'd follow. If the room beyond was empty, they'd be on their way up the stairs in less than a minute.

If it wasn't empty, that would make things significantly more interesting.

"Breach in ten seconds," Rico said. "Here we go."

Brad turned away from the tunnel when the Marines did. His helmet would protect him from the overpressure, but why take this cavalierly?

The breaching charge went off, and even the sound dampers in his helmet couldn't stop it all, though it did keep his ears from ringing. The Marines whirled as a group and raced forward.

The wall where Brad had seen the breaching charges earlier was gone, replaced by a massive hole filled with smoke.

He found out the room beyond wasn't empty when they started taking fire, even before they made it into the residence. Heavy fire, not just a few scattered shots.

The Marine in front of Brad fell, his helmet shattered.

Brad stepped into the smoke-filled room beyond the breach. He saw movement to his left and found himself face to face with an armored man. One not in Marine armor, either.

He fired his shotgun into the man's face. The flechettes mostly bounced, but not all of them were deflected. Some penetrated the thinner material at the man's throat, and he staggered back.

A flicker of blue to Brad's right sent him diving for the floor. A mono-blade swept over his head and took the arm off the injured man Brad had just shot. He rolled onto his back and shot his attacker several times, but wasn't sure if he'd disabled him, as the man leapt back.

All around him, the Marines were in a life-or-death struggle against a heavily armed and armored defensive point. Their plan had officially gone to shit.

CHAPTER TWENTY-SIX

Brad pulled his mono-blade from his hip and activated it. The line snapped out with a hiss. Then, still lying on the floor, he slashed an enemy off at the ankles before following up with a strike to the man's head.

"Up you go, sir," Trista said, pulling him to his feet as she fired on the enemy with her off-hand pistol, not looking as if she'd broken that arm at all. "We need to withdraw."

"Screw that," he snarled. "We advance."

He let his shotgun hang from its strap and grabbed the fallen Marine's automatic rifle and spare ammo. Then, using short, controlled bursts, he advanced into the smoke, looking for people who needed killing.

The initial appearance of heavy resistance proved illusory. While there had been armored enemies, there weren't many of them. Not standing, anyway. Most lay scattered on the floor, taken out by the breaching charges.

The Marines crushed the remaining resistance and led the way up the stairs a few moments later. They left two of their own dead at the entryway and had several more injured at their heels. Now they wanted blood.

It looked as if the area they'd chosen to breach the building had also been the defenders' command post. Well, that should disrupt things for Chandra's people.

Brad had time to look over one of the dead enemies while he waited for the call to proceed down. The similarities to the commandos they'd fought at Jupiter were too great to ignore. These men wore the same armor and carried the same kind of weapons.

These men weren't Chandra's people. They were Mader's. That meant he was still there.

Falcone was going from body to body, collecting wrist-comps and other electronics. Brad left Lisa to guard her and started down the stairs as soon as the Marines gave the all clear, with Trista on his heels.

The main level of the residence looked like a war zone. The other Marine attack teams had beaten them there and obliterated all resistance. It seemed the only heavily armed defenders had been where Brad had come in.

The dead men here were unarmored and carried pistols that they'd seemingly decided gave them some kind of chance against the Marines.

Rico was standing at the base of the stairs while his people proceeded to search into the main part of the house. Like many other in-ground homes, the entrance was at the top of the structure and the floors below housed the residents.

"The other teams haven't hit any strong resistance," the Marine officer said. "They're pushing down pretty fast. If Chandra has an exit, he's probably using it right now."

Brad held his wrist-comp toward Trista. She pulled off her helmet and shook her hair out before dialing the number the detective had given her.

"It's happening," the female mercenary said before killing the call.

If anyone was monitoring the calls, they wouldn't see Brad. He hoped that in all the rush, no one would ask too many questions about who had called that in and what it had meant.

"We should keep the pressure on," Brad said. "Let's help drive them out of the house."

"My people have that under control," Rico said.

"We already had this discussion, Major. My operation. My rules."

The man sighed but stepped out of the way.

Brad went down the stairs two at a time and found the Marines set up at the bottom of the stairwell. Several of them were exchanging shots with people outside while the rest were preparing to break out.

"What do we have?" Brad asked Lieutenant Tomas.

"The classic last stand," she said. "They've got enough cover to protect them from grenades, but we'll rush them. They don't have much in the way of heavy weapons. While I wouldn't call it safe, it shouldn't be a suicide charge."

"Do we know if Chandra and Mader are in there?"

"No," she said with a shake of her head. "We won't know until we've finished clearing the building."

"LT," a man said. "We're ready."

"Go," she said.

The Marine stuck a grenade launcher through the door and started firing. He held it high so his comrades could crawl underneath his fire. Explosions rocked the corridor beyond the stairs.

That pushed the enemy back enough for the Marines to make a bridgehead into the lowest level. Resistance cracked at that point, and the criminal thugs started throwing down their weapons and surrendering.

Not that the Marines trusted them. Each potential prisoner was thoroughly searched for weapons and cuffed.

In all, it took half an hour to be sure they'd secured the entire residence. There was no sign of Chandra or Mader, and no one was talking.

"There has to be a secret exit," Rico said, frustration in his voice. "By the time we find it, they'll be long gone. We'll have to hope that Huddleston and her people catch them before they get into orbit, or that the Commodore's blockade keeps them where we can get at them."

Falcone was making a pass through Chandra's rooms. They were surprisingly austere.

"All the comps are trashed," she complained. "Our people might be able to get something from them, but I wouldn't hold my breath. We need Chandra and Mader."

Brad nodded. "Rico, do you have any extra breaching charges?"

"A few. Why?"

"This room is the most likely terminus for the exit tunnel. I want to trash some walls and find it."

Ten minutes later, they were in the hall and Rico triggered the reduced charges. They rushed into Chandra's rooms and found one of the walls collapsed into rubble, revealing a narrow tunnel.

Brad didn't wait for anyone to lead the way, taking charge of the pursuit himself.

The passage twisted and turned, providing plenty of places where a defender could hold back people chasing him. Brad didn't expect Chandra needed that, so he was surprised when someone ahead leaned back and shot a pistol at him.

The flechettes rebounded off his armor, and Brad stepped back behind the last turn in the passage.

"Whoever you are, we have more than enough force to come through you," Brad said. "Put down your weapons and surrender."

"And what if I'd rather go down fighting?"

Brad recognized the voice. Chandra. Falcone had played a few vids of the man, and he had a very distinctive accent.

"Give it up, Chandra. Mars Security is all around us and I've got Commonwealth Marines behind me."

"Who are you?"

"Brad Madrid. I want the people above you. Give up now and you don't have to die."

The man laughed. "Someone was just talking about you. I told them your reputation had to be overblown. My mistake."

"That was Jack Mader, or whatever his real name is," Brad said. "He got away, but I don't think he'll ever forgive me for ruining his life."

There was a long pause. "I'm impressed. It *was* Jack Mader. I'm willing to make a deal."

"I'm listening."

"My family is here with me. Mars Security has the exit to my tunnel blocked. I will stop fighting if you allow my family away unharmed."

"Mr. Chandra, this is Agent Falcone of the Commonwealth Investigative Agency," Falcone called from behind Brad. "I'm willing to agree to that, so long as your family has no direct ties to your criminal enterprises. And by that, I mean direct control."

"I'm sending them out," Chandra said. "Don't shoot."

Brad covered the approach with his pistol and saw a woman and three children coming hesitantly forward. They didn't seem armed, so he allowed them to pass and Falcone handled them.

"Time for you to come out," Brad called out.

Chandra stepped out, his hands up and empty. Brad walked out to meet him.

"I knew someone would come for me one day," Chandra mused. "I just didn't expect such a dramatic ending."

"Where is Mader?"

The other man smiled. "Gone. He left as soon as we received word the cargo he was shepherding had been traced. He's already left Mars space."

If true, that was a blow. It might be a lie, though. Brad wasn't giving up so easily.

"You work for the Cadre. I want to know where their base is."

The other man's smile widened. "I was never trusted with that level of information. I only dealt with people via coded accounts and cover names. The Cadre jealously protects their base location. Even if I wanted to help you, I couldn't."

Falcone stepped around them and cuffed Chandra. "Then where are these middlemen?"

"I wiped my computers as soon as I realized we were under attack. My people at the warehouse will have done the same. That was an excellent distraction, by the way. Well played.

"No, I'm afraid you're not going to find a way through to the Terror in my organization. It's the only way to make sure the maniac doesn't kill me one fine day to keep my mouth shut."

"Dammit," Brad said as he slammed the heel of his fist against the stone wall. Another dead end. Michelle's time was running out and he was no closer to finding the Cadre base than the day he'd started.

———

Every computer was searched as soon as Lieutenant Huddleston put in an appearance. As expected, her superiors were less than pleased, but the work was done. They could complain now, but it would make them look petty. Not that the prospect seemed to slow them.

No doubt, some of them were on Chandra's pay and would love to find a reason to undo everything, but the amount of illegal weaponry in the residence and the stolen cargo recovered at the warehouse made that impossible.

The smug bastard wouldn't tell them anything about his organization, and no one admitted to knowing anything about the Cadre. It was even possible that most of his minions had no clue who their ultimate employer was.

Brad knew he was going to be there for a while, so he decided to let his people know where he was. If anything did come from this, he'd need them at Mars soon.

The com signals from Mars to the Io Yards took time, but that seemed to be something he had in quantity. He sent an update and waited for their response.

Shelly had a message back to him far sooner than he'd expected. The original signal couldn't even have reached Io yet.

"We picked up your signal, Commodore," she said. "We're on our way to Mars right now. We'll be in orbit in a day or so. And don't think I'm not going to give you shit for slipping out like that."

Bemused, he sent a signal back. "How did you find out where we were? And why isn't the Cadre after you?"

A few minutes later, she responded. "We slipped out after a Fleet destroyer cloned our transponder. They wanted to see if they could lure some of the Cadre ships into an ambush headed up by the cruiser battle group we met at Saturn. I hear it worked wonderfully, by the way."

"Well, I'm glad to see you made it out safely," Brad said. "I'll be back in orbit by the time you get to MOSO. We'll have to transfer Dr. Duvall from *Lion* to *Oath*. She'll be thrilled at the extra space."

So would he.

He'd just sent the last bit when the door opened and Falcone walked in.

"Good news," she said without waiting for him to respond. "I might have a lead on one of those elusive middlemen."

That snagged his full attention. "I thought they'd wiped all the computers."

She grinned. "They missed one of the Cadre commandos. The commander of the detachment, I think. He had a note in his wrist-comp to contact a merchant on Oberon to get passage back to his boss when this was all over."

Oberon. Interesting. That was the outermost moon of Uranus. Definitely not the kind of place upstanding folk did business.

"Was there a timeframe mentioned?" he asked.

"He had passage arranged at MOSO for two days from now, for him and his people. If we hustle, we can be at Oberon before he's expected. If the merchant doesn't know what this guy looks like, you might be able to use that."

Finally, a break.

"My new ship is going to be here tomorrow," he told her. "They figured out where we'd gone. We can boost for Uranus as soon as we move Dr. Duvall."

"We should talk with Commodore Bailey to see if we can get some support, too."

That hope was dashed a few minutes later. It seemed her bosses were less than pleased that she'd gone around them. Until the investigation was done, she was going to be cooling her heels on MOSO.

Well, he'd just have to solve this riddle on his own. He'd have the time on the way out to Oberon to settle on a course of action. One way or the other, he'd make this merchant talk and then he'd rescue Michelle.

CHAPTER TWENTY-SEVEN

THE PEOPLE who'd created the main settlement on Oberon had been—in a word—cheap. There were no domes, no artificial-gravity plates, and not even a real surface spaceport. Oberon City, a grandiosely named trading town of maybe fifteen thousand people, was nothing more than a massive warren of crumbling tunnels.

Finding anything in that maze, Brad had discovered, was hard. He'd found Ferarre's trading company's computer system with relative ease from orbit. While its security was laughable, he couldn't find anything helpful.

Everything Ferarre bought or sold involved clients marked only by numbered accounts. Brad had the number of the client who was paying for the dead Cadre commandos to be brought out, but no transactions in the system for that client had destinations.

If he was going to get the lead, Brad would have to get them face to face.

Which meant he was there, in the labyrinth of tunnels near the spaceport, regarding the door to Ferarre's office through the slit in the black face wrap he wore. In any other place, a man wearing a long cloth strip wound entirely around his head, concealing everything except for his eyes, would've drawn attention.

On Oberon, face wraps appeared to be in fashion. There were even versions suitable for the ladies, so Falcone stood beside him, equally anonymous.

Brad had no desire to hang out in the corridor and draw attention, so they might as well get this over. On the other side of the door was a small, dingy waiting room. Instead of a receptionist, four heavily armed men occupied the chairs, their weapons trained on the door. And Brad.

"I'm Donaldson," Brad said, a small device placed on his throat modifying his voice. "I have an appointment."

Which was true. The security systems on Ferarre's computers had really sucked.

One of the thugs stood and checked a wrist-comp that strained to fit around his wrist.

"She stays here," he rumbled after a moment.

Falcone nodded and found a wall to hold up while she waited.

The man gestured for Brad to proceed him through a door at the back of the room. That led to another roughhewn tunnel.

His trained eye picked out security systems in the tunnel. Even if someone made it past the thugs in the front room, getting through here wouldn't be a picnic.

At the end of the tunnel, a single door stood unguarded. The thug opened it and gestured Brad inside, standing at something remotely resembling attention.

Before Brad could get a glimpse of the man inside the room, he spoke. "Leave us."

A long moment passed as Brad watched the thug depart, and then stepped into the room. The sole occupant was a mild-looking man in a business suit that wouldn't have looked out of place anywhere.

He held a large, ugly-looking pistol trained directly on Brad's forehead.

———

A moment passed in silence. "How stupid do you think I am, 'Mr. Donaldson'? I schedule my own appointments. Those idiots certainly couldn't do it.

"Of course, I'll admit I didn't notice your addition to the schedule until they told me you were here." He gestured toward a folding chair with his pistol. "Sit."

Brad regarded him coldly. "I'd rather stand."

"And I'd rather shoot you," Ferarre replied. "No one would ever know. This room is sealed against sound. Now sit."

Brad smiled as he approached the chair and placed his hands on it, as if about to sit down. The chair was unattached to anything, and he sent it flying across the room to smash into Ferarre's face as he ducked to the side and drew his own weapon.

The man's gun boomed once as he fell backward out of his office chair, the rogue bullet smashing into the wall behind Brad. Ferarre landed poorly and his pistol went skittering off to spin lazily in the corner.

Before the man could recover, Brad had stood. He trained his weapon on the man as he walked slowly around the desk.

"Lovely security, Mr. Ferarre," Brad sneered at the trader. The man seemed paralyzed, his eyes locked on the gun. "Now, I'm here for information and you're going to give it to me."

Despite his seeming paralysis, the trader shook himself. "I don't trade info—*urg!*"

The man's voice cut off as Brad kicked him in the groin. Ferarre curled into a ball and gagged.

Brad considered his options. This man was a fence and likely a murderer. He deserved everything he got. Yet there were limits to what Brad would do, even to scum like this.

A few years before, he'd have started cutting off fingers to get what he wanted. He wouldn't have even felt badly about it later.

Those days had passed. His humanity was once more in control of his behavior. Yet the man didn't have to know that.

Brad drew a knife from his belt and flicked it on. The vibro-blade's high hum echoed through the office as he knelt next to the whimpering trader.

"You supply the Terror's base," he said conversationally. "You labeled him as customer 843837767. Very original. Tell me where the base is."

"I don't know what you're talking about."

Brad shook his head, grabbed the man's hand, and pulled his arm tight. "Care to change that statement? Last chance."

"Fuck you!" the Fringer spat at him.

With a swift, economical slash, Brad cut a long gash down the man's forearm. The heat generating by the vibrating blade's friction with the air and the flesh partially cauterized the wound. Blood began dripping onto the floor.

"Where is the Terror's base?" Brad demanded again.

"I don't know anything about the Terror," the man said, whimpering.

"Second lie, Mr. Ferarre," Brad said softly. He reached higher and made a deep incision on the man's upper arm. The Fringer screamed.

"Tell me and the pain stops," Brad said flatly.

"I honestly don't know," the man sobbed.

"Pity." Brad raised the knife.

"Wait!" the man screamed. "I really don't know! My ship makes a rendezvous with another ship to transfer the cargo."

Brad lowered the knife slightly, regarding the trader. "Where?"

For a moment, the man stopped whimpering. "I can't tell you! He'd kill me!"

Another slash and accompanying scream. "If you don't tell me, I'll keep cutting you. Consider the options. A hypothetical death later if the Terror finds out you betrayed him, or a certain death now if you don't."

Ferarre was sobbing incoherently, nothing intelligible coming out past his burbling. Brad smashed him across the face with the hilt of the vibro-knife. "Consider your choices carefully, but it's time for talking or cutting. Which will it be?"

"I don't know the rendezvous," the trader got out past his sobs. "It's only given to the ship captains and only just before they leave."

"Really?" Brad asked in an inquiring tone, moving the blade over the man's palm.

"I swear to Light!"

"How do I find one of these captains?" Brad demanded, allowing the knife to cut just a little into the flesh to encourage the man. "Who gives them the coordinates?"

"*Amarea,*" Ferarre choked out, his sobs distorting what he said. "She leaves in an hour. I gave her captain the code phrase the customer gave me with the order. One of the dockhands will use it to give her the coordinates. Probably already has."

"Thank you, Mr. Ferarre. It's been a real pleasure doing business with you."

Ferarre was staring at the knife in Brad's hand. "Please let me live."

"Oh, I have no intention of killing you," Brad assured him as he turned the knife off and holstered it. "I'll leave that to the Cadre when they figure out who must've betrayed them.

"I hope you have a fast ship and a deep cover. Have fun looking over your shoulder for the rest of your miserably short life."

With one economical movement, he drew his pistol and smashed the man on the side of the head. It didn't knock him out, so he repeated the blow, sending the man to the deck, unconscious.

———

The thugs seemed a bit surprised at him coming back out, but pleased. Oddly, genuinely pleased, even though Falcone had disarmed them and tied them to their chairs.

"About time you finished up," she said, rising to her feet. "The boys and I have been discussing the situation and how it was going to turn out. We had a bet. If you walked out alive, they got to live. If not, well, let's just say they're pleased to see you."

"It went okay," Brad allowed. "Ferarre wanted to play some games, but we found common ground. I think I have what we need."

"Excellent. Let's get out of here. This place smells like feet."

The two of them made their way into the corridor, not bothering to untie the goons. Either their employer would do so later, or they'd get loose on their own.

As they headed for the dock where he'd left *Oath's* shuttle, he called Shelly on his wrist-comp.

"Shelly," the response came. "Everything work out?"

"Our target is a ship called *Amarea*. She's either a freighter or transport. She should be leaving within the hour.

"I want you to keep an eye on her. Once we get back to the ship, we'll shadow her out and see if we can make new friends. Tell Randall to make sure the stealth system is operating at one hundred percent. That ship is going to be our guide to the Terror's base."

"There she goes," Jason said softly. On the screen, a small freighter had broken clear of the wisps of gases Oberon pretended was an atmosphere.

"Do we have a lock on her course?" Brad asked as he settled into *Oath's* command chair.

He'd planned to have a mostly different bridge crew on the destroyer, but Marshal's death and the ensuing chaos had some of the hiring on hold. He'd figure it all out once they had this matter settled.

"Not yet. They're just leaving orbit. I'll know more in an hour or so."

"Take us out on a different heading and engage the stealth system once we're out of sight. Then we'll circle around and pick her up again."

Three days out from Oberon, they reached what Brad suspected was *Amarea's* rendezvous point: the cluster of asteroids and other spatial debris floating at the third Saturn–Sol Lagrange point.

Following the freighter for three days without being seen had not been fun. Even on standby, ships radiated enough thermal energy to stick out like a sore thumb. *Oath* possessed a great deal of expensive—and potentially illegal—hardware to conceal her presence, but even she had to be careful when she brought her drives online.

Nonetheless, they seemed to have done it.

"There's definitely something in there," Jason confirmed. "I'm picking up a faint thermal signature and what appears to be a metal hull."

"Gotcha," Brad whispered softly. "Can you work out a vector as to where it came from?"

"Negative. They're just sitting there."

"Damn. All right, we watch. When they leave, lock in their vector and follow them."

He turned to Falcone. "I suspect the cargo is going to get dropped here and picked up by the waiting ship. Then it will head for the Cadre base. Odds are good they'll be careful not to pick up observers, so we'll have to move very carefully going forward."

"What is your eventual plan?" she asked from the spare bridge console. "This is a powerful little ship, but she's no match for the Terror's flagship, much less all the other ships he'll have. Oh, and let's not forget the fixed defenses to keep Fleet at bay."

Brad shrugged. "I'm not sure. At the very least, we'll get good readings of everything and send tight-beam messages to Senator Barnes and Commodore Bailey with the encryption codes we worked out. Between the two of them, they'll be able to follow up on what we find, even if we aren't around to enjoy it."

She raised her eyebrow. "You're not going to try and bring the Mercenary Guild in on an overriding contract?"

He shook his head. "The slavers' base was almost more than they could handle. This is a job for Fleet. All we have to do is keep the location under wraps and stop anyone from the Fleet units from telling them who is coming. The Cadre's days are numbered."

Brad hoped that didn't sound as farfetched to her as it did to him.

CHAPTER TWENTY-EIGHT

THE TENSION LEVEL on *Oath*'s bridge rose as they watched the ship concealed in the asteroid cluster bring its drive online and come out to meet *Amarea*. After nearly ten minutes of maneuvering, *Amarea*'s captain clearly thought the other ship was close enough and detached the cargo capsules she carried.

As soon as the capsules were clear, the freighter came about and headed back toward Oberon. *Amarea*'s projected vector didn't bring her anywhere near *Oath*, so Brad wasn't going to worry about her for now.

Whoever was in command of the Cadre transport clearly was not in a hurry. By the time they'd picked up the last of the capsules, *Amarea* was well past the point at which she could detect anything happening in the cluster, barring an exchange of torpedoes.

Despite that, the transport remained motionless once she'd picked up the last capsule. Brad felt his hands clenching as the minutes passed, and forced himself to relax. He could wait. He'd waited three years for this opportunity. He was not going to blow it now.

Finally, nearly half an hour after *Amarea* had dropped off *Oath*'s passive sensors, the transport began to move. And move she did. The instant her captain decided it was safe, she brought her drives online and was blazing out-system at four meters per second squared—not much less than *Oath* herself could put out.

The speed of her engines was a surprise. This must be a former Fleet transport to have this kind of acceleration.

"Watch the bafflers," Brad instructed quietly.

The transport's course would bring her past *Oath* at less than eight thousand kilometers—well within active torpedo range. "You have her vector yet?"

"Another minute at least," Jason replied. "We're still gathering data."

Brad nodded and turned his gaze back to the tactical display. Which meant his eyes were on the screen when the sensors picked up two new signatures and put them on-screen.

"Jason!" he snapped.

His executive officer froze for a long second as he too took in the new signatures. "Two ships. They're on a rendezvous course with the transport, so I'd guess they're her Cadre escorts. My best guess is two destroyers. They were lying out there in hiding, just like us."

"Are there any more?"

The other man shrugged. "We'll find out when they start accelerating."

Brad had made sure that Hiroshi Kawa had made *Oath* punch above her weight class, but the two ships coming their way outmassed —and likely outgunned—*Oath of Vengeance* nearly two to one. This was going to be an unpleasant fight unless he evened the odds.

"How close will the destroyers get to *Oath*?" Brad asked.

"They'll pass the transport before they match its velocity. They'll zero with it about four thousand kilometers away from us."

At four thousand kilometers, there was no way they'd miss *Oath*. They needed to be maneuvering and firing long before the enemy destroyers hit torpedo range if they were going to have any chance at all of surviving this fight.

"Torp the transport with half a salvo," Brad said. "Shelly, take us down the buggers' throats."

Four small icons appeared on the screen, tracking across the thousands of kilometers between *Oath* and the Cadre transport.

As soon as they launched, *Oath*'s icon changed, vector data shifting as the destroyer brought her drives online and surged toward the remaining enemy ships. The data on the enemy ships became a lot better as their scanners went active.

They didn't need to pay attention to the transport. It had no chance of escaping their torpedoes. The unarmed Cadre vessel was already dead. It just hadn't finished running and screaming yet.

As soon as the Cadre warships saw *Oath*, they spread out to clear each other's firing lanes. They didn't bother to stop decelerating, though. They'd want the maximum time possible to blow *Oath* into small pieces.

Or so they thought. Brad grinned coldly and typed a code into his repeaters. "Jason, I've released four torpedoes from epsilon magazine's locked rounds. I want them to be half of your first salvo."

Jason looked up sharply. "I've been wondering what you had hiding in there. Do I want to know?"

Brad ignored the gunnery officer for a moment as he continued to type things into the repeaters, and then he leaned back. "Probably, but I'll let them surprise you."

"You're the boss," Jason said with a grin. "We'll be in active torpedo range in nine minutes."

"All right," Brad acknowledged, his eyes locked on the screen. "When we're in range, I want the first salvo of torpedoes and a couple of salvos of driver rounds aimed at the lead destroyer. Then switch everything to the other one."

"Sir?"

"If it confuses them half as much as it's confusing you, they aren't going to enjoy this encounter one little bit."

***

They were still twelve thousand kilometers clear when the two Cadre warships opened up with their mass drivers. Streams of little red dots began to cross the screen, thousand-kilometer-per-second steel arrows.

Before Brad could say anything, he felt *Oath* lurch as Shelly took them into evasive patterns. A moment later, a green circle appeared around *Oath*, marking her active torpedo range. The enemy edged slowly toward it.

Three minutes passed and the Cadre ships hadn't managed a single hit. The crisscrossing and twisting lines of their fire were beginning to box *Oath* in, though, and Shelly swore as a burst slammed into the hull.

"Damage report," Brad requested of engineering via his com.

"Fuck-all," Randall replied immediately. "But that's not going to last if you keep letting them shoot us."

Brad said nothing, watching the range indicators. In front of him, Jason cleared his throat and looked back at him. "Active range, sir."

"Engage as specified," Brad ordered coolly.

"Four from Epsilon and four regular torps away," Jason responded immediately, as eight small icons marked the torpedoes on his repeater. "Engaging with mass drivers."

As lines of green dots began to appear on the screen, red icons flashed up.

"Enemy launches detected," Jason reported without missing a beat. "Eight torpedoes from each destroyer."

"Route gatlings Five through Twelve to torpedo defense," Brad ordered. "Lock One through Four on the second destroyer and engage with standard torps."

The lines of green dots began to shift as the gatlings' steady round-every-two-seconds changed targets, tracking the incoming torpedoes. The pattern cut off the torpedo's evasive movements, and two of the red icons vanished from the screen.

As the driver rounds began to weave their patterns around the destroyers' first salvoes, a second salvo of torpedoes launched from both Cadre ships, matched by eight more torpedoes from *Oath*, aimed at the second destroyer.

Brad ignored the outgoing weapons, his attention firmly riveted on the incoming torpedoes. The green dots of the driver rounds once again wove their complex pattern across the stars, trying to catch the torpedoes in their net. A torpedo vanished from the screen, then another.

A third was hit, its icon flickering, and then spiraled into a fourth, both vanishing from the screen. Half the salvo was gone, but even as the gatlings picked off a fifth, a third salvo launched from the enemy ships.

"Reset all gatlings to defense," Brad ordered quietly, his gaze still locked on the screen. Jason didn't acknowledge, but the lines on the screen shifted as all of *Oath*'s mass drivers focused on stopping the incoming torpedoes.

As the sixth and seventh torpedoes vanished, the back of Brad's mind noted the lurch of another burst of driver hits. The screen showed the spinning vector cone of *Oath*'s course as Shelly took them into a tight spin that caused the eighth torpedo to flash by the ship, less than eight meters clear of the hull.

Almost simultaneously, the screen suddenly flashed white with an incredible energy signature. Their first salvo had just reached the lead destroyer.

"What the Dark was that?" Jason demanded, staring in shock as the screen cleared from the flash, showing that the destroyer had vanished.

"An abandoned Fleet project that someone gave me the specs for," Brad said with a grin. "Personally, I think someone from the Cadre killed the project, because they seem to work just fine."

He shot a look at Falcone, but she simply shrugged as if she had no idea what he was talking about. It was even possibly true. Brad honestly had no idea who had sent him the plans. Only that Hiroshi Kawa had gleefully agreed to build him some in exchange for the exclusive rights to build more once knowledge of them became more widespread.

"What were they?" Jason repeated slowly. "Were they nukes?"

"Of course not," Brad said. "Fleet would never allow anyone other than themselves to have nukes. Those were specially designed to radiate energy in the scanner spectrum. Lots of it in a very short period of time. They blinded the destroyer, and that meant they couldn't stop the other four torpedoes."

"How did our torpedoes manage to see the enemy?" Shelly asked. "Wouldn't they be blind too?"

"Our torpedoes have a special code in the scanners. There's a little pulse of warning from the jammers before they go off. We can change that up if anyone ever figures it out, but our torpedoes shut off their scanners for a few seconds to avoid being blinded." Brad shrugged. "We could do it for *Oath's* sensors too, but even flash-blinded in one direction we can see everywhere else.

"Now that we've killed the one destroyer, we're back on an even footing. The damned things are expensive, but I'll use them on the other destroyer if we need to. Kill those torps, Jason."

The lines of driver rounds had been sweeping around to take out the next salvos already in space from the destroyers. As the torps got closer, they became easier targets, and three more vanished in a few seconds. Then another.

But four more torpedoes were still burning in toward *Oath*. Brad felt the ship lurch as Shelly threw them into a violent evasive pattern. Jason picked off another torp in the few seconds she bought, two more shot by, missing by meters, and then the last slammed into his ship.

Alarms screeched through the ship as a hundred kilos of high-velocity metal ripped into the hull. The bridge blast door slammed shut, cutting off a sudden rush of air before it began.

Brad's gaze was drawn inexorably back to the screen, watching the last salvo of torpedoes come racing in. For one horrible moment, the gatlings refused to fire as the torpedoes lunged toward them.

Jason cursed, but before Brad could say anything, the guns flickered online again.

Shelly's evasive maneuvers and the motion added by the first impact had pulled them away from the incoming weapons, giving Jason a precious few seconds to begin tracking with the guns.

A tiny red warning suddenly flickered up on the screen, flashing the words SAFETY INTERLOCKS DISENGAGED, and fire began to flash out far too fast from the mass drivers. Brad realized how Jason had gotten the guns to fire.

The gatlings spat their slugs at a rate of fire nearly double the safe "maximum" rate. Their weaving garrote closed around the remaining torpedoes and began to shatter each in turn.

The last torpedo died eighty kilometers short of *Oath,* and Brad breathed a sigh of relief.

"The other destroyer?" Brad demanded.

"Dead," Jason said. "He died right before we killed the last of his torpedoes."

Brad nodded. "And the transport?"

"Clean sweep," Jason confirmed. "All ships destroyed."

That wasn't quite the outcome Brad had hoped for. If they didn't have a useful vector, all of this would've been for nothing.

Brad touched his com. "Randall, report."

Silence answered for a moment and then the engineer came on. "You want the bad news or the good?

"Both, of course."

"All right," the engineer replied with a sigh. "The bad news is that Gatling Five is gone, Drive Three is down hard, and we've lost atmosphere across a third of the ship.

"The good news is that I think I can get at least half of the over-heated gatlings back online from the overload firing, and we still have all our torpedo tubes. If we all work at it, we can restore atmosphere within an hour, but the drive is down until we get to a shipyard."

"Good enough," Brad said, and meant it. *Oath* could've been in a lot worse shape. "I'll meet you in Engineering in fifteen minutes and we can start working on damage control."

"Understood. Randall out."

Brad turned to Jason. "Do we know where those bastards were heading?"

"We got enough data on the transport before we blew it to make a guess, if they hadn't planned to change course later. I think we've got enough vector information on the warships, too. If the two overlap, we have a target."

"Get to working on it," Brad ordered. "I think it's time somebody paid the Terror a courtesy visit."

CHAPTER TWENTY-NINE

Thirty hours later, Brad knew they'd blown it. The vectors hadn't led to anywhere the Terror would hide a base. No amount of toying with the vectors gave them an option that made any sense at all.

He sighed and looked around the wardroom at his exhausted crew. They'd repaired as much of the damage as they could without returning to the Io Yards. Now they needed to decide on their next course of action.

Saburo, Trista, and Lisa had done an admirable job getting the new combat team into shape. Thankfully, all were veterans and they knew what needed doing.

With Marshal gone, Shelly looked more strained. She'd taken up the duties of pilot as well as those of communications officer. Thankfully, with Dr. Duvall on board, she didn't have to be the medic.

That said, he knew she'd been getting more on-the-job training as a medic while they had a true professional aboard. All that left little time to sleep.

Not that he personally knew what sleep was.

Randall looked dead on his feet. While the others had managed to grab some rest in between repairs, the engineer had been working full-out the whole time. His pale, drawn face concerned Brad, who fully intended to order the man to sleep for the next day or two once they'd finished the repairs.

Falcone had been spending her time over on the wrecks of the Cadre ships, looking for any clues. He didn't hold out much hope. Each of the ships had left some fairly large pieces of debris, but the location of the Terror's base wouldn't just be lying around.

Jason was the last crew member at the meeting. His face was as grim and tired as the rest of them.

"We have nothing," Brad said tiredly. "The vectors didn't pan out."

Everyone in the room sagged a little.

"After the first few hours, I was afraid of that," Shelly said. "It should've been obvious where they were going. Only, it wasn't anything more than a waypoint."

The wardroom door opened and Falcone came in just in time to hear Shelly's last sentence.

"That might be okay," the Commonwealth agent said as she took a seat. "I found coordinates that might match the vector in a wrist-comp belonging to the dead transport pilot. It also had a radio frequency and a code to transmit."

"And you think that means it will tell us where the Terror's base is?" Trista asked, obviously holding Lisa's hand under the table.

The similarity to how Jason and Shelly behaved amused Brad.

"There's no other reason for that kind of shenanigans," Falcone said. "Also, we recovered one of the cargo pods intact. It hadn't been secured as well as it should've been and came loose in the last-minute evasive maneuvers. I think you'll find the cargo illuminating."

She commandeered the console and brought a series of images up on the screen. The pod was filled with torpedoes. Ones with a very distinctive golden halo on the tip.

"Are those what I think they are?" Brad asked.

"If you think they're nuclear torpedoes intended for Fleet, you'd be right. We have sixteen of them in the cargo bay."

"So, the Terror has nukes, assuming this isn't the first load siphoned off for him," Brad said grimly. "This is getting more unpleasant by the moment."

"What are your plans?" Falcone asked. "Do we call Fleet in now?"

He shook his head. "We don't know if this is a wild goose chase. Also, the moment we call Fleet, the Terror will find out. He has them too deeply penetrated. We continue as planned."

"One ship is not going to make much of a dent on the Cadre base," Jason objected. "We don't have that kind of firepower."

"We do now," Brad said, gesturing toward the nuclear torpedoes.

That produced a profound silence in the room.

"Using them is an act of treason, I think," Shelly said.

"Not quite," Falcone said, "but even I can't give you permission. That kind of thing is way outside my already-extravagant authority."

Brad smiled. "Think about the names of my ships. *Heart of Vengeance* and *Oath of Vengeance*. Do those leave the impression of someone who'll allow the law to stop him from taking bloody revenge on those bastards?

"I'm more than happy to play by the rules so long as they don't hamstring me. When I can use illegal means to end something like the Cadre, you bet your ass I'll do that, too. Without a single regret, no matter how it ends up for me."

He looked around the room at each of them. "Now is the point where you can choose to walk away. I won't take anyone down with me who doesn't choose to be there. If anyone wants out, we'll make a side trip and drop them off. No harm, no foul. Clear?"

They looked at one another and made a show of leaning back in their seats.

"It looks as if we're staying," Falcone said. "Consequences be damned. The Cadre has to be stopped."

"This might be the end of the Vikings," he warned them. "It will certainly be the end of me being in charge of them. The Guild will have no choice but to expel me, and Fleet will clap me in irons. I'm hopeful they won't go any further, but I can't promise anything."

He turned toward Falcone. "And I can't order you at all. You're as exposed as I am."

She shrugged. "I was looking for a change of pace, anyway. It's going to be a hard call for them. Acknowledge the destruction of the Cadre and then prosecute the people that ended them? That's hardcore and may even be politically impossible.

"In any case," she said with a grin, "I'm willing to roll the dice on this one. Let's do it. Darkness, we might all die in the attempt and we're worrying over nothing."

"I had no idea you were such an optimist," Saburo said dryly. "We're all in for this, sir. If it means taking down the Terror and the Cadre, it's worth it."

"And rescuing Michelle!" Shelly added. "I'd do this for her even without the rest."

Nods from everyone else confirmed he had his command crew.

"I still want everyone to have a chance to head back to our base," he said. "There will be no dishonor if someone doesn't want to go with us. None."

"No one will abandon you," Saburo said. "This is the moment we've all known was coming, even the new people. None will look away; mark my words."

Brad turned to Randall. "What's our overall status?"

"Seven of the gatlings are back up," the engineer replied. "All of the torpedo tubes are functional. The nukes topped off our magazines. I have them loaded up front in Alpha. Drive Three is still down, so we can't pull more than about two point eight mps squared, though."

Brad looked around the table. "Assuming we find something at these coordinates, we'll send word to Senator Barnes and Commodore Bailey, but we won't be waiting for their response.

"This base is protected by secrecy. The Terror likely has only a few warships on station. Most of the defenses should be platform- or asteroid-based. We should be able to isolate those from outside their own range and blow them apart. That will clear the way for us to board the main installation."

"Board?" Doary demanded. "Thirty of us against an unknown number of bad guys. Do we have any other surprises on our side?"

"We have two advantages," Brad said. "Firstly, we're there for two specific objectives. One team will rescue Michelle and any other prisoners near her while I kill the Terror. Once we make that happen, we get the fuck out.

"Secondly, I don't care what we break. We go in loaded for bear and kill anything that moves. Shelly, set in a course for the transport's rendezvous point. It's time to end this."

———

They found an old drone at the coordinates. It readily gave them a new destination once they gave it the right code: a spot in Neptune's leading trojan cluster.

With Drive Three down, that was a week distant. He waited until they were almost there before sending the data to Bailey and Barnes. That meant there wouldn't be any support, but no one would be able to betray their presence.

None of the asteroids clustered at the destination were large. The spherical zone of gravitational stability tended to catch and hold the things, but there had been few large asteroids this far out in the system to be caught.

There were nearly a hundred asteroids floating in a sphere about fifty thousand kilometers across. Most were small, less than a kilometer across, but a single larger rock, perhaps fifty kilometers in diameter, held a place of seeming pride at the center of the cluster.

That rock, according to *Oath*'s sensors, was the site of what appeared to be a small colony. Built off the side of the asteroid but likely linked to the "colony" by gantry-like passage tubes, was a refueling station.

Brad looked at the magnified image on the main viewscreen with grim wonder. For nearly four years, he'd hunted the Terror, and now he was here at the pirate's lair. Vengeance was finally within his grasp.

"This is going to be fun," Jason said, an odd tinge to his voice. "That place is fortified to the Dark and back again, sir."

"Show me."

The view of the base slowly moved out to encompass the whole cluster. An even dozen of the asteroids were now highlighted in red.

"These asteroids are the sites of ground-based sensors and presumably weapons. To take them out, we'll need to literally reduce the asteroids to dust."

Thirty glittering red dots appeared on the screen. "These, on the other hand, are satellite weapons platforms. Each of them masses around a thousand tons. A single standard torp will take them out, but each of them would probably have half of our firepower if we were fully operational."

Two red icons appeared, one linked to the fueling depot and one orbiting above the central asteroid.

"Last, but by no means least, there are two destroyers. One appears to be refueling, but the other is on guard. She's stationary relative to the main base with her drives cold, but she'll see us coming soon enough to come online and hold us in place while the rest of the defenses take us out."

His executive officer might have once been his tactical officer, but that didn't mean he was the end-all of tactical doctrine.

"You're looking at their strengths. I agree, they're tough. Yet they're vulnerable in one very critical way: none of them can dodge."

Jason froze for a long moment, then nodded slowly. "If we send the torps in ballistic—"

"They'll never know what hit them," Brad finished with satisfaction.

He tapped a code into his computers. "You now have complete access to the nuclear warheads and the pulsars in Epsilon magazine. I want you to set up a firing plan that drops a nuke on each of those asteroid platforms, at least two standard torps on each of the satellites, and two nukes on each of the destroyers."

"If we nuke the destroyer at the refueling station, we'll probably take that out, too," Jason observed.

"So?" Brad asked with a cold smile. "I don't care what we wreck. Blowing the fueling station will certainly distract them and so long as we don't nuke the surface, the colony integrity shouldn't be affected."

Brad doubted any other ship in space could have done it. Even launching on ballistic trajectories, they couldn't fire until they were almost on top of the base. They had to be able to see the targets very well to be sure the torpedoes had precisely the right courses.

Oath's thermal baffling was designed for a Fleet cruiser. On their smaller hull, it occasionally blocked line of sight for some of the scanners, but it made *Oath* just about invisible when she wanted to be.

If a cruiser tried to slip up like this, her size would give her away. *Oath* was small enough to not be seen. Barely.

At fifteen thousand kilometers, *Oath* was still nearly invisible. Inching along at less than half a kilometer per second with the baffling on full, she radiated too little to be detected on thermal scanners and moved too slowly to be picked up by visuals.

"They're dialed in," Jason said quietly as the ship continued to drift slowly in. "Firing pattern is ready."

Brad regarded the red icons on the screen in front of him and then glanced down at the repeater, which marked the target designations for almost all of *Oath*'s torpedoes. If this worked, he wouldn't need any more weapons. If it didn't, *Oath*—and her crew—were dead.

"Fire," he ordered softly.

Almost instantly, the first eight icons popped onto the screen and began to slowly fade out. Launching from the torpedo tubes gave them another four kilometers per second on top of *Oath*'s own speed, but that still put them nearly an hour from their targets. Nonetheless, the complete lack of drive power made them even more invisible than the destroyer.

Twenty seconds after the first salvo, the second fired. Slowly and evenly, every twenty seconds, another eight torpedoes entered space. The first salvos—all kinetics targeted on the satellite platforms—were away in just over three minutes.

Jason glanced up at Brad once they were. "Standing by to launch nuclear rounds."

This was it. Everything up to now could be forgiven. Using nukes was going to cross the line between mercenary and vigilante.

Brad typed another code into his computers. "Complete nuclear release granted. Fire."

Jason turned back to his console and launched two more salvos. "Firing pattern complete. We have two salvoes of regular torpedoes in reserve. I have pulsars mixed in with the regular torpedoes to blind the satellites. They won't go off until the nukes detonate, since they aren't set up to account for them."

"Let's hope we don't need the last of our torpedoes," Brad said solemnly. "Keep a close eye on the area. If anyone else shows up, we'll have to deal them in."

"You know I'll support you to the hilt on this," Falcone said from the seat she'd appropriated.

"I appreciate that," he said with a lopsided smile. "I worry more about your future employment than what happens to me. You know what those monsters have done. They deserve what they're getting and I'll willingly pay the price for my revenge."

When she said nothing, he returned his attention to the main screen. By now, the icons marking the locations of the first salvos were only projections—*Oath* couldn't detect them any more than the Cadre could now.

"Time to impacts?" Brad asked quietly.

"Forty-eight minutes and counting," Jason said.

Brad said nothing. There was nothing to say. He simply watched as the torpedoes made their slow but steady way toward the enemy.

As the time slipped by, he began to consider just how insane his attack plan was. There was enough firepower out there to make a squadron of cruisers turn back, and here he was thinking he could take them out with a single damaged destroyer?

It was impossible. They were all going to die because he was an arrogant fool.

Of course, the Cadre hadn't picked up the torpedoes yet, but that didn't mean anything. While the ones targeting the stationary platforms might make it through, but the ones against the destroyers didn't have a hope if the attack was spotted. Darkness, any movement on the part of the destroyers would make them miss.

Even as his brain kept running in circles, the torpedo icons began lighting up, marking their drives coming online. It was too late to worry about failure now. He was committed.

———

The last torpedoes launched—the ones aimed at the destroyers—lit off first. Then, as those surged forward, they passed the torps locked onto the asteroid platforms, and those lit off. The cascade of glittering icons lighting up continued through the kinetics, until all the torpedoes were online.

Then, a bare handful of seconds after the last kinetic torp activated, those targeted on the destroyers hit their victims. For a moment, the screen flashed with the fury of nuclear fire. The flash expanded as the other nuclear torpedoes struck home, annihilating the asteroid stations.

Other icons flashed up on the screen, nearly obscured by the coronas of destruction expanding from the nuke strikes, marking the pulsars going off and blinding any remaining defenses. Seconds later, the last of the torpedoes took out the satellites.

"Everlit, yes!" Jason hissed as the flickering light encompassed the entire central portion of the cluster for a few moments. "Look at the bastards burn!"

Brad was silent, his thoughts grim as the light faded and the scanners began to trawl in their data. Jason flashed the visual of the main base up on the screen, just in time to catch the final side effects of the strike.

The refueling station, holes punched through it by the fiery lances of *Oath*'s torpedoes, was slowly falling under the impact and the slight influence of the planetoid's gravity. As it fell, it became clear that there had been another ship attached to it, but Brad couldn't make out any details in the visual.

The ship was clearly making a desperate effort to escape, its engines burning at maximum power, even burning parts of the station as it tried to run. For a moment, it seemed held by the girders of the station, but then it broke free.

Thankfully, it broke free moments too late.

Even as the girders snapped, an explosion began at the heart of the fuel tanks. The rippling burst of destruction, fueled by the massive quantities of both fuel and oxidizers stored in the tanks, surged outward from the station.

It caught the fleeing ship, broke it in half, and then threw the broken chunks out as a few more pieces of debris upon the wave front of the station's destruction.

"Son of a bitch," Brad said softly. By the time the explosion petered out, that entire side of the asteroid had been engulfed in its fury. Parts of the "colony" had been exposed, but most of the installation had been protected by the curvature of the asteroid and being underground. Michelle should be safe.

"If there were any weapons or sensors on the surface," Jason responded quietly, "I don't think we need to worry about them anymore. As for the pirates, they are going to be *very* distracted for a little while."

Brad nodded, then glanced over to the pilot's station. "Take us in, Shelly. Use the burned side of the asteroid as our shield. Tell Saburo we'll launch the teams on schedule."

Falcone stood. "Then I'd best go armor up. You, too. I hope your arm is up to the challenge."

He did too. Dr. Duvall had done the best she could, but he wasn't back up to his peak performance. That was still weeks away.

Well, he'd do the best he could. That's all anyone could ask of a man.

"Right behind you," he confirmed. "Jason, you have the conn. Go active on scanners and deal with any ships they throw at us. Good luck."

CHAPTER THIRTY

THE LANDING BAY they'd picked on the Cadre base—once they'd finally found one that looked remotely passable—had a half-melted look to it. The bay doors had been ripped off when the blast front had passed over the base, and it looked as if there'd been secondary explosions in the bay as well.

That made things difficult for Brad when he tried to find a place to put *Oath*'s first shuttle down. He was moments away from activating the bow guns and trying to clear a landing zone when Trista touched his shoulder.

"There," she said quietly, pointing at the area near the entrance to the rest of the base. A chunk of the outer door had smashed its way through there, and while it had made a tortured mess of the wall behind the door, it had also swept the area in front of the entrance relatively clear of debris. Better yet, it had room for the second shuttle to land beside him.

Brad brought the shuttle forward with a flick of power. The planetoid's gravity was negligible, and while the place clearly had gravity plates, they'd been disabled by the explosion. With a gentle touch of counterthrust, he brought the shuttle to a stop about a meter above the bay's floor.

With the landing legs fully extended, he brought the shuttle down with a gentle *clunk*. Brad checked to be sure they had full contact and then switched on their gravitic fields, locking the shuttle down. Saburo brought the second shuttle in beside his and landed just as neatly.

He tried to signal *Oath* that they had arrived, but received no response. The base had to be shielded. They wouldn't get any warnings from their comrades overhead if there were trouble. Hopefully Jason and Shelly would recognize what the lack of coms meant—he couldn't spare any of his ground team to take a shuttle back out to let them know.

"We're go," Brad said into his suit's com. He and Trista joined the rest of his attack team in the back of the shuttle. Randall, Shelly, and Jason were holding the fort back aboard *Oath*, standing by to warn them if they detected Cadre warships approaching.

One of the troopers handed Brad a weapon as he reached the shuttle exit. The high-power automatic rifles his people sported were very much out of place in space combat, but Saburo believed in being prepared for everything.

They'd been purchased for the possibility of planetside combat, but they'd do equally well fighting through a station where one didn't care how much damage one did. So long as they only fired at people with guns, the hostages should be relatively safe.

Brad checked the magazine on his rifle, turned the safety to the off position, and faced his strike team.

"Try to keep someone alive to tell us where the Terror is. We'll leave rescuing Michelle to Saburo and Falcone. All right, folks. Let's do this."

The door sealing the landing bay from the rest of the complex was clearly intended to function as an airlock. Two sets of tracks were cut into the deck for the heavy doors.

A fragment of the outer doors had gouged its own trench into the floor, cutting both tracks, and had hit the inner door as well, bending it completely out of its tracks. The combination meant that not only were both doors open, they were exposed to vacuum.

Brad and Trista settled into overwatch positions as the troopers moved through. One of them stepped back into view and gave the all-clear sign.

The pair of officers followed through into one of the eeriest sights Brad had ever seen. Even past the debris from the landing bay, the corridor looked like hell. Power surges had blown out most of the lights, and the ones that still worked flickered intermittently.

Careful to allow each grav-boot to lock on before removing the other from the floor, Brad crossed to a small alcove in the wall. The computer was still operational, though its screen was flickering as badly as the lights. He brought up a map of the station, which carried a status warning on the various corridors on it.

"All right," he said softly into the radio. "It looks as if most of the base has lost atmosphere. The deeper corridors have pressure but no power. This has one of those places marked as detention. Saburo, take Agent Falcone and rescue everyone there."

"Yes, sir. Then we come for you."

Brad shook his head. "Get them to safety. My story will be played out by that point. I'll either be dead or victorious. Return to *Oath* as quickly as possible."

His friend looked less than convinced but saluted. Brad half-doubted the man would follow that order, but he'd done what he could.

"The only major surface area with air and power is an atrium about four hundred meters north and two floors up. That's the most likely place to find the Terror."

A line of text flickered onto the screen, with a pattern marking itself as a repeating service message. "As if we needed the confirmation, the computer is telling all inhabitants to meet at the atrium to plan repairs and defense."

Brad stepped out of the alcove, carefully covering the corridor with his rifle as he did. "No matter what happens, I'm proud of you. Good luck."

They ran into trouble almost immediately. With the power toasted, the elevators were out of commission, and all the shafts they checked were blocked by elevators above their floor.

Stairs were the obvious next step, but there didn't seem to be any. Not that they could easily see, anyway.

Ten minutes after they'd entered the base, Brad's strike team found itself moving slowly down the corridor, opening every door they found, by brute force or otherwise, trying to find stairs.

Brad was trying yet another door when a single *click* came over the radio. He stopped and turned to see what had attracted his people's attention. About twenty meters down the corridor from where his team was standing, a door was opening.

He dropped to one knee, bracing the rifle against his shoulder, and waited. A vac-suited man stepped through the door, followed by three others.

Vacuum doesn't convey swearwords, but the first man scrabbling for his pistol certainly seemed to convey that feeling. Brad exhaled gently and pulled his trigger. A moment later, Trista and the troopers opened fire.

Brad's first three-round burst slammed through the chest of the man who'd been drawing his pistol. By the time Brad tracked to another target, all of them were down.

His breathing was loud inside his helmet as he lunged to his feet, shuffling down the corridor as fast as his magnetized boots would allow.

Just as he reached the door, another man came out from behind it, a pistol in each vac-suited hand. Brad put a three-round burst clean through the man's body and into the asteroid rock wall behind him.

One of the troopers caught up with him at the door and lunged ahead as Brad swapped magazines. He found the trooper grappling with two pirates above the bodies of three more seemingly cut down by point-blank automatic fire. One of the pirates was holding the trooper's rifle while the other jerked free, his mono-blade swinging up.

A short burst of fire from Brad's rifle took the man out before he could swing. A very slight shift of aim allowed Brad to put another burst through the remaining pirate's faceplate.

Brad took a long breath and then glanced around. They were in a stairwell. Wide sets of stairs headed both up and down. He brought his rifle around to cover the way leading up.

A moment later, Trista and the other troopers joined them. He gave the hand signal for *proceed* and then gestured toward the stairs.

Trista and the troopers who'd come in with her settled into over-watch positions again. Brad nodded to them and then gestured the other trooper forward with him. They climbed the stairs and reached the next floor.

Brad surveyed the landing and checked farther up the stairs. He then stepped back to where Trista could see him and gestured *all clear*.

The second set of mercs moved up, past Brad and his trooper to the next landing. For a moment, they scanned the area around them, and then Trista gave Brad's team the all clear.

The strike team reunited at the top of the stairs. Trista stepped over to the door leading to the floor, but Brad gestured for her to step over to him. Touching his helmet to hers, he could speak to her without using the radio.

"The atrium should be about a hundred meters to our right," he said. "Take half the team and find a way around to the other side. When the fight goes down, I'll be counting on you to protect me if he cheats. Also, if I lose, make sure he dies here."

"You'll win, sir," she said confidently. "And no matter what, the Terror dies today."

She opened the door and stepped out, half of the troopers following her. Their weapons swept the corridor and she gestured the all clear again.

Brad and his troopers joined them, their own weapons sweeping the corridor. He checked down to the right and saw, as expected, what appeared to be an airlock sealing the corridor about a hundred meters away.

He waited for Trista to find a cross corridor and lead her people away before he started toward the airlock. He was about ten meters away when it began sliding open.

Brad gestured for his people to take cover but not to fire. He stood alone in the center of the corridor as the airlock finished cycling.

A man in a vac-suit sporting a stylized screaming eagle on its shoulder stepped out of the lock and froze at the sight of Brad.

With a cold smile, Brad activated his suit's com unit on all general frequencies. "My name is Brad Madrid and I'm here to complete my duel with the Terror. Take me to him."

The pirate touched his wrist-comp, activating another channel. He must have left the general channel open as well, though, and Brad could hear his words.

"Sir, several of the intruders are outside the atrium. The leader claims right of combat. It's Madrid."

Silence reigned for a moment, and then a gravelly voice that Brad remembered only too well came out of the communicator. "Bring him to me. Only him and see that he's disarmed."

"I don't think so," Brad said, trusting that the Terror and—more importantly—the other pirates, could hear him. "I claim right of combat and am keeping my weapons. My people are too. You don't exactly have a reputation for keeping your word, after all."

He felt his lips widen into a cold smile. "You're not afraid of the man that destroyed your base, are you? I have seven men with me. Are you so cowardly that you won't finish our duel?"

"I'm no coward," the Terror snarled. "Bring them in, but if anyone raises a weapon to interfere with our duel, my people will cut them down."

"And if your people try to cheat, my men will cut them down. I believe we understand the rules. I can't tell you how much I've been looking forward to ending this. And you."

"Dream on, mercenary. In just a few minutes, you'll be dead. Come meet your master, fool."

The pirate ahead of him gestured toward the airlock. Brad called his people forward, and they all entered the lock.

When it finished cycling, Brad stepped through the inner door and into the atrium. The gravity inside was active but only set to about half of lunar standard. A twelfth of normal gravity. That would make things interesting.

He held himself fully erect as, for the third time in his life, he found himself face to face with the pirate warlord called the Terror.

———

"My chrono tells me it's almost noon Sol Standard," Brad said over his helmet speakers. "High noon. Fitting, isn't it?"

"You really are a fool," the Terror said softly. "You should've run when you had a chance."

"I've hunted you down and destroyed your base. Now I'm going to kill you. Perhaps you should run. Coward."

"Bases can be rebuilt," the Terror snarled. "But you *have* hurt the Cadre. Worse than Fleet has in years of trying. Thousands dead, decades of work destroyed. You've frustrated us at every turn and you just keep refusing to die."

Brad drew his mono-blade and activated it. "I believe you have a chance to make that happen right now. Shall we remove our helmets and duel face to face? I'd like to see the damage I caused last time, One-Eye."

The pirate yanked his helmet off with another snarl and tossed it aside. "Take a good look at the man who will end you, Madrid."

One of his troopers stepped up and helped Brad get his helmet off. That was good, since his off hand was still subpar.

While he did, Brad drank in the damage he'd done to the Terror's face. One of the man's eyes was not just artificial but blatantly so. A metal patch covered two-thirds of one side of his face, with optical receivers where his eye should have been.

The Terror drew and activated his own mono-blade. "Say your final prayers, Madrid."

CHAPTER THIRTY-ONE

Under the atrium dome's flickering lights, the two men circled one another. The dome seemed an incongruous place for a fight to the death, filled with plants and sporting a basketball court.

A circle of pirates had gathered around them, at least a hundred strong. Brad's men watched them closely, but he had no illusions about his survivability after the fight ended.

That didn't matter. Only killing the Terror and saving Michelle mattered.

"It ends today," the Terror told him flatly, raising his blade to guard. "You won't leave this place alive. How's that arm I cut off? Weak? Hard to control?"

Brad smiled coldly, raising his blade, crossing his arms as he did so and touching a hidden spot on the suit's wrist. For a moment, he half-heard the hum of the mono-filament bracer as it spread into specially prepared tubes that lined his sleeve.

From the outside, his shield was invisible. With the tubes controlling the flex of the monofilament, his arm was safe from accidental injury. The only set of circumstances that would reveal it was if he used it to block a strike.

With his hidden defense active and another trick up his other sleeve, one he hoped he didn't need, he was as ready as he'd ever be.

"One of us *will* die here," Brad agreed. "Let's see who the fates have chosen."

Brad was taller and had a longer reach than the pirate, but past experience had taught him that the other man was much stronger and almost as fast. Plus, the Terror didn't have a crippled hand.

Silence descended as the two men continued to circle one other on the marked-out lines of the basketball court, both holding their weapons at the ready and utterly focused on their opponent.

Brad let the world flow away, ignoring the stars overhead, the plants, and surrounding circle of pirates. His world consisted entirely of his opponent.

The slight shift of the Terror's feet warned Brad an instant before the Terror attacked. He deflected the lunging strike to the side as the pirate sailed through the air at him, and then parried it entirely as the Terror activated his boots and stopped abruptly, attempting to convert the thrust into a slash.

The pirate spun away, slightly off-balance, and Brad stepped in, trying to take advantage. He flicked his blade at the pirate, trying to keep the man unsteady, but the Terror parried him three times in a row and then converted his increased imbalance into a spin-kick toward Brad's head.

Brad barely managed to catch the kick in his bad hand, his reflexes nearly betraying him. For a moment, they held a tableau with the Terror's boot in Brad's hand, and then the Terror deactivated the field in his other boot and brought it up in a kick that caught Brad in the chest.

The impact knocked Brad back several steps, allowing the Terror to come to an even landing. Before the Terror had finished, however, Brad was attacking again, his blade flickering out in a lethally complex pattern.

The Terror held his own for a moment and then was forced back a step. Then another. A ripple spread through the watching crowd, but before Brad could press his advantage further, the pirate chief sent his free hand flashing out in a perfect straight-on punch.

Brad's delayed reflexes in his left arm failed to catch the blow, and it was his turn to be knocked off-balance. The Terror, like Brad, pressed his advantage, driving in for a series of blows Brad barely managed to stop.

For a half-moment, Brad regained his balance, just to see the Terror lunging in with the same nearly unblockable attack that had crippled him last time. In one swift motion, Brad deactivated his grav-boots and leapt away from the blade.

He arced over an intervening wall of vegetation and landed in another clear zone. He activated his boots, readied his blade, and waited for the Terror's arrival.

Apparently unwilling to risk the jump, the Terror slashed his way through the plants. For a single instant as he cleared the last of them, he was open, and Brad attacked.

The Terror managed to interpose his own blade and caused the attack to slide off his arm, leaving a gouge through the pirate's suit arm that slowly began to turn red.

"That's just the beginning," Brad promised, pressing his attack. "I'll have your blood even if I have to take it one drop at a time."

The Terror blocked, and for a moment, the two blades locked together.

Unwilling to risk a match of strength, Brad kicked out, catching the Terror in the side of his knee. The pirate's leg buckled and Brad slashed again.

The Terror deflected his strike and pulled himself back to his feet, but Brad continued attacking. The Terror fell back a step. Then another.

Brad intercepted the man's lashing foot with his left hand and sent the Terror spinning away. He followed the pirate, pressing his attack. Blade crashed on blade, but he could feel the older man weakening. This fight was almost over.

"Are you afraid yet?" he asked as his blade took off the hair on one side of the Terror's head.

The Terror didn't reply, desperately parrying Brad's next series of attacks. He stopped them all, but only at the price of a slash across the chest. While shallow, it also began to slowly leak red.

"I'm what you made me," Brad said, driving the Terror back another half-dozen steps with a flurry of blows. "I am vengeance."

The Terror botched a parry and sent Brad's blade into his own leg. Another minor cut, but they were adding up. It was time to end this.

Brad launched the same attack the Terror had used on Blackhawk Station. The attack that was unstoppable if perfectly executed. Brad did it perfectly.

The Terror blocked it anyway.

With a stunningly loud electrical discharge, the Terror's blade slashed through the very top of Brad's mono-blade handle. The filament went flashing across the room to behead a pirate. Somehow, Brad didn't think the dead man appreciated the lethal pratfall.

Brad threw the useless hunk of metal at the Terror and slowly retreated. Time for the plan of last resort. He stripped his gloves off as the grinning Terror swaggered closer.

"You'll die just like all the rest," the Terror told him. "No one will even remember your name, Madrid."

"Not Madrid," Brad said, sliding his right thumb up along his knuckles. "Mantruso. Brad Mantruso."

That made the Terror's natural eye widen. "Well, well. That *is* a surprise. I thought I killed you on your uncle's ship. Sent you Dutchman. This is a right fitting duel after all. We've been enemies all this time. Now you join the rest of your traitorous brood."

The Terror struck. A mighty, two-handed blow from above. Nothing but a mono-filament blade could stop it.

Brad threw his left arm up into the path of the descending strike, praying that his shield held.

With the distinctive *hiss-crack* of blade-on-blade contact, the pirate's mono-blade hit the bracer concealed under the vac-suit's sleeve and rebounded.

Even as the Terror stared at him in shock, Brad activated the mono-claws that Saburo had forced him to learn over the last three years and threw himself at the pirate warlord. He used his shield to block a last-minute strike as he slashed the claws across the Terror's throat. Blood splashed everywhere and momentarily blinded him.

Going totally defensive, Brad staggered back, desperately wiping at his eyes with his left hand. When he could see again, the Terror was miraculously still on his feet—but his shocked expression slowly clouding with death.

The pirate's body hit the floor, and whatever paralysis had held the pirates failed. Dozens of weapons swung up, bearing on Brad with what would surely be lethal finality.

His troopers raised their own weapons, and Brad could see Trista and her people taking aim unseen from behind the pirates.

The momentary freeze wavered but held right up until the airlock behind Brad blew in, utterly vaporized by a shaped charge. Out of the smoke came dozens of white-armored figures, and a voice bellowed over every com frequency.

"Fleet Marines. Drop your weapons or die!"

Brad deactivated his weapon and raised his hands, stunned at the unexpected arrivals. He gestured for his men to follow suit.

The Marines suppressed what little resistance there was with brutally efficient automatic weapons fire. Only once they had everyone on their knees did the Fleet officer in command of the force enter the atrium. It was a man Brad knew…a fitting man to be here at the end of everything.

Captain Mark Fields commanded the cruiser *Freedom* and had saved Brad from the Dutchman the Terror had sent him on when they'd first met.

He held out a hand to Brad and lifted him to his feet. "It's good to see you in one piece, Madrid," he said as he stared at the Terror's corpse. "Though I wish you'd trusted us a little more. You've left us quite the mess to clean up."

"How are you here?" Brad asked. "We only sent word of the base's location a day ago."

"You seem to forget cruisers can be stealthed. We were following you all the way from Mars, just in case you needed help."

"Shouldn't you have mentioned that little detail?"

"Not my call." The Fleet officer looked around at the devastated atrium. "I expected you to find the base and call for help. When we saw how tough this place was, I was ready to hang with you until the help you called arrived. But then you attacked.

"Sweet Everlit, where in Darkness did you get nukes?"

"From the transport," Brad said. "They were bringing a load of them to this base. I'm guessing it wouldn't be the first set, either."

Fields shook his head in disbelief. "You laid out a textbook run on them. Wiped out every defense before they could fire on you. Dark, before they could even know they were in danger. It was brilliant. And so *Darkness-damned* stupid."

With a long face, the Fleet officer gestured for a Marine to approach. "Brad Madrid, under general order seventeen, the unauthorized possession and use of a nuclear device, I am forced to place you under arrest. I cannot tell you how unhappy that makes me."

"We all do what we have to do," Brad said. "Don't be sorry for me. I got the vengeance I wanted. I only hope that I achieved the salvation I craved, too. I was responsible. Leave my crew out of this."

"That's the least I can do, considering."

As the first Marine was cuffing Brad, another came up and spoke to Fields. "We have some people outside the temporary airlock, sir. They insist they be allowed in to see this man."

"Let them in," Fields said tiredly. "And get me an update on clearing the base."

Moments later, two figures in Vikings vac-suits came in with their helmets off. One was Falcone. The other was Michelle.

Brad tried to step toward her, but the Marine holding his shackles held him tight. That did nothing to stop Michelle from rushing to his side and throwing her arms around him.

"Thank Everlight you came for me," she sobbed. "I've been so scared."

"Did they hurt you?" he asked, reveling in the feel of her against him.

"No. The Terror wouldn't let them, though he promised all kinds of things once he'd killed you."

That's when she noticed Brad's arms were restrained. "What the fuck is this? Have you lost your minds? He's a hero. Take those off this very instant!"

"I wish I could, ma'am," Fields said. "That's above my paygrade. You're absolutely right about him being a hero, though."

He gave Brad a sad look. "And that's going to make this a damned mess for the poor bastards who have to sort it out. What a public relations nightmare. Arresting the man who took out the Terror and broke the Cadre."

"I'm not so sure that's entirely true," Brad said quietly. "I haven't seen Jack Mader or the Terror's flagship, much less all those ships they had at Blackhawk Station."

Fields grunted. "True. The Cadre isn't dead, but you've cut its head off."

Brad shook his head. "I cut out its heart. I've suspected Jack Mader was its head for a long while. What happens now?"

"We get your people back to your ship and I take you to *Freedom*. Then we wait for Commodore Bailey to get here and sort this out."

"Just out of curiosity, what is the maximum penalty for violating general order seventeen?"

"Death," Fields said grimly.

CHAPTER THIRTY-TWO

THE ROOM they put Brad in aboard the cruiser closely resembled the room he'd occupied so many years before. In fact, he suspected it was the very same room.

The Marine guards outside his quarters made it perfectly clear that he was a prisoner. There was no anvil-vat this time, and his room's computer was locked down tight. They'd confiscated his wrist-comp along with his weapons, so he had a lot of time to think over the next two weeks.

They did allow his crew to visit and even allowed Michelle to have private time that they assured him was unmonitored. They put those brief moments to good use. Neither of them knew for sure how many they had left.

The time he had to think filled itself with what the Cadre would do next. He'd long suspected that there was no way the Cadre could have survived as long as it had without support somewhere in the Commonwealth's government.

A chill ran up his spine at the thought of the reaction of Cadre's quiet patrons to the violent destruction of the pirate base. They would have their revenge; of that he was sure. They might even get it through the legal process they were about to subject him to.

Well, whatever happened happened. Nothing he could do at this point would change the outcome. He had taken his bloody vengeance and it would have to be enough.

A soft chime announced a visitor. Odd. Michelle had just left and he wasn't expecting anyone until Jason and Shelly came over for dinner. And he normally had no control over the door.

He rose to his feet and pressed the button to open the door. It slid aside. Outside stood Falcone, Commodore Bailey, and Senator Barnes.

Judgement time was at hand, it seemed.

"It seems kind of odd to invite someone into a prison cell," he said dryly, "but please come in."

Once his visitors were in and had seated themselves, Brad closed the door on the Marine guards outside. "I don't have a lot to offer in the way of refreshments. Nothing, really."

"I think drinks are the least of our worries," Bailey said bluntly. "Everdark, but you know how to fuck up a wet dream, Madrid. Nukes. Holy shit." The last was accompanied by a disbelieving shake of her head.

"Admiral Weber sent me out on *Eternal* to make sure we've cleaned the Cadre out of the area and to deal with your violation of general order seventeen."

Brad sat on the edge of his bed. "You must be pleased to finally get out of Mars orbit."

"Is this *really* the time to be snarky?"

He held up his hands. "Sorry. I couldn't help myself. Is this a tribunal set to determine my fate?"

"It is," Senator Barnes said flatly. "General order seventeen isn't just a Fleet regulation. It's also reflected in the Commonwealth charter. That brings me here as the closest handy Commonwealth official. One that is high enough to be able to speak for the Commonwealth as a whole.

"Agent Falcone, though in some trouble herself, has been tasked to speak for the Commonwealth Investigative Agency. They're the closest we have to Commonwealth-wide law enforcement. We three cover all aspects of the offended parties and can render judgement."

"Not that I want to," Falcone said sadly. "I warned you, Brad. Using nukes was something you couldn't walk back."

"I'm told that Captain Fields found the remains of nukes on several of the asteroid defensive stations," he ventured. "I don't suppose there can be an element of self-defense to this, can there?"

"No," Bailey said curtly. "Two wrongs do not a right make. The judgement of this tribunal is only over your own use of prohibited weapons."

He leaned back a little more and looked at them silently for a moment. "Shouldn't I have a lawyer present? If this is an official tribunal, I have the right to defend myself."

"The law allows no defense for what you've done," Barnes said tiredly. "You gave the orders. We have your bridge recordings. The proof is incontrovertible. A lawyer won't change one damned thing."

"Lawyers usually only make things worse," Falcone added.

"I'm not quite sure how one makes a death sentence worse," Brad opined. "If I ask for a lawyer, do you torture me first?"

"Dammit, Madrid," Barnes said. "You have a real mouth on you. The use of nuclear weapons is only authorized by Fleet. Do you deny that you knowingly took possession of prohibited weapons and then ordered their deployment in battle?"

"No," Brad said quietly. "I do not. In fact, I'd do it again, if need be, to wipe scum like the Cadre out of the universe. If you mean to space me for it, I can't stop you. Let that rest on your own consciences, because mine is clear."

"So much melodrama," Bailey said with a sigh. "I take no pleasure in saying that while I personally cheer what you did, you put Fleet in a very bad spot. We literally have no choice other than becoming the bad guys here."

"The Commonwealth government is in a similar predicament," Senator Barnes said. "With the evidence, we have no choice but find you guilty of the charges, though I desperately do not want to be the agency of your death.

"My daughter owes you her life. I owe you so much more, too. Given even the slightest choice in this matter, I would dismiss the charges and fete you as a hero."

"And can you imagine the fucking media circus when your crew starts talking?" Bailey asked. "The public will rightfully point out how impotent Fleet and the Commonwealth as a whole have been at stopping the Cadre.

"They'll rake us over the coals—rightly so—for punishing the one man able to stop the Terror. You've put us all in a terrible catch twenty-two."

"Yeah," Brad said ironically. "My sympathy is a little limited right now. Do I at least get to make a final statement? See my crew one last time? Maybe say goodbye to my girlfriend?"

"That's the very least we can do," Falcone said. "But I thought you might be willing to consider an alternate set of facts that led to these events. Facts that would spare your life but bind your future in ways you might not prefer."

"They say that nothing concentrates the mind like being hung in the morning," Brad said. "What do you have in mind?"

To say that Jason and Shelly were shocked when he stepped onto *Oath*'s bridge an hour later would've been a gross understatement. They'd only been expecting Falcone.

Michelle flew out of the spare seat and raced across the bridge to clutch him tightly. "They let you go? Thank the Light they came to their senses."

Falcone cleared her throat. "Not precisely. We came to an agreement and retconned the ill-fated series of events that led you to this place with the approval and endorsement of Fleet, the Commonwealth Investigative Agency, and the Commonwealth government.

"Basically, we're all lying in a way that makes what you did legal. Unfortunately, it has consequences for all of you."

Brad kissed Michelle and gestured for her to resume her seat. "This affects you, too. Not you, Michelle, but the Vikings."

"How?" Shelly asked warily.

"The only way we could use nukes without violating Commonwealth law was by being Fleet. This probably comes as a great shock to you, but a month ago on Mars, this ship became a Fleet reserve vessel and you all received reserve commissions."

Jason laughed. "That's it? We've been expecting doom for two weeks, and they could have backdated that commission at any time. I'm fine with that, but I'm not so sure how the Mercenary Guild will see it."

"There is precedent," Falcone said. "Three other mercenary commanders were also reserve Fleet officers. One of them commanded a ship that was also a reserve vessel. I have no idea what hoops you'll have to jump through, but someone went down that road already.

"That said, it isn't all you'd be doing. And this includes you, Michelle."

Michelle's eyes widened. "Me? You want me to be a reserve Fleet officer? I was a diver captain, who is no doubt in big trouble for dumping her cargo near Blackhawk Station, blowing said cargo up, and then losing her ship. I probably don't have a job anymore."

"You do now," Falcone said. "Partly because you've become a target for the Cadre and partly because Brad thinks you have some-thing to offer. In any case, I wasn't really talking about that."

His girlfriend's eyes narrowed and she held up a finger, stopping Falcone.

"Before you so cavalierly move on, I want to know what kind of job Brad could have for me. Not that I'm saying no, but a girl likes at least the illusion she has a choice."

"I need a captain for *Heart of Vengeance*," Brad said quietly. "That was going to be Jason, but with Marshal dead, I need him here."

"Me?" Michelle asked incredulously. "Captain a mercenary ship? I was a *diver* captain. I've never fired a weapon in my life."

"Tell that to all the Cadre ships you vaporized," he said. "You've destroyed more Cadre vessels and killed more pirates than the majority of the mercenaries in the Guild. I will have zero trouble getting you membership."

That set her back on her mental heels. Before she could resume, he held up a finger of his own.

"I know you'll have a lot to learn, but we have some good teachers in the Vikings. Don't reject the idea until you hear the whole story. Please."

She considered that before slowly nodding. "I'll hear you out."

He breathed a sigh of relief and turned to Falcone. "I'll have to run the reserve Fleet commissions past everyone to be sure, but I don't think they'll object. Tell them the rest."

"My superiors think Brad is a bit of a loose cannon," Falcone said dryly. "I'm not sure why, but they think he needs more in the way of supervision."

Brad laughed and raised an eyebrow. "Me? I heard it was you they said that about."

She waved her hand dismissively. "Let's not lose sight of the bigger picture. The Commonwealth government and the Commonwealth Investigative Agency have agreed that they both need to keep an eye on Brad."

"What she's tap-dancing around," he said, "is the fact that I was given the choice of becoming an agent or getting that death sentence."

"Talk about *do or die*," Jason muttered. "Are you seriously telling me that they held a gun to his head to take the job? How can you possibly expect he won't be bitter?"

"Because my mission is the same as it has been for the last few years," Brad said. "Find and destroy the Cadre. That included whoever has to be supporting them. Jack Mader escaped. He was off on *Lioness*, the Terror's flagship. He and a lot of pirate ships are still on the loose. And we still have no idea what they are doing with regards to the He3 refining in the Outer System.

"The Terror was a sadistic piece of crap, but Jack Mader is smart. He'll be much more dangerous than any Cadre leader we've ever faced. The fight is changing. It's no longer about one man's vengeance. I can't be a vigilante anymore. That part of my life is over.

"But I won't stop until every last pirate is dead or captured. I'm now an agent for the Commonwealth Investigative Agency, and Kate Falcone is my partner and boss, at least as far as the non-military parts of what I do. Can you work with that?"

Jason and Shelly glanced at one another and shrugged at the same time.

"I don't see why not," Shelly said. "Are we like junior agents? Do we get badges?"

"No," Falcone said with a chuckle. "The stress of having an agent in charge of a mercenary company will cause enough complications, I suspect. He can't hide that from the Guild. It would violate the agreement they have with the Vikings.

"I believe we can make the case to the Guild leadership and get this past them. They're not immune to the public-relations aspects of this story, either. Still, it's best not to push things too far. The Agency will pay the Vikings a retainer for the work we want you to do, by the way. As will Fleet."

Jason perked up. "Does that mean we get to carry nukes all the time?"

"Let's not push our luck," Brad said dryly. "Maybe they'll trust us with them one day, but today is not that day."

"Captain Fields wants to know about the pulsars," Jason said. "He was really interested. Maybe we could trade."

Before Brad could respond, the hatch behind him slid open and Dr. Duvall stepped onto the bridge. "Ah. I was told they'd released you, Commodore. Excellent. That means I can take you in for your final treatment in a less-confined manner."

By that, she was undoubtedly referring to the armed Marine guards who had accompanied him to all the regeneration sessions during his captivity.

"Your timing is good, Doctor. Shall we?"

———

Once Duvall had him back to the sickbay and strapped into the regeneration machine, she closed the hatch and locked it.

That was new.

"I needed to pass along something that I've learned," the doctor said quietly. "About the Terror."

Brad frowned. "I can't imagine anything you could say that would require locking the door."

"You and he were related," she said bluntly. "The gene scan indicates he was almost certainly your uncle on your maternal side."

"My what?!" Brad felt as if someone had punched him in the gut. "Is this some kind of sick joke?"

"I do not *joke* about medical matters," Duvall said stiffly. "I only chanced across the data accidentally. The doctor aboard *Eternal* passed the medical examiner's report on to me as a courtesy. When I imported it, my software notified me of a match in my private database.

"I have no idea what it means, but the man known as the Terror once went by another name: Armand Riggio."

Stunned didn't begin to describe how Brad felt. He hadn't even known his mother had siblings. And the Cadre had killed her when they killed his father. What kind of sick bastard killed his own sister?

"Wait," he said, holding up his free hand. "How could I never have heard of him?"

Duvall shrugged. "I can't imagine. There is no doubt, though. His gene records were on file in the Commonwealth database. That's where the medical examiner made the identification. Perhaps you could ask your uncle why he never mentioned the Terror was his brother-in-law when you find him."

His uncle was still missing, as were the other survivors from *Mandrake's Heart*, but Brad now knew there had been survivors.

Fleet had questioned the captured pirates closely, and Brad had asked them to get the information. Half a dozen people had been captured alive on *Mandrake's Heart*, including Boris Mantruso.

Unfortunately, none of them were here and no one knew where they were being kept or why.

One more mystery to be solved. One more secret to hold.

"Thank you, Doctor," he said with a sigh. "Do you think I'll be able to recover full use of my hand?"

"I do," she said with a smile. "Some of my best work under what I would charitably call trying circumstances."

That was great news. If his guesses were correct, he'd need every weapon at his disposal to stop Jack Mader and the Cadre.

"And, if I might be so bold?" Duvall continued. "Your young lady has been very worried about you. Now that you are free, shower her with attention. She's a keeper."

Brad smiled. "You have no idea, Doctor. She and I have a lot to discuss. A future we never dreamed of."

"You know what they say. 'Life is what happens when you're making other plans.'"

He laughed. "How true. To life, then."

ABOUT THE AUTHORS

#1 Bestselling Military Science Fiction author **Terry Mixon** served as a non-commissioned officer in the United States Army 101st Airborne Division. He later worked alongside the flight controllers in the Mission Control Center at the NASA Johnson Space Center supporting the Space Shuttle, the International Space Station, and other human spaceflight projects.

He now writes full time while living in Texas with his lovely wife and a pounce of cats.

————

Glynn Stewart is the author of *Starship's Mage*, a bestselling science fiction and fantasy series where faster-than-light travel is possible–but only because of magic. His other works include science fiction series *Duchy of Terra, Castle Federation* and *Vigilante*, as well as the urban fantasy series *ONSET* and *Changeling Blood*.

Writing managed to liberate Glynn from a bleak future as an accountant. With his personality and hope for a high-tech future intact, he lives in Kitchener, Ontario with his partner, their cats, and an unstoppable writing habit.

OTHER BOOKS BY TERRY MIXON

You can always find the most up to date listing of Terry's titles on Amazon at
author.to / terrymixon

<u>The Empire of Bones Saga</u>

Empire of Bones

Veil of Shadows

Command Decisions

Ghosts of Empire

Paying the Price

Reconnaissance in Force

Behind Enemy Lines

The Terra Gambit

Hidden Enemies

Race to Terra

The Empire of Bones Saga Volume 1

<u>The Humanity Unlimited Saga</u>

Liberty Station

Freedom Express

Tree of Liberty

<u>The Fractured Republic Saga</u>

Storm Divers

<u>The Scorched Earth Saga</u>

<u>*Scorched Earth*</u>

<u>**The Vigilante Duology** with <u>Glynn Stewart</u></u>

Heart of Vengeance

Oath of Vengeance

<u>Bound By Stars: A Vigilante Series</u> with Glynn Stewart

Bound By Law

Bound by Honor

Bound by Blood

Want Terry to email you when he publishes a new book in any format or when one goes on sale? Go to <u>TerryMixon.com/Mailing-List</u> and sign up. Those are the only times he'll contact you. No spam.

OTHER BOOKS BY GLYNN STEWART

For release announcements join the mailing list or visit **GlynnStewart.com**

STARSHIP'S MAGE
Starship's Mage
Hand of Mars
Voice of Mars
Alien Arcana
Judgment of Mars
UnArcana Stars
Sword of Mars
Mountain of Mars
The Service of Mars
A Darker Magic
Mage-Commander (upcoming)

Starship's Mage: Red Falcon
Interstellar Mage
Mage-Provocateur
Agents of Mars

Pulsar Race: A Starship's Mage Universe Novella

DUCHY OF TERRA
The Terran Privateer
Duchess of Terra
Terra and Imperium
Darkness Beyond
Shield of Terra
Imperium Defiant
Relics of Eternity
Shadows of the Fall
Eyes of Tomorrow

SCATTERED STARS

Scattered Stars: Conviction

Conviction

Deception

Equilibrium

Fortitude (upcoming)

PEACEKEEPERS OF SOL

Raven's Peace

The Peacekeeper Initiative

Raven's Course

Drifter's Folly (upcoming)

EXILE

Exile

Refuge

Crusade

Ashen Stars: An Exile Novella

CASTLE FEDERATION

Space Carrier Avalon

Stellar Fox

Battle Group Avalon

Q-Ship Chameleon

Rimward Stars

Operation Medusa

A Question of Faith: A Castle Federation Novella

SCIENCE FICTION STAND ALONE NOVELLA

Excalibur Lost

VIGILANTE
(WITH TERRY MIXON)
Heart of Vengeance
Oath of Vengeance

**Bound By Stars: A Vigilante Series
(With Terry Mixon)**
Bound By Law
Bound by Honor
Bound by Blood

TEER AND KARD
Wardtown
Blood Ward

CHANGELING BLOOD
Changeling's Fealty
Hunter's Oath
Noble's Honor
Fae, Flames & Fedoras: A Changeling Blood Novella

ONSET
ONSET: To Serve and Protect
ONSET: My Enemy's Enemy
ONSET: Blood of the Innocent
ONSET: Stay of Execution
Murder by Magic: An ONSET Novella

FANTASY STAND ALONE NOVELS
Children of Prophecy
City in the Sky

www.ingramcontent.com/pod-product-compliance
Lightning Source LLC
Chambersburg PA
CBHW021309190726
48288CB00003B/767